TEE with Carly

Taylor James

Copyright © 2010 Taylor James

All rights reserved.

ISBN-10:147826750X
ISBN-13: 978-1478267508

The language of friendship is not words, but meanings.

- Henry David Thoreau

TEE with Carly

Taylor James

Scenes, characters, and events contained in this work are the product of the author's imagination and any similarities to any person or persons is coincidental.

This work is copyrighted by the author. It is licensed for use by the original purchaser only. Making copies of this work or distributing it to any unauthorized person by any means, including e-mail, disk, file transfer, paper print, or any other method constitutes a violation of copyright law. Please respect authors.

Please send comments to: taylorjamesmail@gmail.com

Cover image from Fotolia.com

Author image: *MKO Productions*

CHAPTER 1

Tee had just taken a sip of a fresh beer when she was pulled from her bar stool and hauled onto the dance floor.

"Jesus, Markie! All you had to do was ask!" Tee was laughing though and already moving to the beat. Markie Killigan was her best friend and frequent dance partner when they were out. They were currently at Sue Ellen's, a mostly women's bar on Cedar Springs in Dallas.

"You know I love this song," Markie laughed. She was a voluptuous blond with an hourglass figure and she moved her hips in a way that was the envy of all females. Tonight she wore tight jeans and a top that was cut low enough for everyone in the bar to either worry or hope for an accident to happen.

Tee Reed was immune to Markie's charms, having been friends with her for more years than she cared to admit. They'd met at Southern Methodist University their freshman year and after trying to date they'd discovered they didn't have the necessary spark. They became good friends instead and it was a friendship that had endured through the intervening years.

"I do believe you have an admirer." Markie danced closer and spoke into her ear.

"Yeah?" Tee asked with a smile. "Who?"

"That gorgeous brunette in the middle of the group by the stairs. The one with the great rack."

Tee swept a casual look that way and found a pair of chocolate brown eyes riveted on her. The eyes were attached to a very nice package. Dark brown hair brushed past her shoulders and she had a straight nose with full sensuous lips. Lips made for kissing was Tee's first thought. She smiled at her before Markie turned her away.

"A very nice rack," Markie observed with a laugh. "You should ask her to dance or buy her a drink."

"You think she'd say yes?"

Markie gave Tee a slow up and down appraisal. "Well, let's see, nice thick natural blond hair, the most beautiful blue eyes ever, a very nice smile, and a body to die for. Yeah, I'm thinking she'll say yes. Duh."

"You always say that," Tee laughed.

"Because it's true." Markie slung an arm around Tee's waist as the music changed and they left the dance floor. She pushed Tee toward the brunette and walked away in the opposite direction.

Tee approached the group and locked eyes with the woman. She held out a hand in invitation and the woman stood. With a shy smile, she took Tee's hand and followed her onto the dance floor. Tee dropped her hand but kept close as the music took over her body. Her new partner was an excellent dancer and let the music move her as well. It was a thumping beat wrapped around a sexy saxophone riff that touched just this side of primal. Without thought, they both began dancing for each other, their bodies occasionally brushing, touching, pulling at each other. Tee was mesmerized by the look in her eyes, even more so than by the sensuous body that hinted at pleasures to be had. It was just the two of them, nothing else existed. Their breathing became one, their legs entwined, pelvis to pelvis, and dangerously close to taking the dance to the final inevitable conclusion. Unknown to either of them they had become the featured act and the others circled them to watch. The final chord found them with their hands on each other's hips, legs scissored, their bodies touching along their lengths. The crowd erupted in applause, cheering, and catcalls. Tee saw her partner blush and she quickly stepped away in embarrassment, but Tee wrapped her in an embrace and whispered in her ear, "You were magnificent. Don't be shy." She waved to the crowd with a slight bow and pulled her new partner off the floor with her. "May I buy you a drink?"

"Yes, thank you."

Tee steered her to the end of the bar where she'd been sitting before and offered the lone stool to her. "My name's Tee," she said as she caught the bartender's eye and ordered their drinks.

"Hello, Tee. I'm Carly. Thank you for the drink."

"My pleasure, I assure you," Tee smiled. "Thank you for the dance. You are truly a great dancer."

Carly looked away again. She was not used to being the center of attention, at least not on a dance floor. "Thanks. I think you are too." She took a drink to give herself some time. She'd never had something like that happen to her. Music had always moved her but never to the point of losing it so totally. She looked back at Tee to find her staring at her in frank appreciation.

Tee's eyes dropped to her chest and Carly straightened her spine, pushing her breasts forward blatantly. She was rewarded when Tee went obviously breathless and unable to hide it. Tee moved closer and put her arm around her back before leaning close to her ear. "You, my dear, are lethal and should not be allowed to run free among unsuspecting lesbians."

Carly blushed but was pleased. "You're certainly a sweet talker."

"No, just honest," Tee swore with a smile. "I've never seen you here before." Carly swiveled on the stool and put her elbows on the bar behind her. It showed off her chest rather nicely and Tee fought to keep her eyes on Carly's face. She won but it was very hard.

"This is only the second time I've been here," she said. "Do you come here often?"

"This is beginning to sound like a bad movie script," Tee laughed.

Carly laughed along with her. "Yeah. Well, I'm an attorney." She gave Tee a smile that lit up the room. "What is it you do?"

"I work for Sylar Industries," Tee said easily. She had learned in the years since graduating from the Cox School of Business at SMU not to let anyone know she *was* Sylar Industries. Sylar Industries consisted of a gay bar called Reeders Room on Cedar Springs, the heart of the gay district in Dallas and just down the street. Sylar also owned a five story building on Greenville Avenue in the entertainment district that housed a public restaurant on the ground floor called The Reed House, a private club on the second floor with a bar and meeting rooms, a day spa on the third floor along with several suites for out of town VIP guests, a banquet/ballroom on the fourth floor, and the corporate offices on the top floor. A few women she had dated thought Tee being successful meant they didn't need to work. She learned her lesson and swore she would not be used like that again. "I own the Reeders Row bar." Now where the hell did that admission come from? She smiled and quickly moved on. "Would you like to shoot a game of pool?" she asked. She was usually more adept at avoiding questions about her work.

"Sure," she agreed. With a look toward the adjoining game area she asked, "Are you any good?"

Tee gave her a wicked grin. "Oh yes. Or so I've been told."

Carly shook her head at her but laughed. "Prove it."

A game was just ending and Tee put money up to pay for them. "Would you like to break?"

"Go ahead," Carly said. "Show me what you've got, hot stuff."

Tee was clearly better at pool than Carly but she played soft against her and kept the game close and interesting. This was not a competition as much as a means to get better acquainted. She bent over the table to line up a shot and was almost ready when she felt Carly snuggle up against her ass, a hand softly on her back, pretending to look over her shoulder. Tee felt a familiar tingle shoot through her body. *Oh, this was going to be fun*, she thought. "Uh, no fair," she said over her shoulder.

"What?" Carly gave her an innocent look.

"No fair touching me when I'm trying to shoot."

Carly smiled. That was nice to know. "Why not?"

Tee turned and stood to her full 5'11" height and slowly let her eyes travel up and down Carly's 5'8" frame. "Sweetie, if you don't know then you must live in a nunnery."

"No nunnery." Carly's brown eyes dance with merriment.

"Hmm," Tee mused. "Then you haven't looked in the mirror lately." She widened her stance so Carly was between her legs. "Because if you had, you'd know you were the most beautiful woman in this bar and that's very distracting."

"Oh." Carly hadn't expected that. She looked up into Tee's eyes and time seemed to stand still. She was lost in their depths, the blue eyes darkening to nearly black. She unconsciously leaned forward as Tee reached up to put a soft hand on her cheek.

"Get a room!" someone shouted at them.

Carly was jolted into reality and took a step back. "I'm sorry." She was embarrassed.

Tee grinned and turned back to the table. "Keep your pants on," she said into the crowd. "I have a beautiful woman willing to talk to me, so cut me some slack." She lined up the shot again and managed to sink the six ball in the side pocket. She smiled back at Carly who had retreated to their table. She missed the next shot because she was remembering the feel of Carly pressed against her ass. And along with that thought came the image of a naked Carly bent over another pool table, one in Tee's private club in The Reed House. She lost focus so badly she didn't even remember whether she had stripes or solids in the game. She handed the pool cue to Carly in passing and let her knuckles brush against her breast. She saw Carly smile as she took the stick from her. Tee watched her bend over the table, pants stretched tight over a trim ass. She held back a groan with effort. Damn, this woman was hot! They finished the game but Tee couldn't tell who'd won. It *so* did not matter. She took Carly's hand as she gave the cue stick to the next player. "Dance?"

"Yes."

The music was just changing into a slow song and Tee was grateful beyond words. She held Carly in her arms and hoped she wouldn't step on her toes or do something equally stupid. She needn't have worried. They fit together perfectly and immediately moved as one. Midway through the song Tee pulled Carly tight against her and brushed her lips across her ear, inhaling the delicious scent of shampoo, perfume, and her. It was heady. She was aware of every place on her body where they touched, those places sparking an escalating heat all through her. She felt lips against her neck in a kiss so soft she might have imagined it. Tee's heart was beating wildly in her chest and she hoped Carly couldn't feel it. She wanted to touch her so badly.

TEE with Carly

The song ended and before she could say anything, another woman appeared by her side and took Carly's hand without a word. Tee recognized her as one of those at the table where Carly had been sitting. The woman pulled Carly off a ways and they began dancing together. Tee watched them a moment, long enough to see Carly look at her with a helpless shrug of her shoulders. She inclined her head in answer and left the floor.

Markie was at a table and she gave Tee a sympathetic smile. "Snatched right from under your nose," she observed sardonically.

"Yeah, so it would seem." She slumped in the chair and stretched her long legs out under the table. "I don't think that's her date though." She continued to watch them dance together.

"No?"

"No. If it were, she would never have danced with me in the first place. And there's no way she would have been allowed to play a game of pool with me."

Markie grinned. "You have a point."

"Yes, I do." Tee smiled. "Plus, she's not nearly as into that woman as she should be if that's her date."

Markie watched them dancing and had to agree. She laughed. "That means you have a chance."

"Oh, yes. Definitely."

"So, you want a date with her?"

Tee thought again how it felt to have Carly pressed against her. "I very much want a date."

"What's her name?"

"Carly."

"Carly what?"

"I don't know." Tee had a silly grin on her face.

Markie smiled. Tee was exhibiting the usual signs of lust. She looked like she was absolutely smitten with this woman. "Maybe this woman is interested in her too," she said with a nod at the dance floor. "And she knows her last name and where she lives and everything else."

The silly grin never left Tee's face. "No matter. As long as she's single that's all that counts."

"Well, you'd better get on it before she leaves you with your metaphoric dick in your hand. It looks like the group is on the move."

The five women were all standing and gathering their things at the table. Carly looked toward her as if for one last glimpse.

Tee jumped to her feet and started in her direction. Carly met her halfway. "Hey," Tee said and couldn't stop herself from reaching out and touching her arm. "Are you leaving?"

"Yeah," she nodded. "They all want to go." She sounded disappointed.

"I could take you home if you want to stay," Tee offered.

She shook her head. "No. We all came together and…"

"Okay," she hastily assured her. "Would it be okay if I called you? Maybe next week?"

Carly's smile was one of relief and pleasure. "I'd like that." She dug into her bag and produced a card case. "Here. Call me any time." She rummaged again and pulled out a pen. Taking the card back she wrote her cell phone number on the back. "That's my private cell."

Tee smiled and took the card again. "I'll call. I promise."

Carly looked pleased at that. "Good."

Tee returned to Markie's table and flashed her Carly's card. "Full name, Carly Matthews, and I have all her numbers plus her *very* private cell phone number." She giggled as she sat beside her once again. "And she wants me to call her next week."

CHAPTER 2

Carly shuffled in bare feet across the kitchen floor to the coffee pot. The phone rang just as she poured her first cup. She looked at the read-out and frowned. It was Kim. She sighed but answered it. "Hi Kim."

"Hi Carly. How are you?"

Carly rolled her eyes at the whiny tone of her voice. "I'm good, Kim. How is everything up there? Are you making any progress?"

"It's still about the same," was the desultory reply.

"Have you gotten any offers for the house?"

"There was one that came in Friday but I don't think we're going to accept it."

"Was it too low?" Carly inquired. "You can't be too picky in this economy, you know."

"We can't just sell the house at the first offer," Kim sniffed.

Carly could hear a tissue being plucked from the box. "I'm not saying you should," she soothed her quickly. "What does your sister, Denise, say about the offer?"

"She doesn't think we should take it either," she reported quickly, defiantly. "She thinks we should wait until we get what the house is worth."

Carly clamped down on her ire. "Kim, it's been six months. How long do you plan on waiting?"

"Carly, this was our mother's home for over thirty years! We can't sell it to just anybody!"

Carly knew it was useless to argue with her about it since they'd had this conversation many times before. "Kim, I know your mother's death hit you hard. And I know you're feeling sort of lost these days, but you have to move on."

"I am," she stated, but her voice wavered.

Carly could hear her crying and felt like shit for adding to her misery. "Kim, honey, I'm sorry. I'm sure you and Denise know what you're doing."

"Karen says we should wait until we get the price we want too." It was said defiantly.

The mention of Kim's former girlfriend no longer affected her as it once had. The relationship between Carly and Kim had been over for months. Kim, always fragile, had begun to exhibit a personality disorder and Carly found herself unable to cope. One day Kim was happy and acting larger than life, the next she was despondent and depressed. No matter what Carly did or didn't do, Kim continued to be unpredictable. They talked for hours on end and Carly urged her to see someone, a therapist, or counselor. Kim refused. When Carly accepted a position at Brown, Hardin & Simon, a legal group in Dallas, Kim went in such a depression she thought about refusing the offer. It was the end of them as a couple. In one of her more stable periods Kim agreed they needed to part ways.

Kim's condition changed drastically with the death of her mother. Her sister finally insisted on taking her to the doctor. She was diagnosed as being bi-polar. The prescribed medications worked—when she took them.

Carly hated herself for her lack of compassion but after six months it seemed to her as if Kim was wallowing in self-imposed grief. She often wondered if Kim could survive the loss of a reason to be depressed. She was, more often than not, morose, depressed, and needy. In the past month their relationship had consisted of a series of phone calls where Kim called and cried, and Carly felt rotten for not being there for her. Over the ensuing months it became evident to her that Kim did not want to part with her mother's house at all.

"She did, did she?" She took in a deep breath and let it out.

"Yes, she did. She understands how much the house meant to Mom."

Meaning I don't, Carly thought. "Are you seeing each other?" she asked carefully.

"What do you mean by that?" Kim's voice turned shrill. "Of course, we see each other. We're friends. It's not what you think! You turn everything into something dirty!"

The venom was new, Carly thought, and wondered what it meant. She gave a mental sigh. "Kim, I didn't mean it like that. I just…"

"You mean I should just sell the house and forget about Mom."

"No, that's not what I meant." Carly took in another breath and let it out. "I know you were very close to your mother." She paused a moment. "I just hate to see you so upset, Kim."

"I'm sorry for putting all this on you, honey," she cried. "I am. Really."

"I know, Kim. I know," Carly soothed her. "Maybe you could come down to Dallas for a few days," she said with some trepidation. "I could show you my new firm. There's a lot to see here. I think you'll like it."

"You know I can't leave," Kim wailed. "I can't!"

"Not even for a few days?" Carly fought to hold onto her temper. This was getting so hard. "Just for a weekend, Kim. Two days."

"How can I leave here?" she demanded in a voice that skimmed along the edge of panic. "Tell me how that's possible, Carly?"

"I just thought you'd like to see Dallas, that's all."

"I can't leave here. Not now."

"Okay, Kim. I understand. Maybe I'll see about getting a ticket to Chicago. Okay?"

"Okay," she answered in a small sniffling voice. "That would be okay."

Carly needed to end this conversation before her patience ran completely out. "Tell Denise I said hello, would you? And take care of yourself, okay?"

"Okay. Bye Carly."

"We'll talk later. Bye." Carly hung up and rubbed a hand roughly over her face. *Shit! How could anyone not feel sorry for someone who had lost her last parent? She must be a monster.* She threw the now cold coffee in the sink and re-filled her cup.

CHAPTER 3

Tee glanced at the clock on the wall opposite her desk on the fifth floor of the Reed House building. It was Monday so the first floor restaurant would be dark today. She pressed the intercom button on her phone for her assistant. "Janie, have you gotten the week's schedule for the second and third floors yet?"

"They just came in a minute ago," she answered. "I'm posting the update now."

In seconds Tee hit the refresh icon on her computer and the bookings for the second floor meeting rooms and the third floor spa reservations popped up. She nodded, pleased with what she saw. All but one of the VIP suites on the third floor had been reserved for the weekend of the GLBT annual ball being held in the ballroom on the fourth floor. She absently hit the intercom button again. "Thanks Jane."

"You're welcome."

Tee looked at the clock again before picking up the phone and dialing the number on Carly Matthews's card. It was answered by a woman with a nasal voice asking how she could direct Tee's call. She asked for Carly and waited for the call to be transferred.

"Matthews," Carly's clipped voice came over the line.

Tee smiled into the receiver. "Good morning, Ms Matthews," she purred.

"Good morning," she answered and Tee could tell she was smiling.

"I tried to wait to call you," Tee said, "but I don't have that much will power. Can you forgive me for being impetuous and a bit adolescent?"

Carly laughed lightly. "You goof. I'm glad you called. I've been thinking about Saturday night."

"Oh? And what exactly were you thinking?"

"I was thinking how much I enjoyed dancing with you."

"Yes," Tee agreed. "I liked that too. I also liked our game of pool."

"Oh, yeah, that was fun," Carly giggled.

"Do you think we might get together again?"

"Yes, I'd like that."

"Soon?"

"Yes," she laughed again.

"Tonight?"

"Well, I'm afraid I've already got plans for tonight."

"Oh." Tee was instantly deflated.

"I am free for lunch though."

She brightened. "May I take you to lunch then?"

"That would be very nice," she agreed. "Shall we meet somewhere?"

Tee fingered her business card. "You're downtown, right?"

"Yes, in Thanksgiving Tower."

"How about meeting at Carmen's?"

"Great. Noon?"

"I'll be there."

"Good. I've got to get back to work. I'll see you soon."

"Bye." Tee hung up and grinned. "High five me," she said aloud and laughed.

Carly replaced the phone with a smile. She hadn't expected Tee to call so soon but she was glad she had. There was just something about her that drew Carly like a moth to a flame. It wasn't just that her high cheekbones and flawless skin made her runway model gorgeous. It wasn't the thick healthy blond hair dancing over her collar, her perfectly arched eyebrows, or her very full and kissable lips. It wasn't even the mesmerizing blue eyes that seemed to pull at Carly until she got lost in their depths. It was something totally intangible. A presence she had about her. She was tall and firmly muscled and…sexy as hell, Carly thought. She seemed very comfortable in her skin, as if she knew exactly who she was and where she was going. She was confident and that alone was attractive enough. She was abruptly brought back to the present when her phone rang.

"Matthews."

"Ms Matthews, Mr. Hardin would like to see you this morning at your earliest convenience."

"I'll be right there," she answered, as she knew she was expected to do.

"Excellent. I'll advise Mr. Hardin."

Carly took a second to check her appearance before leaving her small office for the short elevator ride up to the floor where the partners had their offices. On the way she wondered what on earth one of the founding partners could possible want with her. By the time the elevator deposited her on the eighth floor she was more than a little nervous. Junior attorneys were never to be seen above the sixth floor. It just wasn't done. She frantically searched her memory for anything she could possibly have done wrong. Was she billing enough hours? That must be it, she thought. She'd wrapped up her last case too quickly. She'd filed the corporate papers with the SEC too fast or she'd forgotten something important. It must be something devastating to have one of the partners summon her to his office. She entered the outer office of Mr. Hardin and presented herself to his secretary, Mrs. Nolan.

"He's waiting for you," she said with a sniff of disdain. Junior attorneys were not the sort of people she would normally allow near her boss and she made her feelings clear. It was rumored Mrs. Nolan wielded almost as much power as her boss and woe be to the attorney that crossed her. Carly swallowed and squared her shoulders before following Mrs. Nolan into the inner office. "Ms Matthews, Mr. Hardin," she intoned before backing out and closing the door behind her. Carly stood where they'd stopped just a few feet into the huge office. Her entire body was rigid with tension as she stood waiting for him to speak. The office had full floor to ceiling windows on two sides and commanded a panoramic view of downtown Dallas. Carly could see City Hall to the south from where she stood.

Mr. Hardin was watching her silently and finally spoke. "Ms Matthews, please have a seat." He gestured her to an area to her left where a tasteful grouping of leather chairs were arranged around a low table. He came from behind his massive desk and ushered her into one of the chairs before sitting opposite her. He wore an obviously expensive suit of raw silk in a dark charcoal and, while Carly had a fleeting thought that his tie was ugly, his Italian shoes were shined to a high gloss. He could have been the poster child for the successful attorney of today. "You're probably wondering why I asked you to spare me a few minutes today," he said with a smile.

"Yes sir," she nodded.

He sat back in his chair and casually crossed one leg over the other. "Our firm has been awarded a case from the district court." When she said nothing he continued.

"As you know, the court will occasionally assign a case to a prominent law firm when their public defenders are backed up. Of course our firm was happy to sign up for the odd case now and then. We're all for doing our part to aid the legal system whenever we can. It just so happens we've been chosen this time." He noticed her raised eyebrow. "We've been watching your progress, Ms Matthews, and I think you'd be an excellent choice to try this case."

"Me, sir?"

"Yes," he smiled. "Don't get too excited though. It's pro bono so there won't be any billable hours but I'm confident you'll handle the case with your usual skill and expertise."

"Of course, sir."

"Just remember not to let your usual work for the firm suffer because of it."

"Absolutely not, sir. I can handle it," she assured him.

"Fine," he nodded. "Great." He stood and Carly scrambled to her feet. "I knew we could count on you." He ushered her to his office door. "Mrs. Nolan has the case file for you. Good luck, Ms Matthews."

"Thank you, sir." She wanted to say more, to assure him she'd been the right choice, but she couldn't get the words out and the door quickly closed behind her. She turned to Mrs. Nolan's desk with confidence this time only to see her continued disapproval. She simply handed her a file and turned back to her duties.

"Please keep me informed of your progress." It wasn't keep Mr. Hardin informed, it was keep *her* informed. A pro bono case meant they'd be getting no fee for their time and effort on the client's behalf. Evidently that meant it was not worth bothering the almighty Mr. Hardin. Carly was undaunted. It may only be a small pro bono case to them but she'd do a good job, get their client off, and show them what a great attorney she was. She was smiling when she got to her floor again.

"Hey, Carly."

She turned to find fellow attorney, Sharon Williams, coming down the hall. "Hey, Sharon."

"I hear you've been breathing the purified air on the eighth floor."

Carly was not surprised word of her summons had already spread. The firm's grapevine was faster than a drunken celebrity's internet video. "Yeah," she nodded. "It was awe inspiring," she joked.

"So what gives? I heard they were giving you a criminal pro bono."

"Yes," she confirmed. "No billable hours but I haven't handled a criminal case before so it should be interesting."

"Too bad." Sharon gave her a sympathetic look. "I'm sure you won't have to spend a lot of time on it though. They won't expect much anyway."

"Oh, I don't mind," Carly told her. "It's something else I can point to that I can do."

"Honey, the boys don't really care about that stuff. They only care about billable hours."

Carly shrugged. She wasn't going to let Sharon rain on her parade. "We'll see."

"Hey, Terri and I are going to lunch together. Want to join us?"

"You know I would normally, but I have a lunch date today."

Sharon gave her a surprised look. "Really? Who with?"

"That woman from the bar Saturday night."

"The blond from the dance floor?"

"Yeah," Carly grinned. "Her name is Tee. She called me this morning."

"Wow, she certainly moves fast. Well, have fun." She waved as she walked off.

TEE with Carly

Carly settled behind her desk and opened the case file Mrs. Nolan had given her. Maybe Sharon was right when she said the firm didn't care about the case. However, it was her case now and she cared. She spent the rest of the morning going over the material and planning her defense points. She'd have to visit her new client at the Lew Sterrett jail on West Commerce too. His name was Luis Alvarez and he was accused of operating a chop shop and selling stolen parts out of his used car lot, Beltwood Motors. Her heart sank as she read through the file. The evidence against him was overwhelming.

She glanced at her watch and closed the file. She needed to get going if she wanted to be on time for her lunch date with Tee. She stuffed the file into her briefcase and left her office. She checked in with the floor receptionist and told her she was leaving the building and took the escalator down to the tunnel beneath her building. The tunnel system ran under the Thanksgiving Tower on Elm Street up through Thanksgiving Square on Pacific Avenue and beyond. From Pacific she would take the escalator up to street level and then walk only two blocks to Carmen's Bistro. It was a walk but it was easier than driving and trying to find a parking place at noon in downtown Dallas. There were many people who never knew about the tunnels under the city but the occupants of the high-rise office buildings spent a lot of time in them. There were office supply stores, copy shops, full restaurants as well as sandwich shops, express shipping niches, and retail stores. There were weeks when Carly never felt the outside air during her workday and in summer it was a blessing. She entered Carmen's just before noon and stopped inside the entrance to search the tables for her date.

Looking for someone special?" Tee's voice came from behind her and she turned with a smile.

"Yes, someone very special."

"Let's get a table quick before the people behind us form a lethal mob mentality," Tee grinned.

They followed their waitress to a table and accepted menus. "You look great," Carly said. "How is your day going?"

"My day is going well, thank you," Tee answered, thinking it had just gotten better from seeing her. "How about yours?"

"I got a new case today."

"Yeah? Can you tell me about it?"

"It's not anything exciting," Carly hastily told her with a shrug.

"They can't all be Perry Mason cases," Tee said easily. "Tell me."

"It's pro bono," she said. "That means we're not even getting paid for it."

"Does your firm handle a lot of those?"

"No. We only get them when the court assigns us one."

"And your firm gave it to you."

"Yes. Mr. Hardin called me into his office this morning and handed it off to me." She paused while their waitress took their order. "My new client is accused of operating a chop shop and selling stolen goods." She continued at Tee's nod. "I just got the file but it looks bad for him."

"What's his name?"

"I can't tell you any specifics. Sorry"

"I understand," she nodded. "You'll do great," Tee added with conviction.

"I don't know," Carly worried. "I've never tried a criminal case before.

"But you know the law," Tee said.

"Yes," she nodded and laughed when Tee just kept smiling at her. "I do know the law and I'm kind of looking forward to trying this case."

"There you go," Tee laughed with her. "You just keep thinking about your client and you'll be fine."

"I am thinking about him," she nodded and some of her worry eased a little. Their food came and talk went by the wayside while they ate. "The problem is, it's pretty evident my client is guilty," she said finally.

Tee swallowed and took a sip of her drink. "But he still needs someone to defend him."

"Yes, he does," she agreed. "And I'll defend him the best way I know how."

"Damn straight," Tee smiled across the table at her.

They finished lunch and Tee paid, adding a generous tip, before escorting Carly outside.

"Thanks for lunch, Tee. It was great."

"You're welcome." Tee put her hands in the front pockets of her pants because she wanted to take Carly's hand and knew she shouldn't. Not yet. "What are you doing with the rest of your day?"

"I'm going down to the jail and meet my new client right now." She grinned at Tee. "I probably shouldn't be so happy about that though, huh?"

Tee laughed. "Probably not." She did take Carly's hand then and squeezed it gently. "Will you call me later and let me know how it goes?"

Carly started to protest but saw she was serious and nodded. It made her feel good to know Tee was interested in her work. "I'll call you tonight."

"Before you go on your date," Tee said with just the barest hint of a smile.

Carly looked guilty for a moment but reiterated, "I'll call you tonight."

"I'm looking forward to it."

"I only have one question."

"What's that?"

"What's your number?"

Tee laughed out loud. "I'm sorry. Do you have a piece of paper and a pen in your bag?"

"Why don't I just put it in my phone?" Carly countered. She extracted her phone and asked, "What's your last name Tee?"

Tee hesitated for the briefest of moments before saying, "Reed." She waited until Carly had entered it and then gave her own cell phone number.

"Okay then, Ms Reed. I'll call you later."

"Thanks." Tee reluctantly let her go and walked in the opposite direction.

She spent the rest of the afternoon in her office going over reports and operation issues. It was the least enjoyable part of her job. She'd rather be in one of the bars mixing drinks and talking to her customers. Late in the afternoon, right as she was packing up to leave, her attorney called.

"Tee?" Her assistant's voice came over the intercom.

She sighed and her shoulders slumped. She'd almost made it out of the office. "Yeah, Jane?"

"Mr. Carrington is on line two."

"Okay, thanks." She reluctantly punched the button for line two and picked up the receiver. "Hello, Paul."

"Hey, Tee, I'm glad I caught you."

"Just barely," she said. "What's up?"

"I've got the contract for Tri-Star on my desk. So far it looks like a good deal."
"I'm still not sure about this, Paul. I know bars and restaurants. I don't know air lines."

"That's why you have me, Tee," he told her. "This is an investment only. Keep that in mind. You don't have to know how to run a charter airline."

"I'm just not used to owning such a big piece of a company that I don't manage."

"I know," he replied and she could hear him sigh. There was a smile in his voice though as he continued. "Trust me. I won't let you get into anything that isn't a solid investment."

"I do trust you, Paul," she said. "It's just something I'm not comfortable with…yet."

"That's why I'm calling. I'll definitely finish the papers this week so be ready to sign soon. Okay?"

"Yeah, okay."

He laughed. "Look at it this way, from now on you get to fly free. It's part of the deal."

"I'll try to keep that in mind," she laughed. "Have a good evening, Paul, and tell Wayne hello."

"I'll talk to you later in the week.

CHAPTER 4

Tee was using a hand sander on a piece of teak when her cell phone rang. She was renovating a building she owned just off Parry Street next to the Fire Fighters Museum in Dallas. Many of the older warehouses in the area had been empty for years but since the arrival of the DART rail system the area was becoming re-populated with new business. She bought the warehouse before the renewal and lived on the third floor while doing the remodeling herself. She liked working with her hands. It relaxed her to take a raw piece of lumber and make it into something of beauty that was also functional. Therefore, while she lived like a broke college student with only the bare essentials for the first year, she now had a beautiful home on the second floor. She'd hired out the electrical and the new plumbing but everything else she'd done herself. She installed tile floors, a wood burning fireplace, all new appliances, and a lighting and sound system that was on a level with any great club. She'd made her own bedroom furniture and her walk-in closet was resplendent with every imaginable convenience.

She put the sander down and dusted her hands on the front of her jeans before picking up her cell phone from the workbench.

"Hello?"

"Hi."

Tee smiled. It was Carly. "You called."

"I said I would," she chided her.

"Yes, you did." Tee leaned a hip against a sawhorse. "How did your visit to the jail go?"

"It's so noisy in there! I think that alone would keep me from committing a crime."

Tee laughed. "Yeah, but I don't think anybody in there thought about that."

"No, I guess not. I had a nice interview with my client though."

"Will he get out on bail?"

"He says his cousin is working on it."

"I wish you luck."

"Thanks."

"Listen, I really enjoyed our lunch today. Do you think I can talk you into dinner next time?"

"I enjoyed lunch too," Carly said and her voice was soft and silky now.

"May I take you to dinner then?" Tee asked just as softly. "Please?"

"I'd like that," Carly admitted. Tee's rich contralto voice, even on the phone, would have had her saying yes to almost anything.

"When?" Tee asked immediately.

Carly laughed, delighted. "I'm free Friday night."

"Friday night it is," Tee stated. Her heart rate was soaring at the prospect. "Where would you like to go?"

"Hmmm," she mused over the line. "I think you should just surprise me. That way I can get an idea of your tastes."

I'd like to taste you, Tee thought instantly and her body grew warm with the image. "I'll take you somewhere special then."

"It doesn't have to be special," she protested.

Tee smiled into her phone. "Maybe just some nachos and a few margaritas then."

"Oh, you are smooth," she laughed. "I'm going to have to keep my eye on you."

"Shall I pick you up at seven o'clock?" Tee sidestepped the comment. It wasn't the first time a woman had called her that.

"Seven would be fine."

"Great." Tee smiled into the phone. "I'll call you later this week. I don't think I can wait until Friday night to speak to you again."

"Uh huh," Carly said with amusement. "I'll talk to you later then."

"Okay. Goodnight Carly." Tee's voice was a caress across Carly's ear.

"Goodnight," she managed to croak out. Lord, this woman was making her hot with just her voice. What the hell would it be like to have her hands on her—again? Her mind replayed the dance they'd shared last weekend. She'd almost come in her jeans by the time it had ended. Tee Reed was one sexy woman. She couldn't wait until Friday.

CHAPTER 5

Carly absently picked up the phone on her desk and pressed it to her ear. It was an internal call so she wasn't surprised to hear her fellow attorney, Sharon Williams, on the other end.

"Hey, kiddo, are you free for lunch? Terri, Suzanne, and I are going down to Campo's."

"Yeah, that sounds good. When?"

"One o'clock?"

"Perfect. That will give me time to finish up a few things first."

Carly replaced the phone and continued to enter her notes into the case file on her computer. Luis Alvarez had claimed he was not the owner of the business, but had simply been carrying out the orders of his boss. She now knew he was telling the truth about not owning Beltwood Motors. She had spent the week tracking down the real owner. She had to wade through the corporate papers of one shell company after another until finally uncovering the man behind the curtain—Mr. Juan Torres. It gave her a thrill when she had unraveled the puzzle and was finally able to figure it all out. Mr. Torres owned a car wash, an express oil change business, and the used car lot where Luis worked. In each case there were several layers between him and the actual operations managers. He kept himself in the shadows and Carly knew it was a good way for him to claim no knowledge of the criminal activities being conducted on the premises. But she had him now. She had him in her sights and it was just a matter of time before she nailed him. She was smiling as she saved the case file. She was jazzed.

She met Terri and Sharon in the foyer at the elevators and Suzanne joined them just as the doors opened on their floor. While Terri and Sharon had been at the firm for over two years, Suzanne was the most senior of them all. Carly was the baby of the group and always welcomed any tips or tricks the others could share with her. Suzanne was a brunette like Carly but taller and she carried herself with the air of success and dignity that only came with experience. She gave them all a smile as she followed them into the elevator. Her eyes raked over Carly with barely concealed lust before she turned to face the doors as they closed.

"So, Carly, I hear you're about to wrap up that pro bono case. Mr. Hardin will be pleased." Suzanne gave her a smile as they were seated at the restaurant.

Carly took a sip of water to give herself a little time. She wanted to ask how she knew that. She wanted to tell her she had heard wrong. She wanted to tell her what she had discovered about the ghost owner, Mr. Torres. She did none of those things. She needed to keep the case to herself. She shrugged and smiled back at Suzanne.

"I hope he is pleased with my work."

"Getting a pro bono settled quickly pleases him," she nodded. If she noticed Carly's non-answer she gave no indication of it. She allowed her eyes to slide down to Carly's breasts quickly before turning her attention to the rest of the table.

Once back in the elevator of their building, Terri nudged Carly with an elbow. "So, how was lunch with that gorgeous blonde from last weekend?"

Carly knew she must be blushing. "It was good."

"And?" Sharon asked.

"And nothing," Carly smiled.

With the long hours they all worked, they eagerly shared in each other's lives, all except Suzanne. She was the oldest, the most conservative, and their acknowledged leader. They were all out to each other but their little group was a closed circle within the firm.

"Come on, tell us," Sharon demanded. "I haven't had a date in so long even your lunch sounds like a slice of erotica to me."

Carly's smile got bigger. "It was just lunch," she said.

"The look on your face says there's more," Terri laughed. "Spill it."

Suzanne turned to look at Carly and quirked an eyebrow. "You're seeing someone, Carly?"

"It was just lunch," she repeated.

"She met a woman in the bar last weekend," Sharon spoke up. "A very hot woman," she added.

Suzanne turned back to the elevator doors. "Be careful, Ms Matthews. You are judged by the company you keep. It's an old adage perhaps, but still true."

The elevator dinged and the doors slid open on their floor. Terri Dunn gave Carly a wink as Suzanne walked off in the opposite direction. "She's just jealous," she said.

"Of what? The fact that I had lunch with someone?" Carly snorted. "She could find a date any time she wants."

"Who, the attorney for the land of ice?" Terri shook her head. "I don't think so. Besides, it isn't your date she wants—it's you."

"Me? Are you insane?"

Terri laughed at her reaction. "Yes, you. She's been looking at you like a hungry lion lately. Tell me you haven't noticed."

"I haven't," she swore.

"Well, you'd better pay attention." Terri veered off toward her office. "You might just move up in this firm a lot quicker than you thought."

Carly could hear her laughter all the way back to her own office. She didn't know what to do with the thought that Suzanne might be interested in her. She respected Suzanne and her position within the firm but she had no romantic interest in her whatsoever. This might be a slippery slope she was on, she mused silently. If Suzanne was interested in her and made the fact known, she needed to be able to handle the situation in a way that neither encouraged nor embarrassed her. She wished Terri had just kept her big mouth shut. It wasn't until she'd logged back into the system that she saw she had an electronic version of the pink message slip. Tee had called. Her pulse quickened immediately as she dialed the number.

In her office Tee reached for her cell phone on the edge of her desk as it sang out the first notes of one of her favorite songs. She knew it was Carly because she had given that ringtone only to her numbers. She was smiling as she answered.

"Hello?"

"Hi. I just got back from lunch and my message center said you'd called."

"Yes. How was your lunch?"

Carly laughed into the receiver. "You didn't call to ask me that did you?"

"No," Tee admitted, "but I'm interested all the same."

"Lunch was fine," she said dismissively. "What else did you call for?"

"You're such a lawyer," Tee accused her with a laugh. "Cut right to the center—no chit chat."

Carly sighed audibly. "You're right. It must have something to do with being at my desk."

"Yes, it must." Tee was grinning like an idiot. "But I forgive you."

"How nice of you." She was sarcastic but there was playfulness in her tone.

"I'm a very nice person," Tee told her, "as you'll find out. I actually called to make sure you hadn't changed your mind about tonight."

"No, I haven't changed my mind."

"Good. I was so hoping you weren't going to rip my heart out already."

"You are so full of it," Carly told her. "I'm going to have to be on my guard tonight, aren't I?"

"Not at all. My intentions are honorable, I assure you."

"We'll see about that," she laughed. "What should I wear tonight?"

"I thought we'd go casual for our first date so jeans are fine."

"Great. Where are we going?"

"Do you like Mexican food?"

"Yes, I do."

"Do you like country western music?"

"Sure. I like most kinds of music actually."

"Okay, then we should have fun."

"Is that all you're going to tell me?"

"Yes."

"Not even a little hint?"

"You'll have fun," Tee assured her. "I'll pick you up at seven o'clock."

CHAPTER 6

Carly gave a start when the doorbell rang. She quickly gave her reflection one more check and hurried to answer it. She couldn't remember being this nervous before a date in a long time. Somehow, in a very short time, Tee had gotten to her like no woman ever had. She pulled the door open and hoped Tee couldn't see how her heart was racing. Tee wore black jeans, black boots, and a yellow shirt buttoned only at the bottom over a tight pale yellow wife beater. A sharp spear of heat shot through Carly making it impossible to swallow, speak, or even breathe for that matter. Tee smiled at her and suddenly everything was fine.

"Come in." She held the door open for her.

"Thanks."

"Can I get you something to drink?"

"I'd love one but, we're going to Ft. Worth so, I think we should probably get on the road."

"Ft. Worth?" Carly was captured by Tee's deep blue eyes. She fell into her gaze, unable to extract herself, until Tee broke the contact by looking away. She shook her head as if to disperse the last remnants of a spell she'd been under and expelled a breath she hadn't known she was holding. "Ft. Worth?" she asked again and wondered if she'd spoken out loud.

"Yes, Ft. Worth." Tee smiled at her again. "Trust me, you'll have a good time."

"Okay." It was all Carly could get out in her present state. This woman was so compelling Carly might follow her to the moon without question. Carly had on a tight white stretchy top over well-worn blue jeans and a pair of red Roper boots. Her skin quivered and jumped when Tee rested her hand on the small of her back as they walked to the truck. She felt the unreasonable need to have those fingers touch her absolutely everywhere.

Tee stole a look at her ass as they walked to the truck. "Are you hungry?"

"Starving," Carly admitted. "Where are we going?"

"Abuelo's."

"I've heard the food there is really good."

"And they make a hell of a margarita too." Tee looked over at her for just a second, needing to reinforce the connection she'd felt since the very beginning.

"Shall we have one then?"

"It might be disrespectful if we didn't," she laughed.

The trip across the Metroplex on I30 into Ft. Worth didn't take as much time as Tee had anticipated, or maybe it was just because Carly's presence next to her made time fly.

The restaurant was packed and they had to wait for a table at the bar where they indulged in their first margarita. They had another drink at their table and ordered as their server delivered the complimentary chips and salsa. Tee dug in, swiping a chip in the green salsa. She watched Carly use the red salsa and grinned.

"Have you ever tried the green?"

"No way. I've heard it's very hot."

"Come on, just a little bit," Tee urged. "Just put some on a chip and lick it off." She grinned as Carly flushed. "You are a wicked woman. We'll see about *that* later."

"Now who's wicked?" Carly countered. But she couldn't look at her now so resolutely dipped a chip into the green bowl of salsa.

Tee winced as Carly's tongue scooped up the salsa. She squeezed her legs together under the table and barely kept from groaning. *Oh, how this woman affected her*. She couldn't have torn her gaze from Carly's mouth if she had tried as she watched her tongue disappear.

A moment later Carly's mouth flew open again and she was fanning her tongue and reaching for her water glass. "Hot!" she gasped. Her eyes were tearing.

"Not the water," Tee said quickly and stopped her hand as it clutched the glass. "It will only make it worse. Drink your margarita."

Carly grabbed her drink and drained nearly half of it in one gulp. "Oh my God! That was hot!"

Tee laughed. "I only meant for you to take a little taste, that's all. You dove in like you knew what you were doing."

"Why didn't you stop me?" Carly used her napkin to wipe perspiration from her brow and opened her mouth again to fan at her tongue. It felt like it was on fire still.

"I was, uh, distracted," Tee told her.

"By what?" Carly demanded.

"I was looking at…your tongue."

Carly's head snapped up then and her eyes grew wide. "You were looking at my tongue?" she asked in disbelief.

"Uh, well, yeah." Tee grinned across the table at her. "I couldn't help it."

"You are unbelievable," Carly said crossly, but was secretly pleased she could do that to Tee. "I'm on a date with a guy after all."

TEE with Carly

"There's no need to insult me," Tee laughed. "Anyone with a pulse would have been distracted."

Carly tried to keep up the pretense of anger but found it impossible when Tee smiled at her. Tee put a hand over Carly's on the table and squeezed gently. "I have been so under your spell tonight that I completely forgot to tell you how gorgeous you look. I thought it though. When you opened your door I forgot my own name."

Carly rolled her eyes. "You had me there for a minute," she admitted.

"What? You *are* gorgeous." She squeezed her hand again and lowered her voice. "You have no idea what you do to me, Carly."

"Yeah, yeah," she brushed off the compliment and withdrew her hand. "Here comes our food."

When they could eat no more, Tee paid the check and they got back in the truck. "That was good," Carly groaned as she held her stomach. "I can't believe I ate so much."

"I know," Tee agreed. "Me too."

"Where are we going now?"

"I thought maybe we would swing by Billy Bob's and check it out. I think Gretchen Wilson is there tonight."

"You're kidding! Really? Have you got tickets?"

Tee smiled and nodded, pleased beyond measure at her excitement. "I do. Would you like to go?"

"Hell yeah!"

Tee took her hand as she drove toward the famous bar. It was the largest honky-tonk in the country since Gilley's burned down outside of Houston. It boasted an indoor rodeo arena, several large bars, dance floors, a gift shop, a game arcade, and the concert stage. Parking was a nightmare and Tee finally had to take a space in a pay lot where they had to walk several blocks to the entrance. She showed their tickets at the door and they were shown to prime seats in the concert area.

"Tee, these are great seats!" Carly gushed after they'd ordered drinks. "How did you manage to get them?"

"I know some people," Tee shrugged. In fact, she'd traded VIP passes to the Reed House for dinner for two, plus access to the second floor Private Club bar, and had thrown in a spa treatment to the female entertainment manager at Billy Bob's in exchange for their seats and drinks tonight. It was well worth it just to see the excitement on Carly's face.

The concert was absolutely fantastic, one of the best Tee had ever been to, and Carly loved every minute of it. Afterward they strolled through the cavernous building, stopping to watch the caricature artist doing quick sketches of patrons and then on into the arena to see the rodeo. It was just ending so they moved on to the gift shop. Before Tee could stop her Carly bought her a key ring with a miniature replica of bull balls that every red neck in the state of Texas had hanging from their truck hitches. Tee had to laugh when Carly presented them to her saying, "You do have balls now."

Tee gave her a quick hug and palmed them before cupping her crotch. "Oh yeah," she murmured as she made a thrusting motion with her hips.

Carly flushed and turned away as a bolt of heat shot through her. She knew she was playing with fire. She also knew she would get burned if she weren't careful. She didn't care.

"Would you like to go dancing?"

"Here?" Carly was shocked.

"No. I know a little bar just down the street."

Carly found herself nodding. "Yes, I'd love to go dancing."

They walked close as they left Billy Bob's and Tee steered Carly down the street with a hand on her back. It felt proprietary. The feeling applied to both of them.

"It's just down the block," Tee said. "It'll be easier to walk."

"This is fine," Carly assured her. Anything to keep Tee's hand on her body, she thought. "It feels good to breathe clean air for a minute anyway."

"This bar is just a hole in the wall so don't expect too much," Tee cautioned her. "If you don't like it we don't have to stay."

"It'll be fine," Carly told her.

The door to the club was black with no lettering or indication that there was anything behind it. Tee pushed it open and stepped inside. The bouncer nodded at Tee. She nodded back and pulled Carly after her. The bar was to their left with tables and booths along the back. The dance floor was on the right flanked by a dartboard and two pool tables. They were all busy and the clack of the balls hitting each other was muted by the music blaring from the jukebox. A few looked up as they entered but immediately went back to their games.

"If you stake out that booth back there I'll get us a drink," Tee suggested. She took a moment to watch Carly walk away before turning to the bar.

When she returned, Tee set the drinks on the table and leaned in to brush her lips against Carly's. "You are so beautiful," she whispered against her ear.

Carly grabbed her collar in both hands and pulled her back down for another kiss. "I've been waiting to do that all night," she admitted.

Tee grinned and took her hand. "Come dance with me." She led her to the floor and they inserted themselves into the edge of the crowd. Tee watched Carly's hips undulate in a sensual sway as she danced. It drove her crazy and she wasn't afraid to let her see the naked want in her eyes. She licked her lips and saw Carly suck in a sharp breath. She moved close enough to put a hand on her hip and knew with certainty that she would have this woman before the night was over. She slid a leg between Carly's and matched her rhythm. They moved together, grinding into each other, as Tee held her at the waist. She pulled their upper bodies together and felt Carly's hard nipples against hers. She thrust hard against her hip, her eyes glassy with need, her breathing matching the beat of the music. Tee ached to touch her, to taste her, to take her. She could feel her control slipping and knew if she didn't get some separation she'd be sorry. She wrapped her arms around Carly and stopped her movement completely.

"If you keep dancing like that I swear I will fuck you right here in this bar," she whispered harshly. She felt Carly tremble as she buried her face against her neck. She squeezed her eyes closed and forced herself to concentrate on breathing in and out slowly. When Tee felt she could walk, she took her hand and led her back to their booth. She was shaken by how close she had been to losing it. She had always had a healthy sex life and never wanted for female companionship. Women shared her bed willingly and they were mostly beautiful and sexy. None of them had the effect on her that Carly did. It was scary as hell. She took the opposite side of the table and exhaled a shaky breath. Without looking at Carly she drained half her beer in one long swallow. Still unable to look at her, she put a palm against her forehead and kept her eyes on the table. Her hand was shaking.

Carly could see this wasn't an act. It was real, raw emotion and not just designed to get into her pants. Her own hand was trembling as she picked up her drink. *Holy God, how can she do this to me? We haven't even gotten naked yet!* She swallowed with difficulty and let the bottle thunk back on the table. Tee was still not looking at her so she took her hand and laced their fingers together. She took a calming breath when she felt the returning squeeze. It was going to be all right.

TEE with Carly

Tee kept her eyes averted but leaned back against the seat with a sigh. She was in control again—kind of. She flicked a glance at Carly then away.

"I'm, uh, sorry," she managed to get out.

Sorry? Carly didn't want her to be sorry. She wanted her to do what she'd said. She wanted her to fuck her right now in this booth! She wanted to know what that kind of passion felt like. No one had ever wanted her like this. No woman had made her feel so desirable that they could lose control like that. She was a lawyer and she dated mostly other lawyers. By nature they were controlled and sedate. Nothing had prepared her for this wild need to be ravished. What the hell was happening to her?

"I, uh..." Carly didn't know what to say. She tightened her fingers in Tee's hand. "Tee." She leaned forward as she looked up. "Can we leave now?"

"Yes, of course." Tee slid out of the booth and waited for her.

Once outside Tee tentatively put a hand on Carly's back. Carly leaned against her and suddenly they were pressed against the side of the building, kissing and groping each other.

"Stop!" Tee gasped.

"God, Tee!" Carly groaned. "I don't want to stop."

"We have to." Tee pushed back from her. Her breathing sounded like she'd just finished a marathon. "Let's go." She held out a hand and Carly took it. "You might want to keep an eye out for traffic cops," she said as she increased her pace down the sidewalk. "I'm going to be speeding on the way back."

CHAPTER 7

Once inside Carly's apartment, Tee immediately pinned Carly against the door. Her mouth was hot and demanding as she kissed her. The kiss was rough and bruising with need, while her hands tore at her shirt, pushing it up to expose her flimsy lace bra. Tee sucked her way down her neck, nipping and kissing every inch of the way. She leaned back just enough to pull the top over Carly's head and flick the clasp on her bra. She impatiently swept the garments down her arms and flung them to the floor. With nothing between them, Tee captured her breasts, twisting and pulling at nipples that were already hard as rocks. She looked into Carly's eyes and saw the answering need, the hidden need, the need she never acknowledged. It sent a raging rush streaking through her.

She knew this was exactly what Carly was looking for, a woman to control her, to take her hard, and dominate her. Tee was that woman. She kissed her way down between her breasts, stopping to tug at the rim of her naval with her teeth as her hands tore the zipper free on her jeans. Carly's stomach muscles quivered and jumped beneath her lips.

"Get out of your boots," Tee demanded as she pushed her jeans over her hips.

"Tee," Carly panted. She was breathless, her hands fisted in Tee's hair. "I...can't stand..."

Tee stood and pinned her back against the door again. "Take. Off. Your. Boots," she repeated in a low growl. She felt her kick free of her footwear and Tee stooped once again and pushed both jeans and panties to the floor, inhaling her scent as she did. Carly was slumped against the door, mouth slack, eyes unfocused. Without a word Tee ran a hand up the inside of her leg and entered her. Carly gasped and her legs shook. Tee had known she was more than ready. She pumped in and out steadily as she held her upright and watched her eyes. When Carly got too close Tee abruptly pulled out.

Carly cried out in frustration and pushed against her. "Tee...please. I need..." She pulled at Tee's shirt to make her need known. She couldn't form a coherent sentence if her life depended on it right then.

Tee slapped her hands away and reached behind to lift her. Carly immediately wrapped her legs around her waist and her arms around her neck. Tee calmly walked them into the bedroom and dumped her onto the bed. They were both breathing hard. Keeping her eyes on Carly, Tee kicked out of her own boots and reached for the buttons on her shirt. Carly got to her knees to reach for the button on Tee's jeans. Tee threw her shirt off and looked down at Carly.

"Turn around."

"Tee..." It was a plea.

"Turn around," she growled. "On your hands and knees."

Carly's whole body shook when Tee rubbed the rough fabric of her jeans against her ass. She whimpered and felt Tee's hand land with a sharp slap on her ass. She yelped but didn't move. Carly was so wet it dripped down the inside of her leg and she was soon sobbing with frustration.

Tee unzipped her pants slowly, making sure Carly could hear it. She could see her quiver but she did not look back at her. Tee kicked out of her jeans and her underwear and stepped back to the edge of the bed where she bumped against her ass again. She bent over her back, her curls tight against her, and felt Carly jerk and groan.

"I'm going to fuck you now," she growled in her ear. "Are you ready?"

"Yes," she sobbed.

"Ask me, little one. Beg me." Tee rubbed her hands over her ass as she spoke.

"Please! Oh God, please, Tee. Fuck me!"

Tee held her steady with an arm around her waist and entered her from behind. Carly immediately moved into her, pushing back insistently and moaning her name. She pounded into her until she knew Carly was close to coming. Her entire body was tense and quivering with need. Tee dropped the hand from her waist and grazed her fingers over her clit. Carly exploded in a flash, screaming, shaking, and sobbing.

When Carly came to she vaguely wondered how long she'd been out of it. It could have been a few seconds or a week. She had no idea. She felt hands on her ass and groaned.

"No," she whimpered. She'd never survive another orgasm like the last one.

"Shhh," Tee shushed her softly. "It's all right. I've got you."

Carly realized then that the hands were soft and soothing, caressing. She was half on top of Tee, her head on her shoulder and one leg thrown over her. She melted against her and sighed heavily. *Jesus! Had she just passed out from having sex? That wasn't possible, was it? That was just in the movies*. The memory sent a hot flush through her. No one had ever taken her like that. So powerful, so dominate, so in tune with what her secret desire had been. How could she have known what Carly wanted after such a short amount of time?

"You are so beautiful," Tee murmured against her cheek. "I love touching you. Your skin is so soft." She ran a slow hand down her side to her hip and back up as Carly fell asleep.

When next she woke, Carly was once again coherent. Tee still held her, but they were now covered by the sheet and Tee was asleep. Carly shifted and placed a soft kiss against her neck and then another. God, this woman was incredible. She just wanted to devour her whole. She shifted even lower and placed the next kiss on her nipple. Tee drew in a long breath but remained asleep. Carly returned her attention to the breast beneath her. Why hadn't she noticed how perfect Tee's breasts were? They were on the smallish side but anything larger would be out of place. The areolas were a light brown and the nipples were very responsive. They were already puckered. She rubbed her thumb lightly over the other nipple as her tongue circled around the one beneath her mouth. Tee once again took in a deep breath and moved a bit. Carly smiled. She closed her mouth around as much breast as she could and sucked gently.

Tee moved under her. "That's nice," she sighed.

"Mmmm." Carly let the breast slip away and smiled up into Tee's deep blue eyes. "Yes, it is nice. Very nice."

"Were you planning on continuing?" Tee brought her hands up to curl her fingers into Carly's hair.

Carly flicked the nipple with a pointed tongue. "Well, maybe for a little while," she murmured. "I actually had plans to suck on something else soon."

Tee sucked in a breath as her stomach muscles quivered and her clit pulsed from the rush. "Oh man," she mumbled.

Carly pushed up and leaned in to kiss Tee. She thrust her tongue inside and Tee sucked it deep. In an instant they were both breathing fast and hard. Carly finally pulled away and kissed her on the neck before sliding back down her body. She kissed a trail between her breasts then across her stomach. Carly moved a hand over Tee's neatly trimmed pubic hair and Tee lifted her hips in response. She continued lower to touch her soft inner thigh. She heard Tee's frustrated groan above her. *Oh yeah*, Carly thought, *this is what I want to hear, this big strong butch aching for my touch*. She softly caressed the thigh and felt the muscles twitch beneath her palm. She shifted again and just then noticed the small rose tattoo on Tee's right hip. She leaned closer to get a better look. "Well, well," she muttered under her breath. "Who knew?" Tee moved restlessly under her. "It's perfect," she said loud enough for Tee to hear and promptly kissed the rose. When Tee moved her hips in supplication, Carly got the message.

She eased between Tee's thighs and inhaled her musky scent. She parted the folds slick with need and her own juices flowed in response. Tee's legs parted wide, offering herself. Carly stroked her length slowly several times before sliding over her clit. Tee was hard and Carly put a single finger on either side to stroke her. Tee immediately pushed against her but Carly took her hand away.

"Carly," Tee moaned. She put her hands in Carly's hair and tried to push her where she needed her.

"Patience," Carly told her. "Just for a little while." She returned to exploring and pushed into her with two fingers. She was grateful to hear Tee's groan and to feel her push down on her hand. "Oh yeah, honey. I like that. You feel so good. Do you like that?"

"Oh God, yes," Tee rasped out. "More."

"More? You mean like this?" Carly pumped in and out of her, increasing the pace with each stroke.

"Yes," Tee hissed. "Yes."

Carly continued to take Tee higher and higher with her hand until Tee was rigid and straining, her hips arched off the bed. She plunged into her once more and held her there before putting her mouth around her clit and sucking it hard. Tee went off like a rocket, gushing all over Carly's face. Carly sucked her dry while still buried deep inside her. When Tee finally lay boneless and limp on the bed, she raised her head and looked up at her. Tee's face was slack with satisfaction. Her eyes were closed and a small smile played on her lips. Carly eased out of her very slowly and got a soft moan from her. She rose above her and settled against her side, pulling her to her shoulder.

Tee rolled into her and slid a limp arm over her stomach.

"So good, babe," she mumbled. "So good."

Carly tightened her arms around her and kissed her cheek. She felt so full, so satisfied, so complete. It was like nothing she'd ever felt before with a woman. She wanted to keep her next to her and never let her go. She wanted this feeling to last forever. She reached behind her for a corner of the sheet and pulled it over them.

"Carly..." It was a drowsy voice, thick with emotion.

"Sleep, honey," she whispered in her ear. "Let's get some sleep."

Saturday Carly woke up to coffee and breakfast in bed. She would need the nourishment as the rest of the day was spent being sexually satisfied in every way imaginable until she finally begged for Tee to stop. She was weak and sore.

"Jesus, Tee," she moaned, "I can't come any more."

Tee lay on top of her, a position she had discovered Carly preferred. She liked weight on her and the feeling of being possessed, she knew. She fisted a hand in her hair and pulled her head back to expose her neck. She licked and kissed her throat but was careful not to leave a mark.

"You come so beautifully," Tee told her. "I get carried away." She kissed her shoulder. "I didn't hurt you, did I?"

"No," Carly quickly assured her. "If you haven't figured it out by now, I like it when you're rough with me."

"Yeah," Tee grinned. "I kinda figured that out."

Carly looked away as a flush crept up her face. "Yeah, you picked up on that pretty fast."

"Thank God," Tee replied. "I, uh, kind of like that myself. Being rough with you I mean."

"How convenient," Carly grinned.

"Yes," Tee agreed. She kissed her on the forehead. "Are you hungry?"

"Hungry?" Food hadn't entered her mind all day.

"Yeah. I could get you something to eat, you know, to build up your strength again."

Carly rolled her eyes and slapped Tee on the arm. "You have a one track mind. Are you sure you're not a guy?"

"Well now, you would know the answer to that," she laughed. She rolled off her and swung her legs over the side of the bed. "I do think food is a good idea though. What do you say to pizza? We could call and then have enough time for a shower before it gets here."

"That sounds good," she agreed and slid to the edge of the bed next to her. Tee's eyes were automatically drawn to her breasts but Carly stood quickly before she could touch her. "I'll call, you take a shower, okay?"

"Sure, but we could save water if we shower together."

Tee had such an innocent look on her face that Carly laughed. "Nice try but I don't trust you." She slipped into a silk robe and left the bedroom. She called in the pizza order and set two places at the kitchen table. She heard the shower but resolutely stayed in the kitchen and tried not to think about Tee standing naked under the water. Her body felt like it had been used and abused but it was an abuse she had long craved and now could not image doing without.

Tee appeared soon and Carly took her turn in the bathroom. By the time she was done the pizza had arrived and Tee was opening soft drinks for them. She looked up and smiled.

"You look delicious."

"Stop that," Carly admonished but couldn't quite keep the smile off her face.

CHAPTER 8

Carly was at her desk Monday when Terri Dunn peeked in her doorway. She looked up and smiled. "Hey, Terri."

"Hey." She came in and leaned a hip on the corner of her desk. "How was your date Friday night?"

Carly would like to have shrugged nonchalantly but couldn't keep the smile off her face. She suspected she was blushing as well.

"Wow. That good, huh?" Terri laughed. "Tell me all about it."

"It was fun."

"Come on, girl, spill it! You *have* to tell me about that gorgeous hunk of woman."

"Well, we had dinner at Abuelo's in Ft. Worth," she said. "Then we went to Billy Bob's and saw Gretchen Wilson in concert."

"Oh, I love her! Was she good?"

"She was great! And then after that we went to a little bar for a while."

"Boy, you packed a lot into a first date. Did you get a goodnight kiss?"

If you only knew, Carly thought. "Yes, there was kissing," she admitted out loud.

"Are you going to see her again?"

"I think so. She said she'd call this week."

"Well, I'm glad someone is getting some action around here."

"I'm glad it's me," she laughed.

Terri stood up and smoothed her suit jacket. "Suzanne will be upset if you're taken off the market."

"Don't even go there," Carly warned her. "You're crazy for even thinking that anyway."

"Uh huh." She moved to the door. "Want to do lunch with me and Sharon today?"

"Sure." Carly's mind was already focused back on her computer screen. "Let me know when."

She was entering data on her pro bono case when her phone rang. She absently picked it up and tucked it under her chin. "Matthews."

"Good morning, Ms Matthews." Tee's deep voice was like thick honey in her ear.

She quit typing and smiled. "Good morning."

"I miss you."

"I miss you too." Carly leaned back in her chair. "Why didn't you call me yesterday?"

"I didn't want to seem desperate or needy."

Carly laughed in delight. "I don't think anyone would ever accuse you of being either one of those."

"I'm only interested in what you think."

"Man, you are a sweet talker," she laughed.

"So, how is your day going?"

Carly told her she was very optimistic about her chances of getting her client's charges reduced. Since she couldn't violate client confidentiality she was forced to speak in generalities but her tone said it all.

Tee smiled into her phone as she listened to her. Her feet were propped up on the corner of her desk and she leaned comfortably back in her chair in her office. The papers covering her desk were forgotten.

"It sounds like you're on your way to a trial, huh?"

"Maybe."

"Can I come watch you in action?"

"Oh, I'll be so nervous!" she laughed.

"You'll do great," Tee assured her.

"I hope you're right."

"Listen, Carly, I have to go out of town this weekend. It's a family thing. But I would really like to see you again."

"I'd like to see you again too, Tee. Will you call me when you get back?"

"Yes Consider it a date."

"Good. I'll look forward to talking to you then."

Tee dropped her feet to the floor and tried to return to work. Her thoughts kept returning to Carly though and she found it hard to concentrate. She got a late morning call from Markie and Jane automatically put her through to her boss.

"So, give me details," Markie said after a quick greeting.

"Now you know I don't kiss and tell."

"Bullshit," she scoffed. "I remember you recounting several dates with Carol in excruciating detail."

"Yeah, that didn't turn out so well, did it?"

"You need to let that go, hon. Carol was a snooty rich bitch from the start, like I kept trying to tell you. You would not have lasted no matter what."

"Yeah, I know," Tee said automatically.

Markie knew it was a defining moment in Tee's life when her girlfriend at SMU, Carol Kingsley, had unceremoniously dumped her when she discovered Tee's family was not rich and she was on a scholastic scholarship. Tee then discovered Carol had been dating another woman the entire time they'd been together. For a long time after that Tee had questioned her own worth. If Markie hadn't been there constantly preaching to her she would probably have left school.

"Carol was the poster child for bitch behavior, Tee. You know that. Now tell me about your date with Ms Gorgeous and Sexy."

Tee laughed and let the past fade away. "It was great," she admitted. "We had fun at Billy Bob's and all that."

"Was there kissing?" Markie cut to the chase.

"Oh yeah," Tee sighed. "There was definitely kissing. A lot of kissing."

"Ooo, tell me more," she urged. "What else?"

"There was…everything else."

"Oh my God, Tee! It was your first real date!"

"I know," she laughed. "It was incredible, Marks."

"Wow," Markie said softly.

"I know," Tee admitted. "She's…she just does something to me."

She sounded helpless and Markie knew this was not just another woman to date. This was something special to Tee. "I take it the sex was good then?"

"Oh yeah. I didn't get home until Saturday night, or I should say Sunday morning."

"What a dog you've turned into!" Markie cried. "Look, I've got a customer coming in so I'll talk to you later. I still need details!" She hung up.

Tee hung up and had to force herself back to work. There were reports that needed to be read and expenditures to be approved. And there were still details about the Tri-Star Charter deal she needed to review. In addition, there was a bar down in San Antonio she was interested in buying. That alone required a lot of research and inquiries as she completed her due diligence.

CHAPTER 9

"Tee?"

Tee's hand automatically reached for the intercom on her phone. "Yeah Jane?"

"Paul Carrington is on line two."

"Okay, thanks." She pushed the button and lifted the receiver. "Hello Paul."

"Good morning, Tee."

"What's up?"

"I just wanted to let you know where we're at in the Janet Sutherland case."

Tee's jaw clenched immediately, in anger. "Yes?" She barely managed to get out.

"We're at an impasse, Tee. I'm afraid it's her word against yours."

"Paul, you can ask anyone! I never did anything to her!"

"Tee, I believe you," he told her sincerely. "I know you would never do anything to an employee, or anyone else for that matter. It's ridiculous."

"But?" she asked, knowing he wasn't finished.

"But, she insists you tried to touch her inappropriately and also made suggestive comments about her, uh, breasts."

"That's fucking insane!" she roared.

"Tee, please," he begged her.

"Damn it, Paul!" Tee said before she could rein in her emotions. She stopped to take in a deep breath and let it out slowly. "I'm sorry," she continued in a more subdued tone. "I don't mean to yell at you. I know it's not your fault."

"It's okay, Tee. I know this is hard on you. Unfortunately, it's become a common cost of being in business. You become a target for these kinds of people. And because Ms Sutherland is straight, there will be sympathy on her side automatically. That is if we go to trial."

Tee sighed and fought to control her anger. "What's the bottom line here?"

"I think it's best if we can come to an agreement."

"You want me to pay her off?" Tee knew she shouldn't be shocked but was anyway.

"I do," he said, knowing Tee did not want to hear this solution. "I think it's too big a chance if we go to trial." He paused but Tee remained silent. "She's cute, has a nice figure, and a kid at home. Granted, she has large breasts, but that will only work against you, not her."

"Jesus, Paul! She came to me begging for a bartending job. Her boyfriend split on her and she had the baby to support all by herself. I thought I was doing her a favor."

"Why do you think she came to your bar? Did she know it was a gay bar?"

"Yes! She said she had tended bar before and was tired of getting hit on all the time at her previous job."

"Great. That'll really help our cause," sarcastically replied. "Tee, I can't see us winning this in court. There just isn't any evidence you can show that would prove her wrong."

"Fuck! Paul, there is never any evidence to prove you *didn't* do something!"

"I know it sucks, Tee. It's up to you. If you want to fight this, we will."

"I don't know, Paul," she sighed. She swept a hand through her hair in frustration. "Let me think about it."

"Sure," he was quick to assure her. "Just don't take too long. I have a feeling she isn't a patient person."

"Yeah, okay." Tee sighed again. "I'll call you, Paul."

"Okay. I'll talk to you later."

Tee hung up and shoved to her feet. She was agitated and needed to move.

Carly glanced at the clock again. She was anxious for her lunch date with Tee. She shook her head in exasperation at herself. They'd had lunch almost every day and yet her heart rate still kicked up when they were scheduled to meet. She was hopeless, she thought. She felt like a schoolgirl with her first crush. But no matter how ridiculous she thought herself to be, she still looked at the clock every five minutes until it was time to leave.

She fairly flew down the escalator to the tunnel and strode down the center aisle with determined steps until she got to the shipping kiosk. Tee was leaning against the counter, watching her. Carly knew she had a silly grin on her face but was helpless to stop it. Tee smiled back and she felt warmth infuse her. She put a deliberate sway into the last few steps.

"Hi." She pulled her hair behind her ear in an unconscious gesture.

"Hi," Tee answered, her smile getting bigger.

"What are you doing down here?"

"I guess I was a little early," she admitted. "So I came to meet you."

"I'm glad you did," she smiled. "What would you like to eat today?"

"You," Tee whispered in her ear. "And if I can't have that, then I don't care."

Carly didn't trust herself to look at her now and put a hand up to her face. She could feel the heat in her cheeks. Tee's words had the same effect as if she'd touched her intimately. "You shouldn't say things like that in public," she admonished.

"My mother taught me to tell the truth," she replied with a soft smile.

"You're incorrigible," Carly laughed.

They ate lunch at a deli and shared a bag of chips. Carly laughed at Tee's teasing and playful leering as she tried to sneak a peek down her blouse. "I'm afraid I need o get back," she sighed after a glance at her watch.

"Would it be okay if I walked you back through the tunnel?" Tee asked. "I wouldn't want you to get accosted."

"Accosted?"

Tee nodded with a grin. "Accosted. Someone as beautiful as you should be careful. You never know what sort of wolves are lurking down there."

Carly laughed so hard she nearly snorted the last of her tea through her nose. "You're a nut," she managed to get out.

"But you like nuts, right?" Tee gave her a dopey puppy dog look.

"Yes," she giggled. "I like nuts. Now, come on and walk me home like the good butch you are."

When she returned to her desk there was a message to call Mr. Hardin's office. She quickly dialed and got Mrs. Nolan.

"Mr. Hardin would like the paperwork on the Alvarez case so he can close the file."

"Um, I don't have the final paperwork," Carly said. "The case hasn't been closed yet."

"Mr. Hardin was under the impression you were pleading him out, in which case it should have been completed by now." Her tone conveyed all the displeasure of her boss.

Carly swallowed with difficulty but forged ahead. "I am sorry, Mrs. Nolan. I don't know how Mr. Hardin got the idea I was going to plead him out."

"Then am I to assume you are not?"

"No, I am not. I'm going to get the charges against him reduced."

There was a lengthy silence. "Mr. Hardin will be in touch." The phone went dead.

Carly let out a breath and hung up. Why would Mr. Hardin think she would plead her case out? Billing, she immediately thought. They weren't getting paid for her time. She needed to wrap this up quickly. She was certain the judge at the very least, would postpone the trial while the police investigated the situation.

Carly was updating her case file when her phone rang. "Matthews."

"Ms Matthews, do you have a moment?"

"Certainly, Mr. Hardin."

"Would you please come up to my office? And bring the Alvarez file with you. I'd be interested in taking a look at it."

"I'll be right there, sir." She took a minute to calm herself. Her boss wanted the case done. He would be please to see she'd gone the extra mile and exposed the truth. All she had to do was explain the situation to him. She was confident by the time the elevator deposited her on the eighth floor. Mrs. Nolan sniffed when she appeared in her office.

"He called me," Carly defended herself automatically.

Mrs. Nolan picked up the phone and announced her. "Go on in," she said stiffly and turned away.

Carly closed the door behind her and waited for him to look up. He laid his pen down and stood. "Let's sit over here." He gestured toward the sitting area where they'd sat on her previous visit. "Would you care for some coffee?"

"No thank you, sir."

"Well then, let's get down to business. Can I see the Alvarez file please?"

"Sir, I was informed that you thought I was going to plead out Mr. Alvarez."

"Yes, I assumed you would since it was such a clear cut case. What's holding it up?" If he was displeased she hadn't brought the file he didn't show it.

"Mr. Alvarez is being unfairly charged as being the owner of the business."

"Why unfairly?"

"He is simply the manager of the business. The real owner has set this business up for him to take the fall in case the illegal operation was discovered. I've uncovered how he set it up plus the number of times he's previously been arrested for this very thing. Mr. Alvarez is guilty of doing what his boss told him to do. He was trying to keep his job so he could put food on his family's table."

Mr. Hardin sat silently for a moment. "Let me make sure I understand. You want to argue that Mr. Alvarez was only following orders and not to blame for selling stolen goods?"

"Not exactly, sir." Carly wondered if she were being tested. "While Mr. Alvarez is guilty of doing the actual selling of stolen goods, the police should be looking at the actual owner who is in charge of the whole operation."

"Ms Matthews, may I remind you this is a pro bono case."

"I know sir, but Mr. Alvarez is getting a raw deal here."

Mr. Hardin stood. "Ms Matthews, I want you to get this case settled. I want you to plead Mr. Alvarez out. He was caught selling stolen goods. He's guilty as charged. We are not the police and we are not investigators. Do I make myself clear?"

Carly stood with him, now rigid with anger. "Yes sir."

"Good." He walked to the door and held it open. "Think about your career here Ms Matthews."

She left his office and didn't even bother to look at Mrs. Nolan. She was in shock as she rode the elevator down to her floor. When she got to her office she sat in front of her computer and went still. The ringing of the phone snapped her out of the spell she'd been under. She had no idea how long she'd sat there. She regarded the phone with ambivalence. She had no interest in talking to anyone. After a bit her message center pinged indicating she had a message. She finally clicked on it intending on deleting it until she saw it was from Tee. It was exactly what she needed. She grabbed her cell phone and left her office. This was a conversation she wanted to have outside of the building. She looked neither left nor right as she pushed through the revolving door to the street. Once outside she slowed her pace and opened her phone. In less than a minute she had Tee on the line.

"Hello, gorgeous."

"Hi Tee."

"What's wrong?"

Carly swallowed around the lump in her throat before saying, "Nothing."

Tee's voice softened. "Come on, I can tell something is bothering you. Tell me about it."

"Tee, I didn't call to cry on your shoulder," she protested.

"Just tell me," Tee insisted gently.

Carly started walking and talking. She told her everything about how the firm viewed the case and how she felt betrayed. "I know we're not getting paid," she concluded, "but it's not like they're hurting for money."

"They've gotten too big," Tee offered. "They've forgotten about actually being lawyers."

"But what about my client? He's the one that will suffer."

"That's the real crime," Tee agreed.

"Thanks for listening, Tee. I guess I should get back to my desk."

"What are you going to do?"

Carly sighed. "I don't know." She fell silent and Tee just let her think. "I'm getting the feeling that my future growth in the firm is tied to this decision."

"That's brutal," Tee remarked. "Do you really think they'd forget about everything else you've done just because you want to defend a pro bono case? That's insane."

"Yeah, but you don't know how it is in a firm like this one. It's very competitive and anything you do against the norm is duly noted. Even if it didn't hurt me right now, it might come back to haunt me later on."

Tee was astounded. "You're kidding me! Why are these people in business? Shouldn't a lawyer's first concern be the client?"

"You'd think so, wouldn't you?"

"Well, you have to do what you have to do," Tee consoled her. "You need to do what you think is right."

"That's easier said than done."

"Just follow your heart," Tee said softly. "Your heart won't let you down."

"Thanks Tee." Carly pushed through the door to her building and walked briskly to the bank of elevators. "I'm glad I got to talk to you."

Chapter 10

Tee concentrated on taking deep breaths, trying to keep calm. She had acquiesced to Paul's recommendation to settle the lawsuit from Janet Sutherland, but she insisted on a face to face meeting first. She wanted to look Janet in the eye before she wrote the check.

Paul arrived at her office just before she could explode from the tension. She followed him down to his car and they rode in silence up to Elm Street where Paul parked in the underground parking garage.

"Tee, I have to tell you, I don't think this is a good idea. In fact, I'm surprised her attorney agreed to it."

"Paul, I just want that bitch to have to look me in the face while she fucks me over. I don't want this to be easy for her."

"Just don't say anything that I'll have to bail you out of jail for, okay?"

"No promises," she huffed.

She had her first surprise when they exited the elevator. The glass door was etched with *Brown, Hardin & Simon, Attorneys At Law*. This was the firm where Carly worked.

Maybe after this meeting was over she could find her. Talking with her always helped.

Paul spoke to the receptionist and soon a woman came to escort them to a conference room. Tee tried to maintain her calm demeanor by continued deep breaths. The checkbook protruding from the back pocket of her black jeans mocked her. She would be giving a check to a woman she had trusted for something she didn't do. She realized she was clenching her jaw again and forced herself to relax.

Their escort inquired if they'd like coffee and departed when they both declined. Everything about the room screamed of money and Tee wondered how her ex-bartender could afford to hire them until she realized she would be footing the bill for that as well.

"Try to stay calm," Paul said quietly.

She blew out a deep breath and sat next to him. "I'm trying," she murmured.

They waited only a scant minute before she got her second surprise of the day. The conference door opened and Janet Sutherland entered the room. Paul politely stood up.

Chapter 11

Carly answered her phone while continuing to read some research on her computer screen. "Matthews."

"Carly, this is Tom Meyer. I need your help."

Carly was momentarily confused. She barely knew Tom and he was in litigation while she worked mainly in corporate filings. It was why she had been so excited about handling the pro bono case—it was litigation. "Hello, Tom. What can I do for you?"

"I need someone to stand in for me today. It's just the formality of signing off on a deal that's already been agreed upon," he rushed on before she could question him. "Sexual harassment case. I just need you to baby-sit the settlement signing."

"Well…I guess I can do that."

"Thank you! I'm on my way to the hospital now."

"The hospital? Is everything okay?"

"We're having a baby!"

"Great!" Carly laughed but the line was already dead in her hand. She called over to Tom's office and got his assistant on the line. She explained the situation and Carly assured her she'd be there in time to meet the client before the meeting. Piece of cake, she thought. All she had to do was sign off on the paperwork and collect their fee. She didn't think anything of it until she was handed the file and shook hands with their client.

"Hello, Ms Sutherland, I'm Carly Matthews. I'll be sitting in for Mr. Meyer today." She smiled at Janet. "He's having a baby at the moment."

"Oh, that's great!" Janet smiled.

"So, let's see what we have here." Carly opened the file and shuffled through the papers. She sucked in a quick breath when she saw just whom Janet was suing. No, this couldn't be right. She looked up with a frown. "You're suing...Ms Reed?" She'd almost called her Tee.

"Yes."

"It says here she touched you and made sexually explicit comments."

"Yes."

Carly remained silent as she absorbed these facts. Tee had sexually harassed an employee? She was having a hard time wrapping her head around this. She was unaware her hands were trembling as she held the file. "And she's agreed to the settlement?"

"Yes."

Carly finally looked up. The client was answering in monosyllables, a sure sign of something hidden. But what? She couldn't interrogate their client. It would be bad form indeed. "Well, it looks like everything is in order, so let's go get the papers signed." She'd have to think about what this meant later, when she was alone. She led the way down to the conference room and held the door for her. She put her professional smile on as she saw Paul stand up. It quickly faded when her client moved away and she saw Tee sitting beside him. It was extremely rare for the accused to be at this meeting and she was definitely not prepared to face her right now. The question of why Tom Meyer had agreed to it flitted across her mind but, with

Tee facing her, she had no time to dwell on it. She thought the shock on Tee's face was probably a mirror of her own. They stared at each other for long seconds until Carly remembered her job.

"Mr. Carrington, I'm Ms Matthews and I'm sitting in for Mr. Meyer, who's having a baby." Paul shook her hand and when she glanced at Tee she saw her staring murderously at Janet Sutherland. "Let's get this deal done, shall we?" she said and wondered if her voice sounded as strained as she thought it was.

"I'd like to ask your client something first," Tee spoke up.

"I don't think that's…"

"How can you do this, Janet?" Tee interrupted her as if she hadn't spoken. "You know I didn't do anything to you!" Her voice rose in spite of the hand Paul laid on her arm.

Carly leaned forward and placed her own hand on Janet's arm to keep her from responding even though she was staring at the tabletop. "This is not the time…" she began again.

"You can't even look at me and yet you accuse me of something like this? Are you kidding me? This is a total farce! Why the hell would I come on to you?"

"Mr. Carrington, your client…"

"Tee, please…"

"You begged me for a job! Remember that?" Tee stood abruptly and everyone tensed up.

"Mr. Carrington…" Carly implored him.

"Tee, sit down."

"You begged me for a job so you could feed your baby. You said the father left you both. Do you remember that? Or was that a lie too? Do you even have a baby?"

"Ms Reed." Carly stood. "That's enough!"

Tee paused long enough to give her a look that said she'd remember Carly's part in this. "Is the whole story a lie? Because this lawsuit is a lie and you know it! Did you think I'd just meekly hand over this amount of money without a word of protest? Do I look that stupid?"

Paul stood and put a hand around Tee's arm. "Tee, please stop."

"Mr. Carrington!" Carly's voice rose to be heard over Tee's. "Please remove your client from this room at once!"

Tee snapped her head around to glare at Carly. "I need to leave?" She spit at her in shock. "Your lying client should be the one leaving!"

"Maybe you should have kept your hands to yourself if that's the way you feel!" Carly wanted to bite her tongue off the second the words left her mouth.

Tee's mouth hung open as she looked at Carly. There were long seconds where only the sound of a ticking clock disturbed the silence. At last Tee threw her checkbook on the table in front of Paul but her eyes never left Carly's. "Pay the bitch off. It seems my innocence and the truth are secondary to what everyone wants." She turned and opened the door. "I'll find my own way back, Paul."

"I'm sorry," Paul said when the door closed behind her. "I thought she would control herself better."

She probably would have if I hadn't been here, Carly thought. "Let's just finish this," she said to cover her own distress. Her heart was thudding against her ribcage. She had to shuffle through the papers twice before she located the proper document in the folder. She slid it across to Paul. "Just sign here and we're done." The words were said by rote, her thoughts still on the look on Tee's face when she'd left.

She already had the check made out and signed Paul noted when he opened the checkbook. He scribbled his signature on the proper line of the document and passed the check across the table. He took note that Janet Southland had not engaged in any defense or even looked at Tee throughout her tirade. She still sat with her head down. He knew it was a good indication of guilt. Not that he had any doubts of Tee's innocence, but it was good to see some validation. "I'll make a copy of this and be right back." Carly left and Paul and Janet sat in silence until she returned.

"Here's your copy, Mr. Carrington." Carly handed him the copied paperwork in a plain folder and he put it in his briefcase. "I hope this served to show you why we don't allow the two opposing parties to meet once a settlement has been reached," she told him.

"I know exactly why we don't allow it," he told her with an edge to his voice. "But you don't know my client and, from what I've observed, you don't know yours either." He picked up his briefcase and headed for the door. "I hope your client can sleep tonight."

Chapter 12

Tee stalked out of the building, anger fueling her pace as she strode down the sidewalk. She slowed after a mile or so. There was a coffee shop on the next corner and she took a spot in line. Once served, she took her large coffee to a corner table facing the street and sat down to watch the traffic and think. She wasn't sure what she was feeling yet. Her mind had blanked it all out while she walked, unwilling and unable to deal with it yet. It was unreal. She knew Janet was getting free money, but she didn't know if it was her idea or if someone else was behind it. Not that it should matter, but it did. She didn't want to admit she had misjudged Janet so badly. She spent some time thinking it through and, in the end, just couldn't be sure whether Janet or someone else was behind the quick money scheme. She needed to put the word out to the other bar owners in the area not to hire her. She would appreciate it if someone warned her of a similar situation so she could protect herself.

On to the more serious problem, she thought. When she finally allowed herself to think about Carly her stomach clenched and she closed her eyes against the onslaught of pain. Did she actually think Tee was capable of making unwanted advances to Janet Southerland? How could she? What did that say about her? What did it say about Carly? She got another cup of coffee and watched traffic for another hour, but no matter how long she stayed there she couldn't change what Carly had said. '*Maybe you should have kept your hands to yourself'* kept running through her head. That's what Carly had flung at her. It could only mean Carly thought her guilty. And why shouldn't she? Tee was settling out of court for a goodly amount of money. Isn't that what guilty people did? Still, Carly should know her better than that. They'd shared more than just their bodies with each other, hadn't they? *Shit!* Tee crushed the paper cup and threw it away in disgust. What the hell had she been thinking? Had she actually thought Carly would defend her? She was a lawyer. She suddenly realized Carly didn't know her at all. She should have known better. Her life had been going way too great lately. She left the coffee shop and walked down to the Stoneleigh Hotel where she got a cab back to her own office in the Reed House on lower Greenville Avenue.

When Jane saw Tee enter the outer office she looked anxiously up at her. Paul Carrington had called her after he left the law offices and told her what had happened. He made her promise to treat Tee carefully. But the slumped shoulders and weary look in Tee's eyes made Jane's heart go out to her. There was no fight left in her.

"Hey Tee," she said softly. "I heard what happened. Are you okay?"

"Yeah, I'm fine," she answered without looking at her. She continued past Jane's desk toward her own office.

"Can I get you anything? A cup of coffee?"

"No thanks, I'm fine." She went into her office and closed the door, indicating she wanted solitude.

Chapter 13

Carly pressed Tee's number into her cell phone as soon as she could get a free moment at her desk. Unsurprisingly it went to voice mail. She worried about what to say to make her understand her position. "I'm sorry, Tee…I didn't know…I wouldn't have...God, I'm so sorry…Please call me…" The beep indicated she was out of time and she reluctantly hung up. God, what a screwed up day this was turning out to be. She leaned back in her desk chair and sighed. What the hell had happened between Janet Southerland and Tee? She didn't think Tee was the sort of woman who would sexually harass anyone but something had happened to make this woman file a lawsuit. After all, people didn't just up and decide to sue someone for no reason. Not Tee, she shook her head. Not the Tee she knew. Could she have misjudged her that badly? She tiredly rubbed her forehead. She was getting a headache to rival all others and her neck was already stiff from tension. Before she could decide what else she could do her phone rang. She needed to go to the courthouse on Young Street to file papers on another case of Tom's. At least this case was merely a paperwork deal, she thought as she went back to Tom's office to retrieve the file before heading back out of the building.

"Markie, I don't really want to talk about it," Tee said again. She was still in her office even though it was after office hours. Everybody else was long gone but she just couldn't gather up enough energy to make the effort to leave. Markie called wanting to know about the lawsuit.

"Tee," Markie's voice held a note of warning that not many could use with her. "Just tell me what happened. Please," she added.

And Tee finally did, trying not to let her know how Carly's words had ripped her heart out. She was good at hiding her feelings but her best friend was the one who could read her moods even over the phone. "So now I know what Carly really thinks of me," she concluded, trying hard to cover her heartache.

"I'm sorry, Tee. Have you tried to call her and see what she says? I mean, Janet was the client and all."

"No. She called and left a message that was full of 'sorry' and 'I didn't know', shit like that. But I can't get over what she said about keeping my hands to myself. That came out when she wasn't thinking."

"You need to talk to her about it, Tee," Markie insisted. "Keeping it all inside is not healthy. You'll stew about it until you turn it into something worse than it is."

Tee's expelled breath came clearly over the phone. "Maybe," she allowed. "But I know what I heard and no amount of explanation is going to make those words disappear."

Chapter 14

Tee absently pushed the intercom on her desk phone. "Jane?"

"Yes, Tee?"

"Where am I staying in Chicago?"

"I've booked you into a suite at the Drake Hotel. Your flight information is in the packet I sent you along with your reservation number at the hotel."

Tee searched among the scattered papers on the desk until she located the folder. "I found it. Thanks, Jane. What would I do without you?"

"You'd take care of the details yourself," she laughed and disconnected.

Tee was on her way to the graduation of her niece, Jorja Reed, from the Booth School of Business at the University of Chicago. Jorja was the oldest child of her brother, William, and his wife, Amanda. They hadn't been close since she'd come out to her family after their father died. But his wife liked her and they allowed her access to the children who adored her. They had two other girls aged eight and ten. Tee hoped the girls would be able to spend time with her other than at the graduation ceremony.

The minute Tee checked into the Drake hotel she put in a call to Jorja. "Hey Sweetie. How's the new graduate?"

"Aunt Tee! You're here!"

Tee grinned into the phone. "Yep. I'm at the Drake."

"Mom and Dad got in a couple of hours ago."

"I'll be right there with them in the front row," she promised. "I'm going to head over to the University now so I can meet up with them."

"I'm so glad you came!" she cried excitedly. "I'll meet everyone at the auditorium, okay?"

"Okay, sweetie. I'll see you soon."

She and Bill gave each other a quick hug in greeting while Amanda gave her a real hug, patting her on the back before she released her with a smile. "Tee, it's good to see you. You look great."

"Aunt Tee! Aunt Tee!" Both of the girls squealed in unison, clamoring for her attention. They grabbed her hands and pulled her away from their parents.

She bent and enveloped both of them in a giant hug, squeezing them until they laughingly begged her to release them. "Who are you?" she demanded with a frown. "What have you done with my cute little nieces?"

"It's us, Auntie!" they laughed at her.

She gave each of them a loud, smaking kiss on their cheeks, grateful they still allowed her to act silly with them. Soon they would be too old for such nonsense. "When did you get so big?" she questioned them with wide eyes.

"You were at our birthday party!" they reminded her with giggles.

"So I was," she admitted. "Well then, when did you get to be such beautiful girls? Your mother didn't tell me she raising beauty queens."

"Oh, Auntie Tee," the older one, Hannah, said with a big grin. "You're so funny."

"Yeah, Auntie. You're so funny," the younger sister, Lisa, mimicked.

"Let's go inside," Tee suggested. "We need to get a real good seat so we can all see Jorja get her diploma."

Both girls took a hand and they followed their mom and dad inside the auditorium, pulling Tee along with them. They all found seats in the fifth row and the girls insisted on sitting on either side of Tee.

The ceremony was full of pomp and glory and when Jorja strode across the stage to receive her diploma, the family erupted in proud enthusiasm. All in all it took over two hours for all the speeches to conclude and the sisters were fidgeting by the time it ended. They waited just outside the door until Jorja was done talking to her friends and their families. She wore a huge smile as she hugged each of them.

"Congratulations honey," Tee whispered in her ear when it was her turn.

"Thanks, Aunt Tee," she whispered back.

"Where's the party?" Tee asked as they parted. Jorja flicked a glance at her parents. "Come on," Tee continued. "I graduated once upon a time and there were parties everywhere!"

"It's okay, honey," Susan said with a smile. "We know you want to celebrate with your friends."

"I want to have dinner with you guys first though," she hastened to say. "Okay?"

"That's great," her father assured her. "Where should we go? What's your favorite place?"

"Bob's has great food," she answered quickly. "But I can't usually afford it. Can we go there?"

"Absolutely," he nodded with a smile. "Let's go."

Carly was nervous as she took a cab from O'Hare International Airport to Chicago's northern suburb of

Streamwood. Kim's house was a narrow older wood frame with a detached garage at the end of a gravel driveway. There was a car parked in the drive as the cab deposited her curbside. She took a deep breath and shouldered her bag. The door opened before she reached it and Denise smiled at her.

"Hello, Denise."

"Hi, Carly. I'm so glad you could come this weekend."

"How is Kim?" Carly set her bag down just inside the door.

"Kim is just fine," Kim announced as she came into the room with a big smile on her face. She strode across the room toward them and hugged Carly tight. "You look great, Carly!"

"Thanks," she answered. "You look great too." She knew she was holding herself tightly in anticipation of an eruption of anger but she couldn't help it. She looked into Kim's eyes and was relieved to see them clear and calm. "I'm glad to be here."

"You can put your bag in the guest room," Denise said. "Kim and I have lunch started so come on in the kitchen when you're ready."

Throughout the day Carly was pleasantly surprised at how normal Kim was acting. It was obvious she was taking her meds and she was grateful. The three of them had a nice time catching up with news of old friends. It was such a nice visit that Carly wasn't even nervous when Denise announced she was leaving to go home.

"Let's go out tonight," Kim said when Denise had driven off. "We could go downtown to the Liquid Lounge. You know, the one that used to be called the Lost and Found."

"I don't know," Carly hesitated.

"Come on, Carly, please?" She took Carly's arm and squeezed lightly. "We'll have fun. We used to have so much fun. Remember? We used to dance all night. I remember you were a great dancer."

Against her better judgment Carly acquiesced, justifying that Kim was on her meds and stable enough. Then tomorrow she would board her flight back to Dallas.

It was still early but the Liquid Lounge was hopping. Kim led Carly inside, pulling her along behind her as they threaded their way through the crowd to a small table along the side wall. "Wow, this place is great!" Kim yelled when they had given the waitress their order.

Carly thought she detected a bit of manic in her tone and tried to look at her eyes. She could often tell what was going on under the surface by the look in her eyes. But it was dark and she wasn't sure if there was anything there or if she was just being paranoid. They had a few drinks and danced. And it was like old times again. Carly relaxed as she and Kim laughed and joked like they used to. She was enjoying the evening and it was a pleasant surprise.

Chapter 15

Tee entered the nightclub alone and quickly garnered the attention of more than one beautiful woman. She ignored the subtle and not-so-subtle flirtations. None of these women could possibly measure up to the last woman she had been with. Carly. Just the thought of her name made Tee tingle, but it was quickly followed by sadness at her loss. She'd never had a woman affect her the way Carly did. She got a drink and made her way around the room, checking out the design and layout, mentally comparing it to her own bar back in Dallas. It was much better if she kept her mind busy and off Carly. She was just cruising the dance floor when her heart rate kicked up at the sight of a dark-haired beauty. She reminded her of Carly. She shook her head. She missed her so much she was imagining her everywhere. Nevertheless, she made her way through the crowd toward her. As she neared the table the woman looked up and recognition mixed in with shock. It *was* Carly!

"Oh my God! Tee?" Carly's mouth hung open in shock. "What are you doing here?"

"A family thing," she answered, her mind frozen in shock. "What are you doing in Chicago?" Before Carly could answer Tee was pulled roughly back by a pair of strong hands.

"What the fuck do you think you're doing!" The voice was a screech in Tee's ears as she fought to stay on her feet. "Don't touch her! Get away from her!"

Tee finally regained her balance and she swiveled her eyes to her assailant. For such a slim woman she showed considerable strength. Tee swung her eyes back to Carly in confusion. "What…"

"Get out! Get out of here!" The strange woman advanced on her once again. "Carly is mine! You hear me? Stay away from her!"

Tee couldn't believe her ears or her eyes. This crazed woman was screaming at her that Carly was in a relationship with her! She noticed that Carly was standing there doing nothing to stop the crazy woman from grabbing Tee again. "Carly?"

"Kim." Carly reached out to Kim, but cautiously. She knew the slightest thing could really set her off once she was teetering on the brink of disaster. But Tee was looking at her in shock and confusion. She touched Kim's arm lightly. "Kim, please don't do this."

"What?" Kim screeched, her voice rising another notch. "What? I'll take care of this, honey, just sit down."

Honey? Tee began to have a sick feeling about this. "Listen, just…"

"Get out of here!" Kim screamed again. Her face was mottled, her entire body shaking with rage.

Carly saw two security guys approaching through the crowd and knew she needed to defuse this situation before they were all arrested. She took Kim's arm but looked at Tee. "Just leave," she said urgently. "Security is on their way."

Tee stared at her in open-mouthed shock. Leave? *She* needed to leave? What the hell was going on?

"Please," Carly implored her. "Just let it go, Tee."

Tee backed away, her gaze swiveling between the two, before she turned her back on them and pushed through the crowd toward the exit. Fine! She'd leave. If that's what Carly wanted, that's what she'd get. She stumbled her way to the door, her sight hazy with shock. Once outside her stomach roiled and she gulped deep breaths of cool night air to keep from throwing up. She staggered as she made her way to the parking lot. Her vision dimmed until she could barely see a foot in front of her. She was in acute danger of passing out. Cold sweat broke out on her face and she put a trembling hand against the side of the building to steady herself. What had just happened? Carly was with another woman. Another woman? How could that be? It had only been a week since they'd seen each other. Unless Carly worked fast it would mean she had been involved with this woman for some time. That would mean the same time she and Carly had been seeing each other. The same time as she and Carly had been sleeping together.

She finally found her rental car and sank into it. She took one look back at the bar and the tears came spilling down her face. She came up to Chicago to celebrate her niece's graduation and was confronted with a situation she could never have dreamed of. Carly was sleeping with her while involved with another woman. Oh God, how could she have so totally lost her ability to judge a person's character? How could this be happening to her again? She forced her mind into a blank. It was the only way she could function at the moment.

By the time she boarded her flight back to Dallas she was numb. She hadn't slept at all the night before, too upset to think about closing her eyes. She had simply lain on the bed, her mind a kaleidoscope of jumbled thoughts and images. She'd given in finally and thrown up.

The flight seemed endless and by the time she got to her house she was ready to scream. She changed into her work clothes and went downstairs to the workroom. She had projects to finish. She needed to work, to do something to keep her mind occupied until she was too tired to think. She grabbed a beer and turned on her phone to punch in Markie's phone number, knowing she would be working and she'd only have to leave a message. She quickly told her about seeing Carly in Chicago with another woman and that they were done and she didn't want to talk about it. That done, she shut down her phone. The recriminations began immediately. How could she have misjudged Carly so badly? Well that's what she got for moving so fast. She'd let her hormones rule her head. When would she ever learn? She threw herself into refinishing the new headboard for the guest room to force those thoughts away. It was way too painful to think about right now.

Chapter 16

When Markie got Tee's message after her store closed for the night, her heart sank and she groaned. She could only hope she could find Tee before she did something stupid. She knew how devastating this would be to her. She drove to her building on Exposition just off Parry Street but it was dark. She tried to see into the interior of the grounds but a high fence and a gate between the buildings secured it and she was unable to make out if her car was parked there. She sat for a moment before driving to The Reed House to cruise through the parking lot there. She finally went inside but they said Tee hadn't been by that evening. She used her key card to access the upper floors. She stopped on the second floor and entered the private bar. The atmosphere was subdued and quiet. She surveyed the various groupings of comfortable seating areas where women were enjoying drinks and conversation. She spied the president of one of the most influential investment banks in the state and waved a greeting. The second in command of the Better Business Bureau called out to her from another area and she crossed the room to her group. She hadn't seen Tee but offered to buy Markie a drink. Markie thanked her but begged off and left to check the other floors. The spa on the third floor was closed, as was the banquet room on the fourth floor. Tee's corporate offices were on the fifth floor but it took a special key card after hours to unlock the elevator for that floor. She returned to her car and sat thinking. She tried calling her cell phone again and again got her voice mail. She kept her voice calm and simply asked Tee to call her. At three a.m. she finally gave up and went home. She was worried about Tee's physical safety but knew her emotional health was most at risk right now. To be dumped by the first woman Tee had shown any real interest in since her college years was bad enough. To be dumped because of another secret affair was killer. Markie wanted to find Carly and set her straight about what she'd thrown away. She realized she was getting just as angry as she had when the same thing had happened back in college. She took the bad things that happened to Tee to her own heart. She was such a good person and didn't deserve to be treated this way. Why couldn't women see all the things in Tee that she did?

Tee was in pain. She tried to open her eyes but it hurt so bad she quickly closed them again. Her head pounded mercilessly. She had a muddy thought that alcohol might be the culprit. Vast amounts of alcohol. The surface under her was hard and she surmised she was on the floor. It was making her back hurt. And she was cold. She experimented with flexing arms and legs and found additional areas of pain. Areas she could have done without knowing about yet. She turned onto her side and her stomach rolled. She froze, trying to will herself not to be sick. She concentrated on breathing through her nose and eventually her stomach calmed enough for her to relax. She tried to get up but only made it to her hands and knees before realizing her left hand was a source of major pain. It felt swollen and she quickly pulled it into her body to protect it. She was forced to lay back down then as a wave of pain went through her. She wondered how she had come to be injured. The only thing she remembered was drinking.

She didn't remember passing out again but the next time she woke up she was in even more pain. It was enough to drive her eyes open. She was in her workshop on the first floor of her building. The room was in shambles. She moaned but forced herself to sit up. Her stomach rolled but settled. She shivered and her skull felt like it was being hammered by thousands of tiny sledgehammers. She moaned again. After several minutes of self-exploration she discovered both her left foot and left hand were swollen and discolored. She thought her ankle was probably sprained by the way it hurt when she moved it. The real problem was her left arm. It was badly swollen and hurt like hell. She managed to get to her feet and balanced on one foot. She had to stand still for a minute while her head eased its throbbing. She hopped a couple of steps toward the door but had to stop when the pain in her arm became unbearable. She squeezed her eyes closed and gritted her teeth until she could breathe again. She tried limping on her sprained ankle and at least she could hold her left arm against her body for support. At the stairs to the second floor she sat down on the steps and rested. She was perspiring from the effort and from pain. She took deep breaths and tried to think about just doing that. After a minute it seemed to help. Her cell phone rang. She fished it out of her front pocket. It was Markie. She knew she had to answer it.

"Hello?"

"Are you okay?" Markie asked immediately.

"I'm fine," Tee lied.

"Where are you?"

"Home."

"Were you there last night?" she asked anxiously. "I came by but couldn't tell if you were there or not."

"Yeah, I was here." Tee was trying desperately to keep her voice even.

Markie let a moment stretch. "Uh, Tee, I'm sorry about Carly."

"Yeah."

"Are you okay?"

"I'm okay," Tee said, but knew her voice sounded strained now.

"Tee? You don't sound okay. I'll be there soon."

"No," she protested feebly.

"Open the gate for me." Markie commanded and hung up.

Tee closed her phone and laid it on the step beside her. She briefly wondered when she'd turned it back on but it was too much trouble and she gave up. She patted her pockets until she located her keys in her back pocket. She pressed one of the buttons on the extra key fob and unlocked her front door. The second button unlocked the gate to the back lot where the garage was. With that done, she started the laborious job of scooting backward up the stairs, one step at a time. She had managed to hobble into the shower by the time Markie arrived and was thankful she had decided on a walk in stall. She was leaning against the wall wondering if she could make it out without falling down when Markie appeared in her bathroom. One look at her and Markie reached out to lend an arm for support. Tee was past caring and gratefully leaned on her.

"What the hell happened to you?"

"I'm not sure," Tee answered dully. "I think I fell in the workshop last night."

"You've been like this all night?" Markie was dismayed at the thought of her injured and all alone.

"I was passed out most of the time," she said. "I think I hit my head."

Markie propped her against the counter and got a towel for her. She noticed her arm then and covered her mouth with her hand. "Jesus Tee! Look at your arm!"

"Yeah," Tee said weakly.

She looked absolutely gray with pain, Markie thought. She dried her off and helped her to the bed. "We're going to the hospital. Just sit there while I get some clothes for you." She retreated to the big walk in closet and got underwear, jeans, and a shirt that buttoned up the front. Tee was flat on the bed when she re-entered the bedroom. "Tee, sweetie, come on and get dressed. Okay?" She helped Tee sit up and then got her into her clothes. She could only wear one shoe. She put her shoulder under her arm and together they shuffled down the stairs. She glanced into the workshop on their way past. "Tee, it looks like you tried to punch out your house," she observed. Markie grabbed Tee's keys and beeped the door locked behind them.

"Yeah. Maybe. I don't know." Tee didn't seem to know or care.

The very fact that Tee was allowing her to take control was telling. Under normal circumstances she'd never have gone quietly. Markie got her into the passenger seat and belted her in. In less than twenty minutes they were in the emergency room.

Tee cradled her arm against her chest and propped her foot on top of another chair. She had her eyes closed and Markie absently rubbed her hand over her thigh as they waited. It was over an hour before they called her name. The doctor was a surprisingly good-looking woman with blond hair to her shoulders, warm brown eyes, and a kind smile. She gave Tee a careful and thorough examination. Tee gritted her teeth and tried her best to stay still on the table.

"I'm sorry, Ms Reed," Dr. Williams murmured. She finally stepped back and glanced at Markie standing beside her head. "What happened?"

"I don't know," she told her and looked at Tee.

"I fell off a ladder last night."

"This is a lot of damage for just a fall from a ladder," she commented.

"I hit a metal table on the way down," Tee elaborated.

"Uh huh." Dr. Williams lifted her right hand and examined the bruised and scraped knuckles. "Did the table fight back?"

"Yeah." Tee tried to grin. "Until I hit it with my head."

"With no evidence to the contrary I'll have to assume the table gave up after that," she observed with dry humor.

"Yeah."

"May I also assume alcohol was involved?"

"You may."

"Okay. From my initial exam I'd say you've suffered a concussion, probably that table's fault, a sprained left ankle, and a fracture of the left arm." She jotted notes on a chart in her hand as she talked. "I'll have to have an x-ray to be sure and we need to reduce the swelling before we do anything." She snapped the chart closed. "They'll get you into a room as soon as possible."

"I don't want to stay," Tee protested.

"Yes, well, perhaps you should have discussed things with that table instead of trying to beat it into submission."

Markie burst into laughter and Dr. Williams gave her an appreciative smile. "Your friend…"

"Markie Killigan," she supplied.

"Ms Killigan can stay with you until they get the x-rays taken. She'll need to leave after you're settled for the night." She looked at Markie expectantly but it was Tee who spoke up.

"She's probably got a date tonight anyway so that won't be a problem."

"I'll be here until they kick me out," Markie told her. "It's not a problem." She flashed a smile at Dr. Williams. "Don't worry."

"Okay then. Relax and I'll check on you after we get pictures."

Chapter 17

Tee waited impatiently for Markie to come pick her up. She sported a pristine white cast on her arm from her elbow to her fingertips and her foot was encased in a big blue boot. Her headache was just a dull throb now but the pain pills at least kept her broken arm from driving her to her knees when she moved. She shifted the dark blue sling higher on her shoulder just as Markie entered the room with a big smile.

"Hey Slugger. I hear you need a ride."

"Yes." Tee smiled back and grabbed the lone crutch leaning against the bed. "Get me out of here."

"You need any help with that?"

"No. There's not much you can do except open doors."

"That I can do," she grinned. She was glad to see that her friend looked much better than she had the night before. Her color was good and she seemed to be in much better spirits. "Did you get any sleep last night?"

"Yeah," she nodded. "Once the pain killers kicked in I went out like a light."

"Did Dr. Gorgeous send any home with you?"

Tee grinned. "You like that, huh?"

"Oh yeah," Markie laughed and pushed the door open to the parking lot. "What's not to like?"

Tee ignored that. "Where are you parked?"

It was awkward getting her into the car but they managed and Markie got them on the road. "You can't stay at your house alone, Tee. Too many stairs. Want to bunk with me for a few days?"

"Thanks, Marks, but I've thought of that already. I'll just take one of the suites at The Reed House. That way I'll be close to work and the restaurant can send food up if I don't want to go out."

And you'll turn into a recluse up there, Markie thought. She couldn't think of any reason to argue against it though. It was the perfect solution. "Okay, but promise me you'll get outside every now and then."

"Yeah, yeah." Tee's attention seemed to be focused on the passing scenery.

Markie escorted Tee up to the third floor suite and then went back to her house to pack a bag and gather up her briefcase and laptop computer. Tee was on the couch, with her sprained ankle elevated on a pillow on top of the low coffee table, when she returned. She unpacked Tee's bag in the bedroom while Tee set up the laptop on the small table next to the kitchenette.

"It looks like you're all set here."

Tee looked up from the computer. "Yeah. Thanks." She smiled. "This will be a great commute to work." She held out her hand to Markie. "I can't thank you enough, Marks. I don't know what I would have done without you."

Markie took her hand and looked over the scrapes and bruises. "You know I'm here for you, sweetie. Always have been, always will be." She sat in the opposite chair at the table. "Do you want to tell me about it now?"

Tee withdrew her hand and looked away. "No. There's really nothing to tell."

"Tee," she said with a knowing look. "Just tell me what happened. Please."

She sighed. "You know I was in Chicago over the weekend for my niece's graduation, right? Well, once the celebration was over, I went to a bar I know."

"Do you know anyone up there?" Markie asked.

"I used to," she nodded, "but I haven't been back there in years. I just thought I'd get a drink and check things out, that's all."

"Okay. So, what happened?"

"I saw Carly there." Tee looked down at her hand and picked at the edge of her cast.

"What was she doing in Chicago?" Markie asked in surprise.

"It...umm...seems she went up there to see her girlfriend."

"What?" Markie was outraged. "She has a girlfriend in Chicago? What the hell!"

"Yeah. I saw Carly sitting at a table so I start toward her." Tee looked up, then back at her cast again. "I thought I should say hello or something. You know?"

"Yeah...and?"

"And this other chick grabs me and pulls me away and starts screaming at me." Tee raised a hand to her face. "It turns out she's Carly's girlfriend."

"Are you sure?"

"Yeah," Tee nodded, still not looking at her. "She's yelling at me and she looks like she's about to really lose it. She's screaming that Carly belongs to her and for me to get away from her. So then Carly takes her arm and looks me right in the eye and tells me to just go."

Markie gently kissed the bruised knuckles on Tee's good hand. "Do you think you should call her and ask her what the fuck she's doing?"

"No." Tee's voice was adamant. "She called and left messages that night but I deleted them. How can I believe anything she says? I saw it with my own eyes! I'm not going to believe some lame explanation she left in a voice mail."

"Oh man, I'm sorry," Markie moaned in sympathy. She grabbed Tee's good hand and pulled it up to her face, holding it against her cheek. "I'm so sorry, Tee. I know you really liked her."

Tee swiped angrily at new tears with the tips of the fingers on her broken hand. "Yeah. Well, it's over and I'm moving on." Her voice wavered but she swallowed hard and got control. "So, that's it and I'd like to not talk about it again."

"Okay, sweetie, anything you want." Markie patted her on the arm. "You should let me find you a suitable date from now on." Markie tried to lighten things up.

"Okay, you're on. You're in charge from now on." Tee tried a smile. She couldn't stand Markie feeling sorry for her.

Markie could sense Tee wanted to be alone so she stood up. "Promise me you'll have the kitchen send something up."

"I will."

"Tee, if you're on medication, especially pain pills, you need to eat."

"I know." Tee looked up at her and gave her a genuine smile this time. "I promise I'll eat."

"Okay. I'll call you tomorrow."

"Thanks Markie." Tee watched her walk to the door. "I love you," she called as she went out.

"I love you too," she heard as the door closed behind her.

Carly stared at her phone and let fresh tears fall. She'd tried calling Tee's phone a dozen times to explain what had happened but each time she'd had to leave a voice mail. And then a return voice mail had come in while she was on the plane home. A gravelly, vitriol-filled, snarl informed her she was welcome to her old girlfriend and no explanations were needed or even wanted. She could go fuck herself as far as Tee was concerned. Before she'd hung up, she added that since she'd fucked her over twice, it wouldn't be that hard to forget her existence. She wiped her eyes for the thousandth time and once again cursed Kim. While Kim had seemed fine, evidently seeing another woman pay attention to Carly had triggered a manic attack. It took Carly the rest of the night to get her out of the bar and back to her house and calmed down enough to talk. Once she'd gotten Kim to take a sleeping pill she called Tee. When it went straight to voice mail she figured Tee was upset and turned her phone off so she left a message. She tried again and again into the wee hours of the morning, leaving a message each time. By the time she boarded the plane for the trip home she was exhausted, disgusted, and thoroughly pissed off at Kim. While she knew Kim had been diagnosed as bi-polar she could not get past what she'd done. The only reason she'd traveled to Chicago was because Denise promised her Kim was on her meds and feeling fine. Carly called Denise first thing that morning and ordered her to come pick her up and take her to the airport. Denise didn't even bother to ask what had happened, she could tell from Carly's voice that it was serious. The only thing she said before Denise dropped her off was to make it clear she didn't want to hear from Kim again.

She had evidently lost Tee anyway by the angry tone of her message. Carly's thoughts kept going back to how the scene had played out at the bar. She could see how the shock she'd had on her face at seeing Tee there could have been mistaken for the shock of being caught with another woman. Even after she'd explained Tee had told her to fuck off. So, what was she supposed to do now?

We weren't even close to talking about monogamy, she thought with sudden anger. *She doesn't own me! What did she think, that great sex means I belong to her? Ridiculous. If that was what her highness thought then it was a good thing I found out now instead of later.*

Chapter 18

"Ms Matthews," Suzanne said and smiled as she entered the room where Carly was busy doing some copying.

"Hi Suzanne."

"How are you doing, Carly?" Suzanne laid the file she was carrying on the adjoining counter, leaned back against it, and crossed her arms over her chest.

"I'm fine," Carly nodded with a smile. "How are you?"

"I'm good." Suzanne regarded her for a moment before speaking again. "I hear you're having a bit of trouble with that pro bono case George gave you."

"Trouble? No, I'm not having any trouble." Carly could actually feel the confusion of the other woman.

"You know, Carly, Mr. Hardin wants this case filed."

"Yes, I'm aware of that." Carly's tone was defensive and just a touch defiant. She hated to be pushed.

Suzanne moved to her side and Carly was surprised when she ran a hand down her arm. "Are you also aware that I find you very attractive?" she asked in a voice full of desire.

Carly fought not to tense under her touch. "I'm...flattered, Suzanne," she managed to say.

"But?"

"But I'm seeing someone right now." She regretted with all her hear that it wasn't the truth.

Suzanne moved even closer and once again ran her hand over Carly's arm. "But can she do the things I can do for you?" She raised her hand to Carly's cheek briefly. "I can make sure your career path here is smooth. I can insure your rapid advancement up the corporate ladder," she continued. "Just think of it; together we could one day take control of this firm."

Carly's mind swirled in shock and confusion. Was Suzanne serious? She remembered Terri saying Suzanne had a thing for her. Was Suzanne interested in her or was she saying something entirely different? It sounded as if she was offering her a chance at the fast track in the firm along with an intimate relationship with her. Without a doubt the one depended on the other. Carly's mind was lightening quick and she processed all this in a nanosecond. All she had to do was say yes to Suzanne and no to Luis Alvarez. Being a partner in a prestigious law firm had been her dream since entering law school at Yale. On the other hand was a man who was actually guilty of a crime even though it wasn't exactly the one he was being charged with committing. Suzanne was stroking her upper arm and shoulder now, waiting on her answer, a small confident smile on her face. Carly heard Tee's soft voice in her head, ' *follow your heart'*. "I'm sorry, Suzanne, but I am seeing someone and I'd like to pursue it. I'm flattered though."

Suzanne's face hardened in an instant. "I've offered you the chance of a lifetime," she spit at her. "You will regret this, I assure you." She turned on her heel, snatched her folder from the counter, and stalked from the room.

Carly's stomach went hollow. She had effectively shot herself in the foot. Had she shot it off completely? She could only hope not.

Chapter 19

Monday morning Tee woke up feeling much better from having slept through the night thanks to the pills. She had a bit of a problem taking a shower but managed to get most parts clean and her hair washed. She was in her office before Jane, her executive assistant, was even in the building. When she heard voices in her outer office she stopped what she was doing and grabbed her crutch. She would let Jane know she was temporarily living on the third floor and why. When she opened her office door she was surprised to find the head of her IT department sitting on the corner of Jane's desk, their hands clasped together. They both snapped their heads around as Tee opened the door.

"Captain IT," Tee said with a smile. "I see you're in early today."

"Yo," the young woman said with a grin. "What the hell happened to you, boss?"

Tee grimaced. "I fell off a ladder at the house." She pointed her chin at Jane. "I just wanted to tell Jane I was living in the small suite downstairs and beg her for a cup of coffee."

Jane stood quickly, thankful for something to do for her boss. "Certainly. I'll get it right away."

When she disappeared down the hall Tee looked at Fiona Nix, the lone employee and, therefore, the head of the Sylar Industries Information Technology department, aka, Captain IT. She had spiky ginger hair, several piercings along each ear and one through an eyebrow, a tattoo on her left wrist that looked like a bracelet of barbed wire, and flashing brown eyes that sparkled with good humor. She could be the poster child for hackers and was often bored with her job. She was never respectful and Tee liked her for it. It had taken Tee months of begging just to get Jane to call her Tee. "Do my eyes deceive me, Captain, or were you holding Jane's hand just then?"

"Your eyesight is perfect," she grinned. "And her hand is all she'll let me hold."

Tee nodded, pensive. She took in Fiona's torn jeans, boots, tight tee shirt, and the multitude of rings on her fingers. "Jane is a wise woman," she said. "You're lucky she lets you hold anything at all."

"You are correct," Fiona laughed. "I'm grateful for that much."

Jane returned with the coffee and looked from one to the other anxiously. Tee gave her a smile. "I only have one hand so I'd be eternally grateful if you'd put that coffee on my desk."

"Of course." She went past Tee and set the cup on her desk.

Tee followed and eased into her chair. "Thank you, Jane," she murmured as she leaned the crutch against the side of the desk.

"Uh, boss?" Jane stood practically at attention.

"Relax, Jane," Tee said. "I don't care if you and Fiona have something going. It's none of my business."

"We don't have anything going—exactly."

Tee took a sip of coffee. "Whatever you do have going, exactly, is fine with me. I know you won't let it interfere with your job."

"I would never let anything interfere with my work," she protested.

Tee grinned at her shocked expression. Jane was as conservative as Fiona was radical. She couldn't image them together, but to each her own. "It's okay Jane." She sat forward in her chair. "Now, let's get to work. I'll be using the small suite downstairs for a week or so, until my ankle heals anyway. I've sent it to the schedule so today's update should reflect it."

"Got it," Jane nodded. "I'll order lunch sent up from the kitchen for you too. Just let me know when you're ready."

"You're the best, Jane."

When she was alone again she leaned back in her chair and stared at the ceiling. Jane and Fiona? Wow. Never was there a more unlikely pair, she thought. Unbidden, Carly's image came to mind and it was all Tee could do not to groan. Without warning her stomach clenched and she bent quickly over her trashcan. She had steadfastly refused to think about her—until now. Now the physical pain was held at bay. Now she was back at her desk. Now she had nothing to keep the memory from haunting her. Nothing was in her stomach to come up and she sat back up. She shook her head sharply to rid herself of her image and instantly regretted it. Her slight concussion suddenly didn't feel so slight after all. The pain pills were wearing off. She closed her eyes and waited for the wave of pain to pass. When it had, she turned back to her computer. She needed to just keep busy, she thought. She had no interest in that woman after all. She managed to keep her mind occupied until Markie called in the early afternoon.

"Hey sweetie," Markie greeted her.

"Hey," Tee replied. "And before you ask, yes, I had lunch sent up."

"You mean Jane had lunch sent up," she laughed. "How are you feeling?"

"Much better today."

"The pills letting you get some sleep then?"

"Yeah. Even my arm is better today."

"Good. Is there anything I can do for you? Do you need anything?"

"I'm fine, but thanks."

"Tee…" Markie stopped.

"What?"

"I wish you'd talk to me."

Tee didn't need to ask about what. "There's nothing to talk about. Really."

"Tee, you punched out your house!"

"Yeah, well I was drunk. And angry. I was both drunk and angry."

"Well you're not drunk now."

"Meaning what?" Tee asked with an edge in her voice.

"Meaning you're still angry. And don't use that pissy tone on me. I'm trying to help you here."

Tee waited until she got her emotions under control. "I'm sorry Marks. I know you want to help. I appreciate that you want to help. But, really, there's nothing you can do. I got dumped by a woman who I really liked. Why I liked such a…person, I'll never figure out, but there it is. I got drunk and beat up on my workroom. It was stupid and I'm paying for it now. But as far as anything else goes there's nothing you can do. There's nothing that can be done. She has a girlfriend and I don't like to share. End of story."

"I just think it would help to talk about it," Markie persisted.

"No thanks. It won't change anything." Tee absolutely hated talking about emotional issues, especially her own.

"God, you're a stubborn woman," she lamented. She knew when she was beat though and gave up. "I love you anyway, honey. I'll talk to you later."

"Don't give up on me," Tee teased her. She hated having her friend disappointed with her. She just couldn't talk about this one.

Chapter 20

Carly was furious. She'd turned down the offer of a lifetime just to help some ordinary criminal and all because of some stupid advice to follow her heart. Follow your heart? What the fuck did that mean anyway? It was some stupid thing that came out of a fortune cookie no doubt.

After turning Suzanne down she'd spent the rest of the day thinking about it. At that time she'd still thought she'd done the right thing. She found Terri in the hall and followed her back to her office. When Terri heard the story she immediately called Sharon into her office and made Carly go through it all again. When she finished the story this time Sharon and Terri both looked first at each other then at her.

"Are you out of your mind?" Sharon was the first to speak.

"What do you mean?" Carly had asked.

"You just threw away your career!" Terri had practically shouted at her.

"No." Carly thought maybe she hadn't made herself clear.

"Yes." They had both nodded at once. "Saying no to Suzanne is like saying you hate working here," Sharon continued.

"No," Carly had said again. She refused to believe it was true.

"Plus you're holding onto that stupid pro bono case when Hardass Hardin wants it filed. What is the matter with you? You've committed career suicide, Matthews!"

And it had been the truth. By Friday afternoon she was locked out of the company intranet system. She thought she was just having some sort of computer glitch. A call to the IT department yielded no information other than her account was locked. She'd yelled at them to unlock it and hung up. Then her phone rang and Mrs. Nolan informed her Brown, Hardin & Simon were no longer in need of her services. She couldn't believe it. It had to be a mistake. She'd demanded to speak to Mr. Hardin himself.

"I'm sorry, Ms Matthews," he'd said. "You left me no choice. It came to my attention this morning that you have breached the confidentiality of a client. The Alvarez case was posted to everyone on the company intranet. That's grounds for dismissal."

She'd been outraged. "What? I did nothing of the sort! I would never do something like that! He's my client!"

"Yes, so you've said. Nevertheless, his file was on every computer in the company. How do you explain that?" He didn't give her time to answer. "This is a grave matter, Ms Matthews. A breach of trust of this magnitude cannot and will not be tolerated. Brown, Hardin & Simon could easily choose to send this to the Texas board of Ethics."

The threat was not lost on Carly. Her heart had squeezed painfully in her chest. Being turned into the Ethics Committee was something that would follow her forever, guilty or not.

"Do I make myself clear?"

"Sir, I did not do this! You know I didn't!"

"That's exactly what every guilty person says. Please don't make this any harder on yourself. Clean out your desk and be gone in the next ten minutes."

This wasn't happening! It couldn't be happening. It wasn't true. She'd picked up the phone to call Terri but a security guard was already inside her office, took the receiver from her, and hung it up. "Your personal items will be sent to you." Carly had taken her bag and stood up. She didn't know what else to do. There weren't any options available to her.

She'd lost her job. She hadn't just lost her job, she'd been fired. Fired because she'd refused the advances of a senior member of the staff. Or was it because she'd refused to plead her client out? It had been devastating. She'd never been fired from anything before. Shit like this wasn't supposed to be happening any more.

What a cruel joke the cosmos had played on her. She'd been betrayed by her firm and she felt as if she'd been betrayed by her lover. She had nothing left now. No job and no lover. And no friends, either. After several failed attempts to contact both Terri and Sharon she knew her calls were not being forwarded. That had been okay. But when her calls to their personal cell phones went unanswered she got the message. These were her friends? She could see not wanting to let the company know they were in touch with her but not answering their personal calls sent a different kind of message. They didn't want her as a friend. They had abandoned her. They left her with nothing and no one.

She had made her seventh job interview this morning. At each interview she'd been confident and assured. She was the picture of a successful attorney. And each time the prospective employer had been cordial, eager even until the firm of Brown, Hardin & Simon came up. One hiring partner had actually paled when he realized he'd have to contact them before hiring her. Each time she'd explained the situation and assured them she was not at fault. And each time they said they'd be in touch. The interview this morning was more of the same and she was beginning to realize the power of Brown, Hardin & Simon held in this city. Without a doubt they were blocking her from getting a decent job. The word was out. And that's why she was currently furious. She was looking failure in the eye and she was scared.

She looked into her glass but found no answer there—yet. She emptied it and called for another. Why not? It wasn't as if she had a job to go to tomorrow. She remembered coming into the bar hoping the atmosphere might lift her spirits. And maybe, for a few hours, she might forget what a miserable life she had. She knew she had gone too far, had one too many drinks, when she had trouble getting off the barstool. She stood for a moment, unsteady, a hand on the bar for balance. The dance floor was crowded and she watched them for a minute, forgetting why she'd gotten up in the first place. She saw a tall blond dancing and her heart skipped a beat. But it wasn't her. It wasn't Tee. She frowned. She didn't want it to be Tee. Did she? What did she want? She couldn't think. She needed fresh air. That's why she'd gotten up. She kept her eyes on the dancers. She wasn't searching for her. She absolutely was not searching for Tee. She'd get some air and she'd be fine. It was just too warm inside the bar, that's all. She stumbled over the threshold a little and grabbed the frame for support.

"Here, let me help you." A strong hand gripped her under her elbow and pulled her out the door. The voice was deep.

"Thanks." She tried to turn around to thank him but she was pushed roughly face first against the brick wall. "Hey," she protested.

"Shut up," her Good Samaritan growled and pinned her against the wall with his body.

"Come on man!" It was a different voice. "Let's do it before someone comes out!"

The thought penetrated the fog in her brain that she might be in trouble. She struggled but her hands were jerked behind her back and held. Hands ran roughly over her body until they found the money in her back pocket.

"Get her watch and rings too." It was the second mans voice again.

"Shit! She ain't wearing any jewelry. Bitch!" Her head was jerked back by her hair and she gasped in pain. "I ain't leaving with just that! She has to have more!" Strong hands ripped her blouse apart, buttons flying everywhere. "Maybe she's got something in her bra. Stupid women are always putting stuff in their underwear. Dykes probably do too." Different hands tore at her bra and then her breasts were being mauled. She screamed and struggled, panic fueling her. She was immediately slammed against the wall again. Her head swirled, stars blinking behind her eyes. Her legs turned to jelly and she started to sag. "Check her pants," the second voice said. "Here, let me do it. You hold her up."

"Hey!" A third voice came out of the dark parking lot. "Hey!"

Her assailants let go of her and she finished the slide to the ground. There were the sounds of running feet and then silence. She was on her knees trying to get her feet under her when a pair of strong hands gripped her under her arms and she was hauled to her feet.

"Are you okay?" Carly swayed a bit before getting her balance. "Miss? Here, let me help you." Her rescuer put his arm around her and offered support. "Are you okay?" he asked again.

"My money," she said. "They took my money." She realized how she must look then and hastily gathered the gaping sides of her blouse together. "Thank you for scaring them off."

"No problem," he assured her, thinking that maybe she was in a bit of shock. "I have a sweatshirt in the car. Stay here and I'll get it for you." He took a couple of backward steps before turning to the parking lot. When he returned he held a sweatshirt in his hand. He stopped more than an arms length away. "I know you're scared, Miss, but I'm no threat to you. I was in the bar just like you were." He held out the shirt. "Just take the shirt."

The door to the bar banged open and another man came out. "What the hell's taking so long, Wayne?" He took a step forward. "Why does everything take you so damn long?"

Wayne gestured to Carly. "I stopped to help a damsel in distress."

The man noticed her then for the first time. "Ms Matthews? Is that you?"

Carly looked at him closely in the dim light. "Yes. Who…?"

"I'm Paul Carrington," he told her. "I was opposing counsel in Reed Vs Southerland. We met in your office."

She felt her heart do another somersault. Of all the people who could have come out that door it had to be Tee's lawyer. She slumped back against the brick wall in utter defeat. Nothing was ever going to go right for her again. She was sure of it. She struggled to keep the tears at bay.

When Wayne saw how defeated she looked he wrapped her in a hug. She fought but he just kept hugging her and rocking back and forth.

"Wayne, you're scaring the crap out of her." Paul thumped him on the shoulder and when he loosened his grip he thrust the sweatshirt at Carly. "Here. I'm sorry. Wayne is a nurturer. He sees someone in distress and he can't help himself."

Wayne took the shirt and pulled it over Carly's head. "Come on, honey, put your arms through the sleeves," he said gently. "Paul is going to go get the car and we're going to take you home with us."

"Oh no," Carly protested weakly. Her head was spinning, making it impossible for her to think clearly.

"Now don't worry your pretty head about it. We have plenty of room and it's no trouble."

"I can't." She finally found the strength to push out of the big man's arms. She wiped her face. "I need to find my shoe."

Paul had noticed her missing shoe and had already begun a search of the nearby area. "I found it," he announced and held up her left shoe.

She leaned on his shoulder and slipped into it. "Thanks, you two." She wiped her eyes again. "I'll just go now."

Wayne put his arm around her shoulders. "Honey, I think you'll be much better off if you go home with us. You need to have your cheek cleaned up and looked at." He turned to Paul. "You drive her car and we'll meet you at home."

"No, wait a minute," she protested.

"You can't stop him once he gets into this rescue mode," Paul advised her. "It's easier if you just go along with him."

Wayne hugged her again. "Give Paul your keys and you can ride with me."

And that's how Carly made her first two real friends. Wayne and Paul took her to their house where Wayne took care of the scratches on her cheek from when she'd been shoved against the brick wall and Paul made coffee. The kindness of these two strangers made Carly's eyes tear up. One tear fell and it opened the floodgates. Soon she was bawling like a baby.

"Please don't cry," Wayne begged her. "Those two guys were just drunken punks." He pulled her nearly out of her chair and into another bear hug. "We'll find them and Paul will sue them!"

"It's not that," she choked out. She wiped her face with tissues from the box Paul offered. "You two don't even know me and you treat me better than anybody I know."

"Oh now, I don't believe that," Wayne said easily.

"It's true." And that brought on fresh tears.

"Tell us about it," Wayne urged.

And while Paul baked brownies and Wayne held her hand and encouraged her, she told them about being an attorney at Brown, Hardin & Simon. She went on with the story of the Alvarez case, her two fellow attorneys and friends in the firm, Mr. Hardin demanding she just file the case and be done with it, and finally how Suzanne had dangled a place on the fast track in exchange for personal services.

"Paul, did you hear that? That's atrocious behavior from a law firm!"

"Yes," he agreed somberly. He set a plate of brownies on the table between them with a frown. "You know that's actionable," he said to her.

"I'm not finished," she said dully. "I turned her down and by the end of the week the Alvarez case was sent to the entire office, I was locked out of my computer, and Mr. Hardin fired me and threatened to turn me in to the ethics committee."

"Oh my God!" Wayne exclaimed. He turned to Paul. "You have to do something, Paul."

"We can discuss that," he nodded but his tone was not encouraging. "Will any of your friends back you up?"

Carly shook her head, fresh tears threatening to fall. "No," she gulped. "They won't return my calls."

"Oh honey," Wayne squeezed her hand. "That's horrible. How can they call themselves your friends?"

"They aren't now," she told him sadly.

"There isn't anything she can do when it's her word against theirs," Paul said. "She'll need proof of some kind."

"I'm so sorry, Carly," Wayne continued to hold her hand.

"That's not quite the end of it," she said softly. "Right before that I lost my girlfriend too."

"Honey, you've had some really bad luck lately. But it's starting to change right now. Now you have two new friends, real friends, and I'm sure there'll be more."

"Thanks, Wayne. You guys have been great." She hoped her watery smile was good enough to convince him she was sincere.

"It's late. Why don't I find you some old pajamas of Paul's and then you can get some sleep." Wayne stood and Carly followed him into the spare room.

"You two have a beautiful home."

"Thanks. I've done most of it myself." Wayne produced sleepwear and handed them to her. "Use anything you need, hon. Sleep as late as you like and we'll talk tomorrow."

Carly kissed his cheek. "Thanks, Wayne. Really. You saved my life tonight."

He met Paul in their room. "I think she'll be okay tonight."

"Wayne, one of these days you're going to bring home a needy stray who'll cut our throats in the night." He shook his head at his partner but with a smile.

"Well hell, Paul, what was I supposed to do? Two guys were ripping her clothes off," Wayne defended himself. "And admit it, you're as bad as I am," Wayne laughed. "I like her. She's been through a lot lately."

"She has," Paul agreed. He got into bed and waited for Wayne to join him. "Maybe she'll find a job soon."

"I really hope so."

Chapter 21

Carly listened to her date tell her about what life as a dentist was like over dinner at La Hacienda. As they shared a basket of chips and salsa, she was reminded of the hot sauce at Abuelo's with Tee and how she'd felt like she was on fire. She tried to get Catherine, her date, to try the hot stuff but she refused. Carly drained the last of her margarita and wondered if she should risk having another. Catherine was talking about some patient who never flossed and she decided she not only should but would. This was their third date. She'd met Catherine at the GLBT center. They were getting ready for their annual ball and she'd offered to help with the mailing. Catherine had been sitting at the same table and they'd struck up a conversation.

"How would you like to go dancing?" Carly asked now as they exited the restaurant.

"Oh, I don't know," Catherine said. "I'm afraid I don't dance very well."

"You're being modest."

"No," she laughed. "I don't have any rhythm."

"I know where there's a good show tonight," she offered.

"A show?"

"It'll be fun," Carly assured her. "I know one of the performers."

"Oh. That might be okay."

"Great!"

Carly took her to the Rainbow Club in the heart of the gay entertainment district. They featured drag shows that ran the gamut from beginners to near professional performers. They were fortunate to grab a table and ordered drinks.

"Wayne is doing the show tonight," Carly told Catherine. "I've seen him before and he does a good job."

"How did you meet him?" she asked. "Was he at the center the night we met?"

"No. I met both him and his partner at another bar a few weeks ago."

"Do you go out a lot?"

Carly hesitated. "No, not a lot." The truth was she'd been very hesitant to go out, afraid she'd run into Tee. She wasn't ready for that. The lights flickered several times and then went out. The speakers boomed with the announcer's voice urging them to welcome the first act of the evening. The first performer was a vibrant redhead who did a creditable job on a Bette Midler song. After that was the usual line up of Liza Minnelli, Barbara Streisand, Cher, and Celine Dion. Wayne did a good job as Tina Turner and Carly laughed, clapped, and whistled as he performed. She loved it when Wayne was performing. She turned to Catherine as the lights came back up and the DJ started playing music again.

"What did you think of the show?"

"They all look so real," she said in amazement. "I've never seen a drag show before."

"They do look real," Carly laughed. It wasn't long before Wayne joined them at their table. Carly stood and gave him a big hug. "You were terrific, Wayne."

"Oh, thank you," he gushed, still in drag queen mode.

"Wayne, this is Catherine. Catherine, this is my best friend, Wayne."

"I'm so glad to meet you," he said with a sly look at Carly.

"Where's Paul tonight?" Carly asked. "I haven't seen him."

"He's working," Wayne sighed. "He said he needed to get some papers done and filed. You know how he is about his job—nothing interferes with it."

Carly squeezed his arm. "That's a good thing, Wayne."

"I know," he conceded. "He'd be here if he could." He laughed then and slapped his palms together. "So, what are we girls drinking tonight? The first round is on me." They drank. They danced. They laughed. It was late when Carly and Catherine left but Wayne was still going strong. "You girls be careful," he called to them as they left. "And don't do anything I wouldn't do."

Carly strained for release. Catherine was a tender and considerate lover and she was having trouble getting there. It was just seemed so different from the last time she was in bed with a woman. The last time was...Tee. *Oh God.* She came with a vengeance.

Catherine smiled with pride as she held her. Carly felt guilty but she couldn't tell her the mere thought of another woman was responsible for her orgasm. Where Catherine was attentive and considerate, Tee had simply taken her. She pushed the thought away. It was not only unfair to think of another woman to achieve orgasm; it was also painful—to her heart. She forced herself to cuddle for as long as she could and hoped Catherine didn't think she was rude as she dressed and left.

Chapter 22

Carly went through the door of the small office building and down the hall to the office of Paul Carrington, Attorney At Law. She smiled at Wayne as she entered. Wayne kept the books, did Paul's billing, and ran his office. Since he was a CPA it worked out nicely for them.

"Hey honey," she called out.

"Hey sweetie," he answered. "Paul's gone so I can't leave for lunch today."

"No problem," she told him. "I'll go get us something and bring it back. We can eat here."

"You are such a doll. Can we have take-out from Chen's?"

"You got it, big guy."

Carly had gotten into the habit of dropping by the office and having lunch with the boys whenever she could. Since she still hadn't found a job it was more often than not these days. Wayne dug money out of his wallet and handed it to her. "You know what I like."

She returned soon and they spread the little white cartons across the conference table. "So, where is Paul today?" she asked as they dug in.

"He's in a meeting with a client."

"Business must be good then," she commented around a mouthful of sweet & sour chicken.

"Oh yeah. Lately he's been very busy. It's good for business but I miss having him here to talk to." Wayne wiped his mouth on a paper napkin. "And, speaking of missing someone, what about that woman you had at the show? You haven't said two words about her."

Carly tried a nonchalant shrug. "She was okay. We're not seeing each other anymore though."

"Why not? She was cute."

Carly sighed and jabbed her chopsticks into a carton. "I don't know. She *was* cute. And she was nice too."

"But?"

"She was too nice," she told him. "It's got nothing to do with her. I think it's me. I'm just not good enough for her."

"Cut that out!" Wayne said sharply. He stabbed his chopsticks at her. "Don't ever let me hear you say that again. No one is too good for you." He resumed eating. "Maybe she just isn't what you want in a lover."

Carly nodded to appease him but she was unconvinced. "Maybe." She picked up her chopsticks again. "Can I tell you something?"

"Sure."

"She was so sweet she gave me a toothache."

Wayne roared with laughter, throwing his head back and letting go. When he recovered he looked at her fondly. "Ahhhh God, Carly, I do so love you." He wiped the corner of his eye with his napkin. "So you're saying you like more, uh, spice than sweet in a woman."

"Yeah, I guess that's it," she grinned. It was hard not to smile when Wayne was around.

"Was your last girlfriend spicy?"

Carly busied herself with her food and didn't look at him. "Yeah, I guess so."

Wayne let it go for a minute but couldn't keep from asking, "How spicy was she?"

Carly didn't match his grin this time. She frowned. "Wayne…"

"It's a simple question," he defended himself. "What's her name?"

Carly shook her head. "It doesn't matter. After everything that happened she wouldn't give me the time of day."

"Do you want her to?"

Carly shook her head. She couldn't even think about it. "It doesn't matter. It ain't gonna happen."

"Why not?"

"Christ Wayne! I told her about Kim. I told her she was not my girlfriend. I told her she was bi-polar and off her meds. It didn't make any difference. She doesn't want anything to do with me. Plus, I don't even have a job."

Wayne shrugged. "But you said you didn't actually talk to her directly. Have you thought about trying to talk to her again?"

"No." Carly closed up the empty cartons and stuffed everything back into the sack.

"But, you'd welcome her back?"

"Shut up, Wayne," she laughed. That was a thought she tried never to have. But some times late at night, when she couldn't sleep, she allowed herself to wonder about Tee. It always ended with her in tears, her sorrow for the lost opportunity at happiness and the pain she knew she had caused her.

Wayne sensed the subject was closed for now. "Hey, are you going to the GLBT annual ball this year?"

"I have a ticket but I don't know." She wanted to go but was afraid. What if Tee attended the ball too and she saw her there? What would she do? Would Tee tell her to fuck off? She didn't think she could stand having to face her yet.

"Come on, it'll be fun," he urged her. "The Reed House is hosting it this year so the food will be good. You can go with Paul and me. We'll be your dates."

"Okay," she nodded. "Thanks." She couldn't think of a decent reason not to take him up on his offer.

Chapter 23

Tee was checking on the preparations for the ball on the fourth floor. The tables were arranged and the crew was busy with the place settings and glassware. The podium was ready and the decorations were up. It looked good, she thought. She wanted this year's ball to be the best ever. She would check on the kitchen and then it would be time to start getting ready herself. Her phone rang as she descended in the freight elevator to the first floor. She dug it out of her pocket as she went down the back hall and entered the kitchen.

"Hello Markie."

"Hi. Where are you?"

"In the kitchen. Are you here?"

"Yes."

"Good. Just press 214 on the elevator keypad and it'll take you up to the third floor. I left the door unlocked and a keycard for you inside. I'll be there soon."

"Okay. Thanks."

Tee surveyed the kitchen staff who worked around the catering staff. The pace was frantic but every person there had a job and knew what to do. She nodded in satisfaction and gave the crews a thumbs up before leaving. The liquor had already been taken up to the ballroom to the portable bar there. She had four extra bartenders working the ball plus a crew chief to make sure everything ran smoothly. Satisfied that all was under control she returned to the elevator and went up to the third floor.

"Honey, I'm home," she called as she went in.

"Hey," Markie grinned at her from the couch where she was putting the last coat of polish on her nails. "What do you think?" She held up both hands for her inspection.

"Well…" Tee looked at the color of her nails then at the color of her lips. "You'll be the most devastatingly attractive woman at the ball," she proclaimed.

"You're such a bull shitter," Markie grinned at her.

Tee laughed and went to the small refrigerator where she pulled out a bottle of Champagne. "How about a little something to get us started?"

"Excellent," Markie exclaimed.

"Can you open it please?" She lifted her cast in a parody of helplessness.

"Of course. Bring it over here."

They shared the sparkling wine; Markie on the couch, Tee slouched in a chair opposite her. Markie waved her hands in the air to aid the drying process between sips.

"Have you driven your staff crazy yet?" she asked.

"Pretty much," Tee laughed. "I try not to get too crazy. I do trust them."

"But you can't help it," she said.

"I can't help it," Tee laughed again. "I really want this ball to be perfect."

"It will be," Markie assured her with confidence. "Quit worrying." She sipped again. "You are going to wear your sling tonight. Right?"

"Yes, I'll wear the stupid sling—even if I don't really need it."

"How's the ankle?"

"The ankle is fine," Tee sighed. "I can even dance tonight."

Markie gave her an affectionate smile. "Then you can dance with me first."

"You're on."

"Oh, and thanks for letting me use the suite to get ready tonight, Tee. I really appreciate it. It's so convenient."

"No problem." She drained her drink and stood. "I guess I should get ready."

"Are you wearing the black tux tonight?"

"Yes." She disappeared into the bedroom. "Does that meet with your approval?" she called back through the open door.

Markie laughed. "Yes dear. You'll look fabulous, as always."

When Tee re-appeared she had on the tuxedo pants and black boots, but she was struggling with the buttons on the shirt.

"Come here," Markie commanded. She buttoned the shirt, inserted the cuff link in the right sleeve, and unzipped her pants.

"Oh baby," Tee joked. "Action tonight."

"You should be so lucky," Markie smirked. "Hold still." She tucked Tee's shirt in and zipped her back up. "Now, where is your cummerbund? Maybe if you play your cards right you can get somebody else to untuck you tonight."

"Sure," she answered tonelessly. "I'll be sure to give that a try."

"Honey, you have to get out there and at least look," Markie chastised her gently.

"I will," she automatically answered. She turned the French cuff of her left sleeve back over the cast on her left arm and searched out the sling she'd abandoned earlier. She found it on the table and slipped it over her head. "Do you think I can get David to introduce me as Tee tonight?"

Markie grinned over at her. "No. He loves saying your full name for some reason."

"It'll take me a month to get everyone to stop," she sighed.

"I'll go get into my dress and we can go upstairs."

Tee whistled when Markie came out of the bedroom. She was beautiful. She twirled for Tee's inspection. The back of her form-fitting dress plunged low, held up by the thinnest of straps. Her throat was adorned with a diamond choker and she wore matching earrings. "Oh darlin', you are going to be the main attraction in a lot of fantasies tonight."

"You're so sweet," she giggled.

"Tell me why you're not tied down again," Tee said as she gave her a one armed hug.

"Because I'm having too much fun," she laughed. "Here, let me help you with your jacket." She held the tux jacket while Tee slipped her right arm into the sleeve and then adjusted the left side to hang from her shoulder. "Talk about being someone's wet dream," she murmured as she stood in front of Tee and smoothed the jacket out.

"Cut it out," Tee snorted.

"Are you ready?"

"Yes. Let's go play with all the other lesbians." She held out her arm and Markie slipped her hand through the crook of her elbow.

Chapter 24

Carly took the afternoon to pamper herself. She had her hair done, a facial, and a massage. She took a long bath and dressed in a long midnight blue gown with a slit up the left side to mid-thigh and matching heels.

Paul and Wayne picked her up and they all went to The Reed House together. "Have you ever eaten here?" Paul asked as he guided her past the restaurant to the elevator.

"No, but I've heard it's great."

"You'll get a taste of the food tonight," Wayne told her. They joined a small group of others in the car and it rose swiftly to the fourth floor. The elevator had been programmed to allow access to that floor only tonight. There were two officers of the GLBT foundation who checked their tickets and then they passed through into the ballroom. A six-piece ensemble played on a raised platform at the far end of the huge room. Tables seating ten people apiece were arranged on either side leaving the center open for dancing. It was filling up fast as the trio made their way to their table.

"What can I get you to drink?" Paul asked.

"Scotch."

"Rocks?"

"Yes, please."

"Wayne, what are you drinking tonight?"

"I'll have the same, honey."

"I'll be right back."

Wayne and Carly entertained themselves by people watching while he was gone. There were every sort of dress in the crowd from leather to men in drag and women in tuxedos. There were long gowns, short dresses, and jewelry galore.

"Oh honey, you put these other women to shame," Wayne whispered in her ear.

"You're so sweet," she giggled at him.

"Let's dance," he said and took her hand.

The ensemble was good and Carly danced easily in Wayne's arms. "You lead pretty well for a total queen," she teased him.

"Paul likes to think he leads," he grinned at her. "We all know it's the women who really do."

The ballroom was full by the time they arrived and Tee swept her eyes around the room making sure everything was as it should be. They stopped to greet David Mitchell, the president of the GLBT organization in Dallas.

"David," Tee shook his hand. "Please, if you must introduce me tonight, the name is Tee."

"Sure," he grinned at her. "And thanks for everything. You have been more than generous by donating the ballroom as well as the food. We really can't thank you enough."

"You've got quite a full house tonight," Markie remarked. "The donations should reflect that. It'll be a good night."

"I think so too," he smiled. "People are networking like crazy already."

"I like the ensemble," Tee said, nodding her head at the musicians on stage. "They're very good."

They were interrupted by one of the board members seeking David and she and Markie drifted to the head table and found their seats.

"What can I get you to drink?" Tee asked.

"I'll get them," she laughed. "How do you think you can carry two drinks in one hand?"

"My hand works," she protested. "I don't even need this stupid sling."

Markie ignored her. "Scotch?"

"Yes," she sighed then added, "Please."

Tee was in conversation with two board members when Markie returned with her drink. They showed no inclination of leaving so she deposited Tee's drink in front of her and left her to fend for herself. She knew they were trying to pressure Tee into joining the board. Tee gave the GLBT her full support but had never wanted to be a part of the reigning hierarchy. She hated anything that was run by committee. One of her business principals was if there had to be a vote to do anything she was out.

Tee glanced around her desperately looking for a reason to get away from the two board members who were relentless in their pursuit of her. She gleefully spied Fiona and Jane entering the room. She pushed her chair back.

"Would you please excuse me? I need to speak to one of my employees a moment." Without waiting for an answer she left the table and crossed the room.

"Fiona. Jane." She greeted them. "It's nice to see you both here."

Jane was in a dove gray dress with heels to match. Her hair was done up exposing her neck and showing off diamond earrings. She looked elegant. Fiona wore a black suit with a red shirt and a matching red handkerchief expertly folded into the breast pocket. The eyebrow stud tonight was a sterling silver post with a diamond on each end. Tee wondered how that worked. She was dapper; there was just no other word for it. She had her left hand at the small of Jane's back but held out her right to shake with Tee.

"It looks like a great party."

"I want to thank both of you for all your hard work this past month. The success of the ball is as much yours as anyone else's."

"Thanks, boss," Fiona grinned.

"Thank you Tee," Jane said more formally.

"The drinks are on me tonight so have a great time." She started away but turned back. "Oh, and Jane?"

"Yes?"

"Behave yourself tonight."

Fiona laughed and Jane turned a light shade of red. Fiona gave her a thumbs up while giving Jane a peck on the cheek. Tee laughed and caught up with Markie at the bar.

"I see you managed to escape the board," Markie observed. "Unscathed?"

"Yes," she grinned, "but it was close." She nodded and smiled at several people around them. Before she could order, a drink was placed in front of her and her bartender gave her a big smile of thanks. Working this event was a plum assignment. The tips would be bigger than working a normal shift at one of the bars. She smiled back and nodded. The lights briefly dimmed twice.

"Dinner is about to be served," she said to Markie. "Are you still sitting beside me or have you met someone already?"

"I've met several someone's but I'm still eating dinner with you," she grinned. "They're for later."

"You dog!" Tee laughed. She guided Markie back to their table as everyone else did the same. There was general noise as chairs were pulled back and people sat until all were settled. The waiters and waitresses began serving and the room settled into a cacophony of multiple conversations amid the clatter of silverware. The ball had officially begun.

Dinner was served and as Tee and Markie ate they chatted with the people at their table, laughing and making new friends. Tee was trying to just enjoy the event instead of continually checking that all was going as planned but it was difficult. She wanted anything with her name on it to be perfect.

As the dinner wound down the podium was rolled onto the stage and David tapped the microphone until he had their attention. It was time for awards, speeches, and pleas for donations of both time and money.

"Ladies and Gentlemen, thank you all for coming tonight. It has been a great turn out." He waited for the applause to quiet. "As most of you are aware, I'm David Mitchell, your president." There was more applause. "Before we get into our program we need to take a moment to thank The Reed House for not only hosting this event but also for donating the food as well. Please give a hand for Thelonious Sylar Reed."

Carly was applauding along with everyone else as Tee stood up from her place at the front table. She froze and her mind went completely blank. Tee? Tee Reed. Reed. The Reed House. Tee was *that* Reed? *Holy Shit!* She knew Tee owned the Reeders Row bar but she never said a word about the Reed House. Tee sat back down and the president continued with his comments but it was all lost to her. She strained to see around all the other people to get another glimpse of her. She let out a long breath and wondered how long she'd been holding it.

"Are you okay?" Wayne whispered in her ear.

"What?" She looked at him in confusion.

"You're white as a sheet. Are you feeling all right?"

"Yes," she nodded and took in another deep breath. "I'm fine."

He continued to watch her and knew she wasn't. He whispered something to Paul and then took her hand. "Come with me." She resisted initially but then allowed him to take her out into the hall. Once there she took several deep breaths and leaned against the wall. "Maybe it's just warm in there," he offered. "It wasn't the food, was it?"

"No, the food was great," she assured him. She wished he would leave her alone. She needed to think but she couldn't do it with him hovering over her. In a few minutes she did relax a little as the shock wore off. The color returned to her face and she pushed away from the wall. She wasn't going to ruin their friends evening just because she'd been slapped in the face with the worst mistake of her life. "Let's go back inside," she said with a small smile that she hoped looked normal. "I feel much better now."

"Are you sure?" His concern for her made her feel guilty.

"I think you were right. It was a little too close in there but I'll be fine now."

Paul looked up when they returned. "Everything okay?"

"Yes," Carly nodded and resolutely turned her attention to the podium again. There were several speakers but it was all a blur to her. She applauded when everyone else did and kept a smile on her face. When it was finally over the music and the dancing began once again.

People used the time to see and be seen and to strengthen their networking. Paul left to talk to another attorney and Carly searched the dancers when Wayne went to get them a drink. She found her on the fringe of the dance floor. She was dancing with the buxom blonde she'd been with the night they'd first met. She looked great, Carly thought. Her tuxedo fit her tall lean frame well and she was as beautiful as ever. They turned and she saw the limp sleeve hanging from her left side and then the slice of blue sling that held her arm across her chest. She was hurt. Carly's breath caught in her chest. It hurt her to think of Tee in pain.

Wayne returned with their drinks. He followed her line of sight and smiled. "You have good taste," he laughed in her ear.

"What?" She hastily averted her gaze.

"She's gorgeous," he grinned. "And she's just as nice as she is good looking."

"You know her?"

"Yeah, a little."

"How?"

"Paul handles some legal work for her," he said. "Remember? The woman she's dancing with is her best friend, Markie Killigan. They've known each other forever."

"Oh yeah," she nodded. "What happened to her arm?" Her eyes were glued to Tee again.

"I don't know," he shrugged. "Maybe Paul does." He put his arm around her shoulders. "Would you like to dance?"

"No," she quickly shook her head. She couldn't risk having Tee see her. She would definitely die of embarrassment. What would she say to her? No, she couldn't risk it. But she couldn't keep her eyes off her either. Even with only one arm she smoothly guided Markie around the floor. "Is she with anyone?" she forced herself to ask.

"I don't think so. Rumor has it she doesn't date much so I would have heard."

"She's gorgeous," Carly said without thinking. "Why doesn't she date? There must be thousands of women who would jump at the chance." *And I blew mine*, she thought bitterly.

"Paul said she got burned in college by some woman who cheated on her and then dumped her because she didn't have any money or something like that." He shrugged. "I don't know the whole story."

Oh great, I treated her like the one she loved before and probably never got over. Could I have been more of an asshole?

They contented themselves with watching the dancers until Paul returned to their table. "Did you make some new clients?" Wayne asked him with a smile.

"I handed out some cards," Paul admitted. "What have you two been doing?"

"Carly's been drooling over Ms Reed," Wayne giggled.

"Good choice," he smiled over at her. He had hoped she would forgive Tee for her behavior at their meeting in her office. He turned back to Wayne. "And who have you been drooling over?"

"Me? You know you're the only one for me, hon."

Paul rolled his eyes but he was smiling. "You're such a sweetie."

"Okay, you two, no public display of affection."
"There's no better place than here," Paul laughed and gave Wayne a loud smacking kiss.

Chapter 25

The ensemble had been replaced by a 5-piece band and the music was more contemporary. Time to party. The bar was immediately flooded as everyone needed a fresh drink. Tee leaned across the table and shook David's hand.

"You did a fabulous job, David."

"Thank you. Did any of our board members coerce you into joining us tonight?"

"No," she shook her head. "And thanks for the full name intro. I *so* like being called Thelonious." Her tone dripped with sarcasm.

"My pleasure," he laughed. "Seriously, Tee, thanks for everything. You've been more than generous this year above all others. This has absolutely been the best ball ever!"

"Don't mention it," she waved the compliment off with a flip of a hand. She took Markie's hand. "Can I have this dance, beautiful?"

"You may." She stood and they made their way to the floor. They danced easily together and Markie kissed Tee on the cheek as the song ended. "I have someone you should meet," she said.

Tee raised an eyebrow at her. "Really? I need a drink."

Markie went with her and together they made a path to the bar. "You remember you put me in charge of your dating?" she reminded her. "I have someone who wants to meet you."

Tee repressed a sigh. It wasn't as if she didn't know how to engage in small talk. She was quite good at it under normal circumstances. She'd endured so much of it as she was building her businesses but she just wasn't in the mood for it tonight. She took one look at Markie's face though and relented. "Who is it this time?"

"Don't take that tone," Markie warned her in a murmur. "Her name is Michelle Hollis."

"Where do you know her from?" Tee was careful to keep her tone even and non-judgmental.

"She's a CPA."

"I could use a good CPA," Tee kidded her with a smile.

"There you go," Markie grinned back. "She's fun and I think you'll like her. Kathleen knows her."

"And who is Kathleen?" Tee asked archly.

"Kathleen is a woman I've been seeing lately." Markie didn't look at her when she said this.

"Ooo, tell me more," Tee urged her instantly.

"There's nothing to tell," she said shortly. "And it doesn't matter who I'm seeing. We're talking about you seeing someone here."

"I'd rather hear about Kathleen. Is it serious?"

"Tee…" she warned again.

"Okay," she conceded. "Tell me about Michelle. Kathleen's friend."

"She has reddish brown hair down to her shoulders. She's around 5'7" so she's shorter than you. She has a great figure too."

"What's the but?"

"What do you mean?"

"If all of that is true and she's single then there must be a but."

"You're still single," Markie pointed out.

"Yeah, you're right," she nodded with a grin. "So, when have you arranged for me to meet her?"

"She's here tonight."

"You were pretty sure of yourself."

"Yes, I was. You put me in charge. Remember that."

"For how long?" Tee wanted to know. There was a worried frown on her face now.

Markie laughed. "Until you find someone."

"Oh man," she groaned. "What have I gotten myself into?"

They'd reached the front of the line and the bartender set fresh drinks in front of them automatically. Tee smiled her thanks and stuffed some bills into the tip jar before turning with Markie to walk away. They stepped to one side of the dance floor and out of the way.

"Where is she?"

Markie searched the room, finally finding Michelle at one of the tables talking to a small group of women. "There she is. She's the one on the right side in the green dress with the pearls."

Tee followed her sight line and observed the woman in question. Nice, was her first thought. She did, indeed, have a good figure as far as Tee could tell. She had a nice figure was her second thought. She gave Markie a nod. "Looks good," she said.

"Let's go talk to her." Markie led her to the table and put a hand on Michelle's shoulder to get her attention.

"Oh, hi Markie," she looked over her shoulder and smiled up at them.

"Hi. Michelle, I'd like you to meet someone."

"Okay, sure." She pushed her chair back. "Excuse me girls."

"Michelle, I'd like you to meet my friend, Tee." She turned to Tee. "Tee, this is Michelle."

Tee held out her hand. "Nice to meet you, Michelle."

"It's nice to meet you too," she smiled up into Tee's eyes. "I hear this is your place."

"Yes," Tee nodded reluctantly. "May I get you a drink?"

"That would be very nice," she agreed. "Thank you."

Tee escorted her to the bar and noticed when they got there they'd lost Markie somewhere along the way. She should have expected that. She ordered a rum and Coke for Michelle but shook her head on a refill on her scotch. "Let's get out of the crowd," she suggested.

They moved away from the bar and commandeered a small open space where it was a bit quieter. "So Michelle, what do you do?"

She leaned a little closer and began telling her about the company she worked for as a CPA. Tee listened politely until a flash of leg on a passing woman caught her eye. The dress was a deep blue and the slit up the leg was very revealing as the woman walked. Tee couldn't help herself—she looked. She immediately lost concentration on Michelle's story as she let her eyes follow the woman as she went toward the bar. She should have thought about the possibility of Carly attending this function. She should have been prepared. She was not. And because she was not, she was helpless to control her body's reaction to the sight of her. There was the instant blazing heat searing her core, the tensing of every muscle in her entire body, and the undeniable rush between her legs. She licked dry lips unconsciously.

"Don't waste your time on her," Michelle said in her ear. "I hear she's a real loser even though she does have nice legs."

"What do you mean?" Tee forced her attention back to Michelle.

"She's unemployed and I heard nobody will hire her. She got fired because of insubordination or something like that." It was obvious to Tee that she enjoyed relating the juicy details of someone else's misfortune.

"Do you know her?" Tee needed any information she could find.

"Not personally but I know some of the people she worked with and they told me the whole story." She gave a little laugh before continuing. "She thought she knew more about being a lawyer than her boss and refused to plead some case or something. Can you image anyone being that stupid? She deserved to get fired."

Something crawled up the back of Tee's neck and she swiveled her eyes to the bar. "What's she doing now?" She tried to keep her voice casual.

"I don't know," Michelle shrugged. "Still looking for a job, I guess. Like I said, I don't know her personally, I just know the story." She put her hand on Tee's arm and squeezed, trying to regain her attention.

Tee searched the crowd at the bar again but couldn't find her anywhere. She mentally gave herself a head slap. *Stop thinking about her!* She turned back and feigned interest in Michelle's conversation even though she couldn't have told anyone what they were talking about later. She asked Michelle to dance and they moved to the floor. Since Tee had only one working arm it meant Michelle had to put both arms around her neck. Generally this would have been a good thing but Tee couldn't shake thoughts of those legs from her mind. They were legs that had been wrapped around her once, thighs quivering and toes curling. She pushed it roughly from her thoughts and tried to focus on Michelle. She let her right hand move along her spine to the small of her back and, while it may have looked like she was caressing her dance partner, it was herself that needed soothing. She needed the feel of soft smooth skin under her hand, the feel of a woman in her arms to ease the ache, a moment of respite from…her. She hated her. She hated her more than she had ever hated anyone. She had let her in, deep inside, where she existed. It was the first time she'd let anyone in so deep. Not since Carol had left her back in college had she felt so humiliated. There must be something she lacked, some essential chemical that everyone else had and she didn't. Or maybe she just had '*sucker*' written all over her face. She pulled Michelle tighter into her one armed embrace. This woman was what she needed. Michelle was exactly the kind of woman she needed. There were no surprises here. And if they didn't love each other so what? It wasn't about love. Love didn't exist. At least not the kind of love she had always wanted. She had been living a fantasy. It was time to let fantasy go now and live in the real world. She had the fleeting thought that Markie would be glad to see her giving up on a fantasy life. At least someone would be happy.

"So how are you and Michelle getting along?" Markie eased up beside her near the bar where she was waiting for Michelle to return from the ladies room.

"You haven't been keeping tabs on us?" Tee asked in mock shock.

Markie grinned. "Well, maybe for a little while. It looked like you were getting along. I saw you dancing together."

"Yeah, we danced."

"But?"

"But nothing," she shook her head. "She seems like just the right kind of woman for me. She already knows I have money so there won't be any mistake there. She's pretty direct in what she wants." Tee looked at her for a moment. "And I'm sure I qualify as a prospect."

"But you're not going to see her again."

"Oh, I'm going to see her again," Tee nodded. "I'm going to see more of her tonight. I'm going to see a lot more of her tonight." She smiled archly at her good friend. "You might be welcome to join us. I haven't asked but she seems like she might be the type."

Markie looked at her long and hard. Her words said one thing but her tone said another. "As fun as that sounds, I think I'll pass this time." She gave Tee another look and saw the resolute but sad glint in her eyes. "You don't have to date her you know. I don't really care."

"No, I think she's perfect for me. No worries at all."

"You don't really seem to like the idea all that much," she remarked. "I'll keep looking for someone for you."

"No," Tee shook her head. "Really, she's perfect. I know what to expect with her. I've decided to give up the fantasy. It's going to be me living in the real world from now on."

Markie looked into those sad eyes again and finally understood. "You saw her tonight, didn't you?"

"Who?"

"You know who. Carly." Markie cast a quick scan around the room. "Is that what this is all about?"

"I don't know what you're talking about."

"Tee, if she's here then maybe you should talk to her; find out what went wrong."

"She thought I wouldn't mind sharing her with another woman, that's what went wrong," Tee said with a bite of anger. She took a deep breath and calmed herself. "It doesn't matter. Thanks for introducing me to Michelle." She walked off leaving Markie both sad and fearful for her.

Chapter 26

Carly returned to their table with drinks from the bar for her and Wayne. She resolutely kept her head down not wanting to call attention to herself in any way. She refused to search for Tee in the crowd again and didn't know where she might be. When she reached their table she sat with a relieved sigh.

"Is Paul networking again?" she asked.

"Yes," he rolled his eyes dramatically but smiled. "I don't know why. He's already got more business than he can handle now."

"Business comes and goes though," she reminded him. "It's not something you can predict."

"Don't look now but there are a couple of women to your left that keep looking your way. Maybe you know them?"

Carly frowned. "Are they looking now?"

"No. Take a quick glance."

She did and immediately stiffened. "Nobody," she snapped.

"Wow, that's some reaction for nobody," Wayne murmured. "I'll assume you do know them."

"Unfortunately, yes. They are my former friends. And I emphasize *former*."

"From BH&S?"

"Yes." She took a hefty pull from her drink. "Selfish bitches," she spat.

He sighed and took her hand in his on top of the table. "Honey, don't even waste your time on them, let alone any of your energy."

She squeezed his hand. "Thanks."

"We should get you a hot woman to dance with to show them you're doing just fine without them."

Carly laughed bitterly. "I was with a hot woman right before I got fired."

"Tell me again who that hot woman was."

Carly looked sideways at him. "Nice try, Wayne. I didn't tell you who it was."

"Yeah, I know," he nodded. "Why is that?"

"Because it doesn't matter and because…I don't want you to think I'm an even bigger fool than you already do."

"Honey, it doesn't matter," he started to say.

"Let's just drop it, okay?"

"Okay." He took a sip from his drink and gave the crowd a searching look. He knew a lot of people and he was sure he could find someone to dance with her. His gaze settled on Gail Smithson, a former colleague of his. He pondered how to go about getting her to ask Carly to dance. They were interrupted by the return of Paul once again. He gave Wayne a kiss on the cheek before plopping down in his chair. "I might have just made headway in getting some work from Metro Energy," he proclaimed with a big smile.

"So that's who you've been talking to for the last hour," Wayne observed.

"Yes," he nodded happily.

"Well, I'm going to dance with our lovely friend here. Will you be here when we get back?"

"Probably. I think I'll go get a drink though. You two have a good time." He rose with them and started back to the bar while Wayne and Carly headed for the dance floor. He took her in his arms and they waltzed their way into the crowd.

Wayne steered her to the area where he'd last seen Gail and found her by accident as they bumped into her. "Hey, Gail. It's been a long time," he gushed.

"Hey Wayne," she smiled at him. "How have you been?"

"Good. Paul and I are doing very well. Have you met Carly? This is Carly Matthews. Carly, this is a friend of mine, Gail Smithson. We used to work together."

Carly shook her hand and wondered how he had maneuvered her into this. Gail was smiling at her though and looked genuinely pleased to see both of them. She smiled back. "Nice to meet you, Gail."

"Hey, why don't you two finish this dance while I go find Paul?" Wayne walked off without giving either of them a chance to refuse.

"Well, Wayne has spoken," Gail said with a smile. She held out her arms and Carly automatically moved into them. What choice did she have?

They danced rather smoothly for it being their first time and Carly relaxed as Gail took control of their movements and led her around the floor. "Have you known Wayne long?" Gail asked after a moment.

"Not too long," she admitted. "I met both him and Paul about six weeks ago. He said you used to work together?"

"Yeah, we both started at Sterling at the same time. We hired in the same day and recognized each other as family right away so we sort of bonded."

"He's a sweetie," Carly said.

"That he is," she agreed.

Tee stood near the edge of the dance floor with a drink in her hand. Michelle had disappeared into the ladies room. Her mind was blank as she stood there watching other people have fun. She felt nothing herself. She had reached a place where nothing existed inside her, a place where nothing mattered. She would wait for her new companion to return and they'd dance, drink, and then go down to her suite at the end of the night. They would not make love. They would have sex. It might not be much of a distinction to some but it was a distinction nonetheless. Her gaze was caught by the flash of a blue dress in the crowd and she looked. If she thought the first glimpse of her had been difficult this one was devastating. She was in the arms of another woman, a woman who was holding her, smiling at her, laughing with her. The kick of a horse to her gut could not have hurt worse than this. She closed her eyes in helpless pain. When she opened them again Carly was looking right at her. Tee held her breath. She wanted to flee but couldn't move. She wanted to look away but was held in place by the force of her gaze. And then Carly's lips moved in a silent plea. 'I'm sorry'. Tee opened her mouth but nothing came out and Carly was turned by her dance partner and was swallowed by the crowd.

Tee was finally able to move and strode quickly into the foyer. She took several deep breaths and only then noticed how badly her hand was shaking. The scotch was in danger of sloshing over the rim. She hastily set it down on a nearby table and shoved her hand into her pocket. *God damn it! How could such a self-absorbed bitch still have the ability to affect her like this?* She fumed at her inability to control her own emotions. *Sorry? She was sorry? That's what she had to say? Fuck! Fuck! Fuck!* She wanted to smash her fist through the wall. *Oh, by the way, I'm sorry for ripping your heart out. That was just great.* She paced across the foyer, more agitated than she could ever remember being. She brought herself up short as she spied Michelle coming back from the ladies room. She took several deep breaths, willing herself to calm down, and stepped back into the ballroom.

"There you are," Michelle smiled at her.

"Yes," Tee nodded. She resolutely kept her eyes off the dance floor and on Michelle. "Are you ready to call it a night here?"

"Oh." She hesitated but recovered quickly. "Yes, of course. If you are."

"I am." Tee put a hand around her waist and guided her out into the foyer. "I have some nice Champagne in my suite downstairs."

"Oh, that sounds good."

Tee pushed the down button on the elevator and they were soon exiting on the third floor. She slipped a hand into an inside pocket and swiped the key card and the door opened. Michelle went inside and Tee followed, locking the door behind her. She went to the mini fridge for the wine while Michelle looked around. Tee set the bottle on the small table and shrugged out of her jacket. She pulled the sling over her head and tossed it on top. She still wore a cast but at least she had the use of her whole arm now. She picked up the bottle and went into the small sitting room. "If you can help me open this I'll go get us a couple of glasses."

"Of course."

With the wine poured Tee held her glass up to Michelle's. "To you." It was simple and yet didn't mean a thing.

Michelle gave her a big smile. "Thank you."

By the time the bottle was empty, Michelle was in Tee's lap, her shoes off and her dress riding high on her thighs. Tee slid her hand up under the hem and caressed the creamy thigh as Michelle kissed her again. Michelle lifted her lips from Tee's and brushed against her ear. "Is there any more of that delicious Champagne?"

"I think I have another bottle," she responded slowly. "I'll get it." She eased out from under her and stood up. There was one last bottle and she brought it back to the couch. Michelle reached for it. "This is really good stuff," she told her as she filled both glasses.

As well it should be at over a hundred dollars a pop, Tee thought. "Shall we see how it tastes in the bedroom?"

"Ooo, yeah," she giggled. "I like that." She stood and Tee reached out to help her.

"Why don't you go ahead and I'll bring the bottle and glasses? I'll be right in."

"Okay, but don't be too long. I'll be waiting."

Tee watched her disappear into the bedroom and went into the kitchen. She took her time putting the empty bottles in the trash and cleaning the immediate area. Finally she picked up the fresh bottle and nestled it in the crook of her left arm and then grabbed both glasses and entered the bedroom. She set the glasses down on the nightstand first and then the bottle. She could see Michelle was already in bed, her clothes strewn across the floor in a trail. She had obviously been in a hurry. She pushed up into a sitting position and the sheet fell, baring her breasts.

"Hey," she whispered. "I've been waiting." She reached a hand out and Tee put a glass in it and then filled it.

Tee kicked off her boots and unfastened the cummerbund. She used the fingertips of her left hand to remove the cufflink from her right shirtsleeve and then it was easy to unbutton the shirt and unzip her trousers. She stood close to the side of the bed and gently took the glass from Michelle's hand and set it on the nightstand. She instinctively knew this woman would want to be brought along slowly, petted, stroked, made to feel beautiful and precious before giving in to her more base and carnal desires. Ordinarily it would not have been a problem but she couldn't get the thought of Carly out of her mind. How different their first time was from this. There had been no games between them. They wanted each other and weren't afraid to acknowledge it. And Tee knew Carly would have done anything with her or to her that night. With Michelle she would need to curb her more…enthusiastic actions. She could do that. She'd done it with other women. Right? No problem.

Gail put her hand on the small of Carly's back and escorted her off the dance floor and to the bar. "What would you like to drink?"

"Uh, scotch is fine, thanks." Carly couldn't resist giving the entrance a swift search while Gail was getting their drinks. There was no sign of Tee. Disappointment stabbed her. Of all the times to have them see each other, it had to be while she was dancing with another woman. Just great. It probably looked to Tee as if she'd moved on to someone else and was just apologizing for forms sake and not very well at that. How was she ever going to make this right? Could she even make it right? Gail returned and handed her a glass with a smile.

"I'm glad I ran into Wayne and you on the floor tonight," she said. "I haven't seen him in ages."

"I adore both him and Paul," she nodded.

Gail was a very nice woman and Carly would probably have been interested in getting to know her better at any other time, but right now all she could think about was Tee. How she looked, the fact that she had been injured, how she'd lost weight, and the shock on her face when she'd seen her dancing. These were the things she was thinking about instead of listening to the woman in front of her. It finally penetrated her foggy brain that Gail was waiting for an answer.

"Sure," she said without thinking.

"Do you have a card with you tonight?"

She got it then. Gail wanted her number. She thought back to a time when she would have whipped out her business card, proud of where she worked. Maybe she should get some cards printed up that simply said, 'Unencumbered by the restraints of business hierarchy'. That should do it. She shook herself back to the present.

"I'm afraid I don't," she said.

"That's okay. I'll just give you my card then if that's all right."

"That's fine."

"Oh, there's Paul. Can we go say hi? I haven't seen him in ages either."

"Certainly." Carly was glad to get a buffer between them right then. She couldn't seem to concentrate on Gail or what she was saying. She led her back to their table and everyone fell into hugs and kisses. She took her seat next to Wayne and tried to act interested.

"Jane," Fiona said in a low voice against her ear, "you're killing me." They were the only two still sitting at their table. Fiona had her chair as close to Jane's as possible and she had her arm draped along the back of it, her hand cupping her shoulder.

"Whatever do you mean?" Jane asked in wide-eyed surprise, but the corners of her mouth twitched. She had her hand on Fiona's thigh under the tablecloth and was rubbing gently along her inseam.

"You know exactly what I mean," Fiona growled. "You need to either quit rubbing my leg or let me take you somewhere where you can rub everything."

Jane's hand stilled. "Oh. You want me to stop?"

"No!" Fiona groaned. She took in a deep breath and then another until she could speak normally. "I never suspected you were such a tease."

"What? You thought I was just a sweet little girl?" she laughed.

"Well, no, not that exactly," Fiona said. "I just didn't expect...wicked." She said the last with a grin and she tightened the arm around her shoulders pulling her against her.

"Wicked, huh?" Jane smiled. "Yes. I like that."

"Oh man," Fiona groaned again. "What have I gotten myself into?"

"You might get yourself to second base tonight," Jane said casually, "or maybe even third if you play your cards right."

"Don't play with me, Jane." Fiona's tone was desperate.

Jane laughed. "Really? Are you sure you mean that? I thought that's exactly what you wanted me to do, Fee."

"Oh God." She groaned again and put her forehead on Jane's shoulder. "I'm overmatched," she said to herself. "I should have known, but I didn't have a clue. I'm in over my head." She looked at Jane and her soft brown eyes were like melted chocolate. "I'll play my cards any way you want, Jane. Anything for you."

"Aw, you're so sweet." Jane leaned closer and put her lips to Fiona's. It was a nice kiss, a sweet kiss, a pure kiss. Fiona wanted to take it a step farther, to use her tongue to delve deeper and discover what lay beyond. She wanted to devour her. She didn't. She held onto her wants and settled for feeling how nice Jane's breasts felt as they pushed against her chest. She was rewarded for her patience when Jane gave a small moan and reached a hand up to cup Fiona's cheek.

Chapter 27

A week later Tee was at her desk early. Her inter-office phone line chirped and she looked up in surprise. The read out said it was the IT department which meant it was Fiona. Tee picked it up.

"Good morning, Captain IT."

"Good morning, boss." There was a pause and then she said, "I was just wondering if you were in the office early today."

"As you can tell, I am." Tee waited, knowing there was more.

"I wanted to talk to you about…something."

"Would you care to come to my office and talk?"

"Yes," she said on an expulsion of breath. "If that would be all right with you," she hastily added.

"I'll see you in a minute," Tee smiled and hung up. Less than five minutes later there was a knock on the door that opened into the back hallway. It was Tee's private entrance. "Come on in Captain," she called out.

Fiona opened the door and entered with a sheepish look on her face. Now that she was here she was having second thoughts. "Hey, boss."

"What's on your mind, Fiona?" Tee leaned back in her desk chair and nodded at one of the chairs in front of her desk for her to sit down.

"Uh, well, I thought..." She faltered to a stop.

"Is this about Jane?" Tee asked gently.

"Uh, yeah."

"I'd love to help you out but you're going to have to tell me what you need."

"Yeah," she nodded quickly and inhaled a deep breath before continuing. "You know Jane."

When she stopped Tee nodded. "Yes, I do."

"You know I like her. Well, more than just like her." She finally raised her eyes to look directly at Tee. "The problem is I'm not quite sure what it is she wants from me."

"Ah. I'm not sure I can help you with that," Tee said quickly.

"No, I didn't mean it like that," Fiona said. "I mean you know what she's like, what she likes and doesn't like, how she wants to be treated. You know, things like that."

"Oh. Well." Tee looked at the ceiling for inspiration. "Jane is a practical type of woman. At least here in the office."

"I know," Fiona said quickly.

"But that doesn't mean she's like that in her personal life," Tee continued. "I need you to be just a tiny bit more specific in what you want to know."

"She's such a tease," Fiona blurted out. "At the ball last week she's rubbing my leg under the table and saying she might let me get to third base. I *so* want to get to third base, boss. I just need to know what I can do to improve my chances. And if you know something I shouldn't do that would sure be a big help too."

Tee hid the smile that threatened to break loose. "I'm going to assume you want to not only get to third base but beyond." She waited until Fee nodded yes. "Is it because it's a challenge? She says no so you want her to say yes. Is it that kind of thing?"

"No," Fiona shook her head vigorously. "I really like her, boss."

"Okay." Tee cleared her throat. "There are no guarantees or tricks, Fee. All I can tell you is pay attention."

"Pay attention?" She looked at her in disbelief. This was Tee's secret with women?

"Yes. Pay attention," she nodded with a smile. "Pay attention to what she talks about. Pay attention to what she looks at in a store. Pay attention to the noises she makes when you kiss her and definitely pay attention to how the noises change when you kiss her in a different place. There is a lot of information to be had if you just use your ears. And then there are your eyes. Watching is just as important. Watch how she reacts."

"How she reacts to what?"

"To everything," Tee grinned. "Like how does she look when you smile at her. Like how she looks when you say something sweet. How does she look when you hold her hand or open a door for her. How she reacts to where you touch her or where you kiss her. Is she purring or growling? Look in her eyes most of all. The eyes don't lie." Tee grinned. "And while she appears to be a practical woman here at the office she's obviously attracted to a heavily pierced and tattooed punk-geek like you."

"Yeah," Fiona grinned, "she is." She nodded. "Okay. I think I see what you're saying."

"Just remember, it's all about her. If you think about her first, last, and in between, then you'll be fine."

Fiona looked at her in awe. "You are my Goddess," she said with reverence.

Tee laughed out loud. "Stop it. I only told you because I think you really care for Jane and want her to be happy."

"I do," she nodded quickly. "Thanks, boss."

"Oh, and doing something nice for her for no reason always goes a long way," Tee added and Fiona stood to leave. "And Fiona?"

"Yes, boss?"

"Be true to yourself. No woman, not even Jane, is worth trying to change who you are. Remember that."

"Any time you need anything, boss, call me. I'm there for you. I owe you big."

Tee laughed. "You may want to wait until you cross the plate before vowing any debt of gratitude, but I'll keep it in mind." She stood herself, preparing to get a fresh cup of coffee. "It goes without saying, Fiona, that I will be most disappointed if you hurt her." It was said with a smile but the tone was stern and the smile didn't reach her eyes.

"I won't," she swore and left through the private entrance to go back to her domain of bits and bytes and computer parts.

Tee went down to the break room and refilled her coffee cup with a smile on her face. She never thought she'd be the go-to person for the office lovelorn. What a joke. She couldn't keep a woman herself but Fiona thought she had the answer. She thought about her dates with Michelle. Their night together after the GLBT annual ball had gone well, mostly because Tee adhered to her own advice about listening and watching. She also always made sure her partner was satisfied first. She took a sip of coffee while leaning her hips against the kitchen counter and staring into space. Michelle had been an adequate lover she supposed. She had had an orgasm anyway. Her mind glossed over how she'd had the briefest flash of Carly dancing upstairs and that had been the impetus to put her over the edge. Michelle was content to cuddle after that and had soon fallen asleep. It seemed she was a one and done girl. Tee shoved off the counter and went back to her office. It was best not to dwell on Michelle. They dated, they slept together, and that was about all there was to it.

No big deal. And that was just what she'd been looking for, right? No hassles, no strings, just good times. She sat behind her desk again and put the coffee on the corner. She could hear Jane in the outer office and pushed the intercom button on the phone.

"Good morning, Jane."

"Good morning," her voice came through the line light and cheerful. "Can I get you some coffee?"

"No thanks, I already have some."

"What can I do for you? Is your arm doing all right?"

Tee's doctor had taken the cast off her arm a few days earlier and it had been wonderful to finally be able to scratch. And, while it looked just a little smaller and whiter, it felt fine.

"It's fine, Jane. Thank you. I just wanted to say good morning. I know you'll update my calendar as soon as you have all the data but don't hurry. I'm doing some research so I'll be busy for a while."

"You'll get the update as soon as I do," Jane assured her.

Tee returned to her computer and her research on the bar and restaurant in San Antonio she was interested in buying. It was on the famous River Walk and it was currently named The Sports Room. They served ribs, chicken, and steaks and boasted over 50 kinds of beer plus the most lethal margaritas anywhere. A note on their menu warned patrons they were only allowed two margaritas. After that, if they ordered another one, they would be escorted from the premises. No exceptions. That alone would intrigue the average margarita drinker. It was situated between a New Orleans style seafood restaurant and a Tex-Mex restaurant. They seemed to be doing a good business and so far she couldn't find anything to indicate why the owner was looking to sell. If everything was as good as it looked on paper he should want to hold onto it. He said he wanted to relocate to the east coast because of a family matter. At least this business was something she had experience in and she could read between the lines on a balance sheet. She also knew a business like this would need to be investigated in person. The profit and loss sheet was good to see and the rating on Dunn & Bradstreet was good to know, but Tee knew all the paper in the world wouldn't tell the real story of how a business was actually doing. The books he sent to Paul looked sloppily kept and she wondered whom he was using as his CPA. Tee was tired of sitting at her desk. She was tired of looking at a computer screen. It seemed like every day was the same—boring. She needed to get out of the office and do something. So a trip down to San Antonio was in order. She smiled as she thought about it. It would be good to get away for a few days. She picked up the phone and got Jane on the line.

"Jane, could you get me a flight to San Antonio and book me a hotel?"

"When do you want to leave and where do you want to stay? And do you want a rental?"

"Tomorrow, whatever hotel you can get near the River Walk, and yes to the rental."

"How long will you be staying?"

"Book the hotel for a week. That should give me enough time. I may be back sooner though so let the troops know the cat will be away but not for too long. And could you please get Paul Carrington on the line for me?"

"I'll put it through when I get him."

Tee went back to her research and it wasn't long before Paul was on her phone. "Paul, I've been doing some research on The Sports Room down in San Antonio today."

"How does it look?"

"On paper it looks great."

"So, you're ready to get started on the sale?"

"Not quite."

"You have reservations about the deal?"

"It's just that it all seems too good to be true," she told him. "It makes me wonder."

"What are you thinking?"

"I'm going to head down there and just nose around," she said. "I want to get a feel for what's going on. Weekend business in a bar pays the bills but business during the week is what makes your profit." She blew out a breath. "I don't know, Paul. I think I just need to see things for myself."

"Then by all means go down there," he urged her. "I don't want you to make a decision about buying this place unless you're satisfied. Let me know if you need me down there and I'll be happy to join you or send the papers, whatever you need."

"Thanks, Paul. I'll let you know how it goes."

"Good luck."

It was only an hour later when Jane informed her she had a ride on a Tri-Star Charter Learjet 31A the next day. The 31A held seven passengers and had a range of 1,400 miles. She was booked for a week into a suite at the Regency Hotel and there would be a Ford Mustang rental waiting for her when she arrived at the charter airport. All she had to do was check in at the counter.

"If you'll call me when you want to come back I'll arrange a return flight."

"You're the best, Jane," Tee told her. "Remind me to give you a big bonus."

"No problem," she laughed.

Chapter 28

Markie stepped into Reeders Row on Cedar Springs and looked for Kathleen Tinley, her date. She was at the bar and waved when she saw Markie. She took the empty seat to her right. Kathleen leaned over to kiss her on the cheek.

"Hi. What are you drinking?" Kathleen asked with a big smile.

"Well, I've been thinking about a martini ever since I got your call today," Markie admitted.

"A martini it is then." Kathleen gestured for the bartender and ordered an apple martini and a refill on her beer. "How was your day?" she asked as their drinks were placed on the bar in front of them.

"It was good," Markie nodded. "Sales were good and all the clerks came to work for a change." She sipped her martini. "How was your day?"

"Boring," she said with a smile. "Some days I wonder why I ever thought being a lawyer would be exciting."

"So I'm guessing it was a paperwork kind of day."

"Yep." She slid an arm around Markie's shoulder. "But the evening seems to be looking a lot better."

Markie laughed and wondered why the obvious line made her warm with pleasure. "You're so full of it," she remarked automatically.

Kathleen was only slightly taller than Markie with thick, curly, light brown hair with natural highlights that hung to her shoulders. She had brown eyes that were very expressive. Her eyes were what had attracted Markie in the first place. They danced with humor and made her look like she would break out in laughter at any second.

"I only speak the truth," she vowed solemnly while holding a hand over her heart. "I've looked forward to seeing you all day."

"I've looked forward to this too," Markie admitted with a smile. "Should we go get something to eat before we get drunk?"

"Whatever you want," she said easily. "What do you have a taste for tonight?"

You, she thought, but said, "How about just going down to Snookie's for a burger?"

"You got it. Whenever you're ready."

They finished their drinks and went down the street for dinner. Conversation was light and lively as they ate, each relating moments of their day, comfortable with each other. Kathleen was attentive to her and Markie realized she reminded her of Tee. She treated her like Tee always treated women, with respect and deference. It felt good to be the absolute center of someone's attention. They returned to Reeders Row for after dinner drinks and took a table this time.

"Would you like to dance?" Kathleen asked as the music turned slow.

"Yes." Markie took her hand and followed her onto the floor and into her arms. She rested her head against Kathleen's shoulder and sighed in contentment as she followed her around the floor. It felt good to be held like this. They reluctantly left the floor when the music changed again and returned to their table. Kathleen scooted her chair close to Markie's and put her arm around her just as a waitress approached them.

"Can I get you two another drink?" She looked at Markie and smiled. "You know your drinks are free."

"I'm fine," Markie shook her head. She looked at Kathleen's beer. "Would you like another?"

"No, I'm good, thanks." Kathleen waited until the waitress moved on before asking, "Why are your drinks free?"

"Because I know the owner," she said with a small laugh.

"And who would that be?" she asked archly.

"Tee Reed."

"Ah, yes," Kathleen nodded.

"What?" Markie asked sharply.

"I've heard about her is all. She owns this bar?"

"She's my best friend," Markie said with emphasis on 'best'. "And yes, she owns this bar. What have you heard?"

"Nothing really," she assured her. "There was something going around at the firm about her. I'm not sure exactly what it was but I got the impression it wasn't good. The cool kids were definitely looking down their noses at her for something."

"Cook kids?"

"Yeah," she laughed. "A few of the girls that hang around together and think they're on the fast track to the ivory tower in the firm."

"And you're not one of them?" Markie asked with a smile.

"No, not me," she shook her head. "I saw the light a long time ago. The boys that occupy the ivory tower right now are never going to allow any woman to become a member of the boys club."

"So what's the thinking about Tee? I don't get it." Markie picked up her drink and then stopped halfway to her mouth. "What firm did you say you work for, Kathleen?"

"Brown, Hardin & Simon."

Markie dropped her head into her hands. "Oh shit."

"What?"

"Uh, I think I know what you heard. Are you sure these women aren't your friends?"

"No. I'm working in a different department and I was already there when they were hired. They seem to be aligning themselves with another woman though. I think her name is Suzanne Phillips. They think she's their ticket up the ladder." She took Markie's hand. "What's going on?"

"Tee was dating a lawyer in your firm, one who was friends with these other women. I don't know what happened exactly but it seems she also had another girlfriend she forgot to mention. She broke Tee's heart. I heard she got fired from there too. One of these days you'll meet Tee. It might be better if you didn't tell her where you work."

"Don't worry," Kathleen said quickly. She sipped her beer. "Do you want me to see if I can find out what happened?"

"I don't think it'll help anything," Markie shook her head.

"What's her name?"

"It's Carly Matthews but don't stir things up. It's over now."

"I'm sorry, Markie. I didn't mean to upset you." Kathleen pulled her hand up to kiss it. "Let's talk about something else."

"Yes, lets."

"Let's talk about where we're going from here."

"As in after we leave this bar or as in our ultimate destination after life?" Markie grinned.

"As in after this bar," Kathleen said and her eyes held hers with a knowing look.

"Is this a 'my place or yours' situation?"

"I believe it is," she nodded, still holding her eyes.

"Then I would say 'mine'." Markie could feel the rush of Kathleen's released breath on her cheek at her answer. "What would you say?"

"I would say, let's get out of here." Kathleen took her hand and stood up, pulling her with her. "Now would be good. Yes?"

Markie laughed. "Yes, now would be good." They drove both cars and it wasn't long before she was leading Kathleen into her apartment. "Make yourself at home." She continued through the small foyer into the living room and on through to the kitchen. "Can I get you a beer?" she called back over her shoulder.

"That would be great," Kathleen answered from where she'd stopped in the living room. She stood and looked around the room, trying to get a sense of Markie from her living space. The room was tidy and comfortable, warm tones on the walls and furniture alike with splashes of color coming from throw pillows on the couch and chairs. She was looking at the bookshelves on one side of the room when Markie returned carrying two beers. She set them both on the low coffee table between the couch and the twin chairs.

"See anything you like?" she asked.

Kathleen turned from her perusal of book titles and looked at her. "Oh, yes. I most definitely see something I like."

Markie felt heat crawl up her chest as Kathleen crossed the room to her. She suddenly felt all tongue tied and awkward. She fumbled for something to say but Kathleen was upon her and she no longer had time to do or say anything before she was pulled into her arms and thoroughly kissed. "Oh my," she managed to gasp when she was released. Kathleen was still holding her and Markie couldn't tear her eyes away from her lips. They were warm, soft, full lips that beckoned to her. She leaned in for another taste. The kiss was full of anticipation, want, and a little fear. When they parted, Markie was limp with desire. She tried to step back and get control but Kathleen was running soft hands up and down her back and all she could think about was how they would feel against her skin. "Kathleen," she whispered.

"Please tell me I'm not the only one who wants to take the next step," she murmured against Markie's ear.

"You're not the only one," Markie answered immediately. "But are you sure?"

"I've never been more sure of anything," Kathleen said. She eased away and took both of Markie's hands in hers. "Show me your bedroom."

Markie led the way down the hall and into her room. She looked around quickly, hoping she hadn't left any dirty clothes on the floor. She snapped on the small bedside table lamp. It looked clean and she sighed in relief. "So…" she started.

"So," Kathleen smiled and took her hands again. "May I have another kiss? You know just a little something to get us started again. Not that I need anything. Just looking at you gets me going."

"You're so full of it."

"Maybe, but you like it." She embraced Markie and kissed her softly. It quickly escalated into a more intense kiss with both of them probing each other's mouths. "Oh God, Markie," she breathed as they parted for air. "I'm not so full of it. You do get me going." She reached up to kiss her neck, letting her tongue glide a path down to the hollow at the base. Markie arched her neck back to allow her better access. Kathleen held her tightly around her back with one arm while she brought the other between them to cup her breast.

"Jesus, Kathleen."

Kathleen cupped her breast, letting its weight rest in her palm, while running her thumb over her nipple. It puckered and tightened into a hard nub, straining against her clothing. Kathleen brought her other hand up to slowly unbutton her blouse. She went agonizingly slow, stopping to kiss each bare spot she uncovered. When she got to the last button Markie had her hands twined in her hair, urging her on. She freed the final button and kissed the area at the top of her jeans.

"Oh baby, you are so lovely," Kathleen whispered as she rose to nuzzle her neck again. She swept the sleeves of Markie's blouse off her shoulders and let the garment fall behind her. With a quick and deft twist of her hand the bra fell loose and she softly eased the straps over her arms and dropped it on top of her blouse. Markie stood naked from the waist up and Kathleen pulled her against her, kissing her while a hand cupped her face. When they parted, her hand went to the button on Markie's jeans and, with a flick of her wrist, she opened them.

"Oh, you are slick," Markie murmured against her mouth.

"No," she protested. "It's just what you do to me." She rubbed her hand down the zipper and cupped her, squeezing her lightly through her jeans.

"Jesus, Kathleen," Markie said again. She was breathing hard, as was Kathleen.

"Come on, Markie," she said with just a hint of desperation. "I want to see all of you."

"Yes. God, yes."

Kathleen took her zipper down and tugged on the waistband of her jeans until they dropped to pool around her ankles. Markie kicked out of them and Kathleen's hand was quickly between her legs, finding her panties moist and warm. "Oh man," she groaned. She kissed her hard as her fingers played along the waistband of her underwear before finally easing them over her hips to fall to the floor. "In bed, honey. Please." She eased Markie down onto her bed.

Markie threw the covers down to the foot of the bed as Kathleen quickly undressed. She eased on top of Markie and felt a shiver of desire run the length of her body. She tried to slow down and kissed her softly, holding her head in both hands, framing her face. Markie moved a thigh between Kathleen's legs and pressed up into her center causing her to rub against her unconsciously.

"Jesus, Markie, I'll go off if you don't quit that," she groaned. She struggled to breathe as she put her weight on her forearms and stared down into her eyes. "You are so beautiful," she whispered.

"No, it's you who's beautiful," she answered. "It's okay if you want to go ahead and ravage me now."

Kathleen laughed softly and kissed her again. "Yes Ma'am." She loved that Markie was forthright and honest about what she wanted. She dipped her head and covered a breast with her mouth, flicking the already puckered nipple with the tip of her tongue. She heard Markie moan above her. Kathleen put her hand on her other breast and squeezed while she used her teeth to capture the nipple in her mouth. She pulled gently. Markie moaned louder and both hands went into Kathleen's hair to hold her. Kathleen gripped her by the sides and turned them over, putting Markie on top of her. "Oh yeah," she breathed as Markie's impressive breasts were at face level.

Markie levered herself onto her elbows and looked down into Kathleen's eyes. "Is this what you want?" Her breasts were mere inches from Kathleen's mouth.

"Oh God yes," she whispered, unable to take her eyes off them. One hand went immediately to one breast and her mouth to the other, sucking in as much as she could take. She ran her free hand down Markie's back to the hollow at the base and then on down to caress her buttocks. She was so soft, so smooth, and so wonderful. She licked and sucked her breasts, totally immersed in the act until Markie pulled up and away from her.

"No no no no," she whined.

"Yes," Markie told her. She put a thigh between Kathleen's legs and rocked against her. "I love your mouth on me but I want more." She continued her thrusts, pushing her own center against Kathleen's thigh, riding her, coating her leg with her wetness.

"God, Markie," she hissed. She tightened her thigh under her while matching her pumping action. "Jesus baby, don't come yet. Please." She struggled to speak as waves of pleasure coursed through her. "I want to taste you. I want to be inside you."

"Don't worry," Markie panted, "I can go more than once." She continued thrusting.

Kathleen flipped them over so Markie was on the bottom once again. She smiled down into Markie's eyes. "Oh baby, this is going to be great," she said softly. "May I touch you?"

"Yes," Markie groaned. "Please." She was moving under her as she spoke and her hands were busy caressing Kathleen's neck, her back, and her ass.

Kathleen worked a hand between their bodies and looked into her eyes as she slid fingers over her curls and through the hot slickness between her legs. A white-hot rush shot through her with the force of a tsunami. She struggled for control, afraid she would lose it right then. "Wait," she gasped as Markie pushed against her hand. "I...I can't..." She lifted her body off Markie and gulped air. "Jesus, Markie," she said through gritted teeth. "I need a minute."

Markie grabbed her by the wrist and pulled her hand back against her. "No, you don't," she hissed. "I need you here."

Kathleen forgot about her own feelings of impending climax and returned her attention to what Markie needed. "Okay baby," she said softly. She moved her fingers up and down through her slick folds and circled around her clit. Her touch was firm and Markie responded.

"Uhhh," Markie lifted her hips and spread her legs wider. "Come inside."

"Oh yes," Kathleen breathed. She circled her opening, massaging her for just a moment before pushing into her with two fingers. Markie cried out as she was filled and Kathleen, once again, almost lost it. This woman was making her so hot. She pulled out and massaged her again, loving the feel of her beneath her fingers. But Kathleen wanted her inside and made her wishes known. She pushed back inside, all the way this time. Markie grunted and pushed back at her. "Do you need more?" she asked breathlessly as she set up a rhythm, rocking her body into Markie's.

"No. Like that. Just like that," Markie panted.

Kathleen concentrated on what Markie needed in order to stave off her own climax. She could feel it coiling in her center edging closer with every soft cry of pleasure that came from Markie. Those sounds drove Kathleen closer and closer while giving her a sense of power she had never known. The look on Markie's face was almost her undoing. Her eyes were unfocused and a little bit wild, her head thrown back, her neck stretched taut. Kathleen increased the force of her thrusts and let the heel of her hand bump against her clit with each stroke. Markie lifted her hips and began making sounds that let Kathleen know she was close. She indicated she needed the pace to increase and Kathleen obeyed, her hand flying in and out. It was only seconds before Markie's legs quivered and tensed and she went over the edge into a powerful climax. Kathleen continued to slide into and out of her but at a much slower pace, coaxing as much out of her as she had to give. Finally Markie was limp on the bed and reaching out for her.

"Oh God, baby, you are so wonderful," Kathleen told her as she took Markie into her arms and held her tight. "You are so beautiful."

"Umm," Markie sighed into her neck as she was wrapped in a tight embrace. She was limp with satisfaction.

"Take your time, sweetie, enjoy it," Kathleen murmured in her ear as she rubbed soft circles on her back.

Chapter 29

Tee took a long pull from her beer and stretched her legs out beneath the wrought iron table. The evening was cool but with her leather jacket the March temperature was tolerable on the patio of The Sports Room. The famous River Walk flowed a few feet in front of her and the occasional tour boat floated by filled with tourists with cameras and sunburns after a day of visiting the Alamo. The bar looked like they were doing a good business for a weeknight. It was March Madness though and that accounted for a lot of the male population. She gave the bar credit for posting a huge board with the NCAA bracket and keeping up with it. At least two of the plasma TVs around the room showed the current game in progress. She'd seen more than a few dollars change hands at the end of the last game. She wanted to go inside for the Texas A&M game against BYU next. She liked the atmosphere in the bar—but that could be because she hadn't had a break from her office in so long.

Unbidden, her thoughts strayed to Carly—as they always seemed to do. She thought about how soft her lips were, how sweet her kisses had been, and how she could reduce Tee to a puddle with just a look. She thought about how they had fit together so naturally. Everything about them had been natural, in fact. Except that Carly had turned out to be a bitch who couldn't be bothered to be honest with her. Fuck her, Tee thought for the millionth time. It lacked the heat it once had though. She was replacing the anger with resignation. She had learned the lesson once before, she could learn it again. The fact that she had to learn it again was the most disturbing aspect of it all. What the hell was wrong with her that she couldn't see what Carly had been? They had talked for hours and she'd never gotten even a hint of anything dishonest from her. She literally shook her head at herself. Stupid, that was all. Just stupidity on her part. She stood and took her beer into the bar. She was tired of thinking about it. The Purdue game against Washington State game was in the last minutes of play and it was clearly going to be a win for Washington. Tee took a seat at the end of the bar and watched as fraternity boys threw money at each other, some scowling, others laughing. There was a pocket of older guys across the room that seemed more serious about the game in progress and Tee gave them her attention while seeming to be bored by it all. While the sports announcers wound down the game and prepared to gear up for the next one she saw one of them separate from the rest and approach the bar. The bartender at that end immediately walked his way and they conferred for a moment. The bartender turned to make drinks and slipped a wad of money into his pocket. He handed the customer his order plus a slip of paper. Evidently there was some betting being done with the bar, Tee mused. As she watched she also noticed he was 'knocking down' at the register. He took the money, made the correct change for the customer but the register showed less than it should. The bartender pocketed a couple of bucks on the transaction. Over the course of a busy night it would add up to a very tidy sum. This would be one pissed off dude if she bought the bar, she thought. She didn't need that kind of trouble. She watched him disappear into the back room only to return within a minute. Bet made and recorded, she thought. Interesting. She'd give anything to know who was in the back room right now. *Not my business—yet.* This was her second night at the bar and she'd learned quite a bit so far. However, she was getting tired of having to fend off misguided boys who had beer-fueled courage. Maybe tomorrow night she'd give herself a break.

She gave up on the A&M game at half time and left the bar. The fresh air outside was a welcome change and she breathed deeply as she walked back down the River Walk to her hotel. As fun as it sounded, sitting in a bar for hours on end every night was exhausting. She had just reached the hotel entrance when her phone sounded its text message tone. She dug it out of a pocket and looked down. It was from Fiona. 'Out of the Park Homerun', it read. She smiled first and then started laughing as she crossed the foyer to the bank of elevators. She continued to laugh all the way to her room. Thank God someone was getting what they wanted. She hoped Jane was happy as well as Fiona.

She stripped down and took a quick shower to get the bar smell off before going to bed. She was about to turn the light off beside the bed when her phone rang. It was Michelle. She repressed an urge to sigh and finally answered.

"Hello?"

"Hello sweetie, how are ya tonight?"

"I'm good," Tee said. It sounded like Michelle was slurring her words slightly. "How are you?"

"I'm great," she laughed. "Really great."

"It sounds like it," Tee commented dryly. "Are you partying?"

"Yeah! Party!" she yelled and Tee jerked the phone away from her ear. "It's girls' night out," she continued loudly.

"Is girls' night out being held at a bar?" Tee asked.

"Oh yeah. You spent the night at a bar, didn't you?"

"Yes, I did. I'm thinking of buying the bar."

"Yeah, we're thinking of buying all the liquor in this bar!" There was a chorus of yells and whistles behind her and Tee envisioned a group of women causing a scene in some bar back home. She hoped someone was looking out for them all and they had a designated driver. "You still there?" Michelle's voice blasted her eardrums.

"Yes, I'm still here."

"Did you meet any cute girls down there?" she asked with a giggle.

"Not so far," Tee said. She waited, knowing Michelle wanted something.

"Yeah, right," she said with a huff. "Just remember, when the cat's away…"

"Michelle, do you have a ride home tonight?"

"I'm sure I can arrange one," she said coyly. "Are you worried about me?"

"Yes. I don't want any of you driving after you've had too much to drink." Tee could not make herself give her what she wanted.

"Well, you don't need to worry about me," she snapped. It was ruined when she giggled again. "I can take care of myself." She let the anger show through. "You just stay down there as long as you want. Don't give me a second thought."

"Michelle, I'm here on business," Tee told her again even though she knew it wouldn't make a difference to her alcohol-fogged brain. "Please get someone to take you home tonight."

"Well, that's an idea," she laughed so hard she dropped the phone and Tee could hear it clatter on the floor.

"Hello? Michelle?" She listened to muted laughter and shouts until the phone went dead. Either she had hung up or someone else had. Tee closed her own phone and put it back on the nightstand. Michelle was becoming too possessive. It wasn't as if they were committed to each other. They'd had a handful of dates, been to bed together, but that was it. They had agreed there would not be anything more serious than that. Tee had made sure that was clear. She would need to address this issue and soon. She did not intend to let Michelle think she owned any part of her. She switched off the light and stretched out. She was restless and edgy, her thoughts skipping here, there, and back again. She needed this new project, she thought. She needed to buy the bar and begin integrating it into her holdings. She would definitely need to hire new bartenders, that was a given. Yes, she would get this deal off the ground. She'd give Paul Carrington a call tomorrow and see if he could arrange a meeting with the owner and bring the papers down. With that settled, she closed her eyes and was soon asleep.

Chapter 30

Paul Carrington signed the papers on his desk with a flourish and grinned happily. He'd just hired Carly Matthews as his first employee. He didn't count Wayne as Wayne was actually running is own CPA business while managing the office for him. He reached over the desk and shook Carly's hand. "Welcome aboard."

"Thanks, Paul. I won't let you down."

"I already know that," Paul said. "Otherwise, I would never have hired you. Besides, Wayne has been after me for a long time to get some help in here. Now that Metro Energy has given me a chunk of business, I *really* need the help. You'll earn your keep, believe me."

"Paul, I need to ask. What about Brown, Hardin & Simon? What will happen when they hear you've given me a job? I don't want to get you into trouble. I love you two guys."

"Don't worry about that," he scoffed. "I'm just a one man operation. They'll figure if you got a job here, it's the bottom of the barrel, and you've been properly beaten down. They won't give you another thought."

"If you're sure," she sighed.

"I'm sure. I'm not even on their radar." He looked intently at her across the desk. "I know this isn't the kind of firm you were hoping to work for but…"

"Don't," she interrupted him. "Don't belittle yourself. I'm honored to work for you."

"Okay." He smiled and stood up. "Let's go tell Wayne the good news and then I'll show you your new office."

He opened the door to the outer office and Wayne looked up expectantly. When he spied the smile on their faces, he jumped up and hugged Carly. "Oh, girl! I'm so happy! This will be so great!" He jumped up and down in his excitement and Carly laughed aloud as she hugged him back. "Paul, can I show her the office?"

"Please, go ahead," he laughed. "I've got some work to do anyway." He turned to Carly. "Come see me when you get settled and we'll get you started on something."

"Will do…boss." She grinned over her shoulder at him as Wayne led her across the foyer toward her new office.

"Carly, I'm so happy you're going to be working here," Wayne gushed again as they entered the second office. "I told Paul so many times he needed help but he didn't want to hire just anyone. It had to be someone he liked and trusted. You're a life saver!"

"I just hope he really needs me and isn't doing this just because he feels sorry for me." Carly voiced her worst fear.

"Don't you fret about that, honey," Wayne waved away her concern. "He's needed help in this office for quite a while. And now that Metro has given him some of their energy business, he's really going to be swamped."

"Oh good," she breathed. "I want to be useful." She looked around the sparsely furnished office and nodded. *God, it felt good to be employed again.* The oak desk held a phone, a computer, and a legal pad. There was a matching file cabinet against the wall and a leather swivel chair behind the desk. She slid a hand along the top of the chair with a small sigh. Her new chair behind her new desk.

"Go ahead, sit down," Wayne urged her. "It's yours now." Carly sat and adjusted the height to her shorter frame and rolled up to the desk. She tapped the keyboard and the computer jumped to life. "I took the liberty of setting up the computer in hopes you would be joining us," Wayne confessed. "It's ready to go. You can set it up with your own preferences, of course, but all the programs are there." He perched a hip on the corner of the desk. "There are all the usual paper forms in the filing cabinet out in the reception area but most of what you'll need is already loaded into the computer." He grinned. "And we can go shopping for office accoutrements. Won't that be fun?"

"Yes," Carly laughed. "I'll need your help with that, for sure." She touched him on the arm. "Just promise me nothing in pink. Okay?"

"You got it."

Tee chose a booth in the restaurant and opened the San Antonio Express-News. She was not one of those people who couldn't eat alone in a restaurant. When the server appeared she ordered pancakes with bacon and coffee. She read the paper while she ate and lingered over a final cup of coffee. She noted the NCAA line up for the day and figured the bar would be crowded again. She nodded to herself. Even though the town didn't have a baseball team or a football team, it still considered itself a sports city. They lived and breathed Spurs basketball during the season and after that, they split their alliances between the Dallas Cowboys and the Houston Texans for their football fix. Most of San Antonio citizens were Houston Astros fans in baseball but there were a few Texas Rangers fans too. She drained her coffee cup and went to pay the cashier.

The sky had turned overcast and was threatening rain by the time she stepped outside. She hunched into her leather jacket and flipped up the collar as a fine mist began to fall. What to do on a dreary day, she mused. She went back inside the restaurant and asked the woman behind the counter where she could find the library. It was time for some local research. She was in luck as the library was only a few miles away. She asked for directions to the newspaper archives and soon found herself ensconced behind a microfiche machine. At the end of two hours her eyes were bleary and she was yawning. The only thing she'd learned about The Sports Room was that the police had been called several times, mostly for drunk and disorderly complaints and once for suspected drug dealing. There was no further information on any of the calls but that was normal. She rubbed her eyes. She needed a break. She left the library and walked down the street to a coffee shop. She sat in the window and absently watched people on the street as she enjoyed the caffeine. A buxom woman in a short skirt wearing heels caught her eye across the street. As she watched, her brown hair blew into her face in the light breeze and she brought a hand up to brush it away and tuck it behind an ear. She had nice legs, Tee thought. She walked as if she knew someone was watching, smooth, and sexy. She had legs like Carly's, she thought absently, legs that would wrap around you and hold you tight. She jerked. *What the hell? Where did that come from?* She looked away from the window quickly. She needed...what? Someone in her bed, she finished the thought. That brought Michelle to mind and she wondered if she'd made it home safely. She felt guilty for not having given it a thought until that moment. She took out her phone and scrolled down to her number. It rang several times before going to voice mail. She left a quick message and hung up. She should get back to the library. There were still things she could learn. The Sports Room looked good so far though and she was getting excited about getting her hands on it. She knew she would have to replace the one bartender and thought she'd probably have to replace all of them just to be sure. The owner had sent the balance sheet and profit and loss statements to Paul but she knew that didn't tell the whole story. She wanted to take one last look at the bar before she called Paul to get the deal going. She spent the next couple of hours back in the library then drove back to the River Walk. It looked like all the bars were busy along the whole walk and she wandered slowly along, enjoying being outside despite the wet weather. She spent the time nursing two beers and watching two basketball games. This time she sat in the back corner and tried to be invisible to everyone else in the bar. It was mostly college boys again so it was easy enough to accomplish. By the end of the games she'd had all she could take and left. Back in her hotel room she called Paul Carrington. He was out of the office but she talked to Wayne.

"Wayne, just tell Paul I want to go ahead with the San Antonio deal for The Sports Room. I need him to make an appointment with the owner and his lawyer, and he needs to bring the papers with him so we can get it done."

"No problem, Tee," Wayne assured her even though he knew Paul was in the middle of some complex legal negotiations with Metro Energy that would require much of his time. He'd let Paul figure it out. "I'll tell him."

"Thanks, Wayne. How are you guys?"

"We're good, Tee. That was a great ball you threw, by the way. We had a great time that night. Thanks so much."

"I'm glad you had fun," she grinned into the phone. "I thought it went rather well."

"It did," he assured her. "You're going to have to come over for dinner one of these nights. It's been too long."

"That sounds good. Are you cooking?"

"I could be persuaded," he laughed, pleased by the compliment.

"It's a date," Tee agreed. "Just tell me when and I'll be there."

"Great. I'll give Paul your message. I hope it works out for you down there."

"Thanks, Wayne. I'll talk to you later."

Wayne made a note on the office message system and sent it to Paul's in box. He'd also tell him when he called in later. Carly was busy with some work for another client who was involved in a lawsuit over property rights with his neighbor and Wayne was in the middle of auditing the books for an auto dealership on Central Expressway. Business was definitely looking up for them. He idly wondered if Carly would like to meet Tee. Maybe he'd invite her for dinner along with Tee and see what happened. She'd noticed her at the ball after all so maybe they'd like each other. He really wished Tee had somebody to love her. She had so much to give and Carly was such a sweetheart. They'd be good together. With that settled, he went back to work.

Paul called the office in the late afternoon. He was between meetings. He wanted to tell Wayne he'd be late—again. Wayne gave him Tee's message and he groaned. "Man, I can't get away right now."

"I know. I didn't tell her that. I just said I'd give you the message. We could call down there to his attorney and maybe he'll want to schedule it later."

"Good idea. I'll give him a call right now. Thanks, Wayne."

He hung up just as Carly opened her office door and brought a sheaf of papers out to be filed. "Was that Paul on the phone?"

"Yeah. He's in meetings with the energy people. We have a client down in San Antonio who needs some papers delivered and a deal negotiated. He's trying to get things set up now."

"Have I told you how much I love working here?" She opened the file cabinet and began filing the papers. "I don't even mind filing."

Wayne laughed. "In that case feel free to file everything." He made a notation in the daily log he kept of the office activities. "Hey, would you be up to a trip to San Antonio? Paul can't get away right now and he's not sure when he will be able to either."

"Sure, I guess so," she shrugged. "What is it he needs done?"

"It's a contract to buy an existing business." Wayne smiled to himself. He'd let her find out for herself what a great client she would be meeting. "I'll give you the papers to review if he thinks it's a good idea."

"Okay, just let me know."

Chapter 31

"Hello?"

"Wayne? I need your help." Paul's voice betrayed his anxiety. "I called Gene Wilkins in San Antonio and his client wants to get this done as soon as possible. I told him I'd call him back but he's pushing for a meeting tomorrow."

"Don't stress, honey," Wayne soothed him. "I think Carly can go. I asked her earlier if she'd consider it and she said yes. I mean, if that's okay with you."

There was a pause as Paul considered the suggestion. "You may have something there," he finally said. "I'd forgotten I have an employee now."

"It's settled then," Wayne said with satisfaction. "You stay with your people there at Metro and I'll get Carly to go to San Antonio and do the deal there. Problem solved."

"I knew there was a reason I loved you," Paul laughed. "Call me back if she can't go for some reason. I'll send the particulars of the meeting to your e-mail. Call Mr. Wilkins and confirm a meeting for tomorrow. Please."

"Will do. Go back to your meetings and don't worry. See you tonight." He hung up and the phone rang instantly. It was one of his clients wanting some free information on their taxes. He firmly guided them to on-line resources for the answers to their questions. His knowledge cost and his time was not free. The phone got busy but when he finally caught a free minute, he brought up his e-mail and got the number of Mr. Wilkins. He called and spoke to his secretary and firmed up the details for a meeting the next day. He printed out the details and put them into the case file. It was getting late by then and Carly had gone home already. He put in a call to her cell phone.

"Hello?"

"Carly, it's Wayne."

"Hey Wayne, what's up?"

"How would you like to see beautiful San Antonio tomorrow?"

"Road trip," she grinned. "What's the particulars?"

"I'll have the file here for you to pick up. I just finished putting it all together. You can read it on the plane or pick it up tonight. I have your plane reservations all set too. Southwest Flight 1554, leaving at nine-thirty-five and arriving at ten-thirty. That should be enough time for the meeting at one o'clock tomorrow afternoon. Paul didn't expect any complications but feel free to call him tomorrow if you have any questions."

"Sounds good. I'm on my way out so I'll probably drop by tomorrow morning and pick up the file."

"Okay. Have a good night. I'll see you in the morning."

Carly settled into the rear of the plane. She retrieved the file and then stowed her briefcase beneath her seat before buckling the seatbelt. She was looking forward to going to San Antonio for the day. Maybe she'd have dinner on the River Walk before coming back. Her ticket was open ended so she could always grab a flight back since they ran practically every hour. She opened the file as they took off and a scant minute later gasped in shock. *No!* This was insane! She must be hallucinating. That was it—she was out of her mind. She was still asleep and this was a dream. No—a nightmare. She dropped the file onto the seat tray and pressed the heels of her hands against her eyes. This can't be happening! How the hell was she going to get through a business meeting with Tee Reed? Tee would absolutely freak. Her stomach was rolling and threatening to empty itself. She tried deep breathing to settle her nerves. Maybe she could fake sickness and postpone the whole thing until Paul could finish the deal. She knew that wouldn't fly as soon as she thought it. She sighed and picked up the file again. Well, if she had to go through with this then she'd better be prepared. She needed to know her stuff inside and out if she was going to represent Tee.

Once they landed at the airport Carly debated what to do. She ordered a latte at a coffee kiosk and sat near an empty gate. She had plenty of time before the meeting. Normally she would have gone to the client's hotel to discuss the deal. She hesitated this time for obvious reasons. Would it be better to let it be a surprise in the attorney's office where she wouldn't make a scene? Or should she let Tee know she was her attorney first so she could get over the shock and maybe cancel the meeting? She sipped her coffee. She knew what she should do. She sipped more coffee. She was a wimp, a chicken. She was procrastinating and she knew it. There were a few points she needed to clear up though if this sale was going to be completed. She pulled out the file again. She went over the notes she'd jotted down during the flight until she could recite them verbatim. When she could delay no longer, she went outside and hailed a cab. Once at the hotel she stopped at the desk and asked for Tee's room. She was informed that Ms Reed was currently in the restaurant waiting for her attorney. She took a deep breath, squared her shoulders, and went to the restaurant.

"A table for one?" inquired the hostess.

"Actually, I'm looking for a guest. I'm supposed to be meeting Ms Reed."

"Yes, she's waiting. Please follow me." The hostess led her to a booth along the wall. Tee had her head turned and was watching the street traffic as they approached and Carly had time to observe her. Her stomach did a flip at the first sight of her. Blond hair fell in thick waves to the collar of her polo shirt and she looked mouth wateringly sexy in black jeans. A black leather jacket was on the seat next to her.

"Thank you," Carly nodded to the hostess. She moved away and the beginning of a smile froze on Tee's face as she caught sight of her. Carly held her breath. They stayed that way for what seemed like forever as Tee tried her best to comprehend the sight of Carly standing before her. "May I sit down?" Carly asked quietly.

Tee snapped to then. "What are you doing here?" she hissed as Carly slid into the booth opposite her.

"I'm your new attorney," she answered. "I'm sorry for springing it on you like this but I didn't know myself until I was on the flight down here."

"How can you be my attorney? I *did not* hire you." Tee's clenched jaw made it difficult to get the words out.

"I work for Paul Carrington and his firm handles your legal work. That's how," she explained. "I'm sorry, Tee, really. If I had known…"

"What?" Tee demanded. "If you'd known it was me you would have what?"

Carly closed her eyes. She knew this would be bad but she wasn't prepared for the absolute fury she found in Tee's eyes. "Tee, please," she implored. "Paul is busy with a big case and couldn't get away. He sent me." She took a deep breath and resolutely continued. "I'm a good lawyer,

Tee. I know what this contract is all about and I can handle this job. Either let me do my job or delay this meeting until Paul is free." She kept her eyes on Tee by a sheer force of will.

Tee shook with repressed anger. She dropped her eyes to the table and drew in several deep breaths. She couldn't think right now. Her mind skittered along without direction. She finally got up, threw some bills on the table, and stalked out of the restaurant.

Carly's heart dropped into her stomach but she scrambled after her. She wasn't going to let Tee keep her from doing her job. She couldn't go back to Dallas and tell Paul and Wayne that Tee didn't want her help. That would be the end of the only job she'd been able to get. She went after her as she pushed through the door onto the sidewalk.

"Tee, please wait," she called. She was in low heels whereas Tee was in boots. She'd never catch her. A red light at the corner saved her. "You don't have to like me, Tee. Just let me do my job, that's all I ask." Tee kept her eyes straight ahead and stepped off the curb when the light changed. Carly resolutely kept up with her this time.

By the time they'd covered four blocks Tee's pace began to slow. She finally blew out a big breath and ran a hand through her hair. She stood for a moment before finally looking at Carly. She was unprepared for how Carly's eyes held hers and drew her in. It was just as it had been the first night they'd slept together. Everything seemed to fit, to meld, to be exactly right, like they were very strongly connected. She mentally shook her head. She had to fight this. She wouldn't—couldn't be a sucker again. It was just too painful.

"Okay. Just get this sale done." She shot her wrist from her jacket to check her watch. "We still have enough time." She turned around and started back.

By the time they got back to the hotel Carly was breathing heavily. She hadn't dressed for a race this morning and her briefcase was not light. Tee led the way to the parking garage and beeped the doors open on a red Mustang. Carly gratefully sank into the passenger seat. She hoped the meeting was far enough away that she would be able to catch her breath.

She was reasonably calm by the time they entered an office building across town. Tee hadn't spoken another word but Carly did not let that deter her.

"Tee, could we talk after this meeting? We need to get some things out in the open." Carly stood next to her in the elevator as they ascended.

Tee didn't even turn her head. "I don't see a need to talk about anything. Your situation is very clear."

"Please," she said quickly. "I really need to talk to you." Her hopes sagged as Tee made a motion that might have been a shrug or not. She remained silent. The elevator opened and they stepped out into the hall. They looked at the floor guide and turned to their left. She put a hand on Tee's arm as she reached for the door. "Please let me do the talking in here," she said. "Don't let them know how much you want this deal. Please?"

Tee looked down at the hand on her arm and then nodded slightly. She opened the office door and they stepped inside.

The receptionist looked up and smiled. "May I help you?"

"We have an appointment with Mr. Wilkins," Carly said with a warm smile. "Reed."

"Have a seat and I'll let him know you're here." She spoke into her headset and Carly moved across the room and took a seat. This was her area of expertise. This was her playground and she was comfortable. Carly cleared her throat as Tee stood in the middle of the room, her stance wide, looking anxious. When Tee looked at her, she tilted her head at a chair. Tee looked like she would continue to stand but then moved to sit beside her. She crossed one boot over the opposite knee and clasped her hands in her lap. Carly's hand trembled with the need to reach out and put a hand on her knee, to stroke her thigh, to make contact with her. She remembered how strong those legs were, how they had wrapped around her while the thighs trembled in passion. She jerked her mind away from those thoughts. She was here to do a job and she needed to keep a clear head.

"Ms Reed?" A tall man in a tan suit appeared in the foyer from the hallway. He was overweight with a gut that hung over his belt and he had thinning brown hair. He was in his shirtsleeves and held his glasses by one earpiece as he waited to see who the buyer was.

Tee stood up and Carly rose with her. "Mr. Wilkins?" She met him halfway across the room and extended her hand. "I'm Carly Matthews. I'll be representing Ms Reed."

"It's nice to meet you, Ms Matthews." He turned to Tee and held out his hand. "You must be Ms Reed then."

"Yes. Nice to meet you, Mr. Wilkins."

No one else would have noticed how tight Tee's voice was or how stiff she held herself but Carly was aware of it. She hoped Tee would stay calm.

"This way, ladies," Mr. Wilkins said with what he probably considered gallant charm. He led them to a small conference room. "This is Mr. Dooley, owner of The Sports Room," he introduced the man waiting there. "Jason, this is Ms Reed, the prospective buyer and her attorney, Ms Matthews."

"Nice to meet you."

Jason Dooley was a man who looked like he was more at home in a bar than in an office. He was of medium height with brown hair that was too long and in a wild tangle. He also needed a shave. His hands were surprisingly soft and Carly noticed a slight tremor. Maybe Mr. Dooley sampled his product a little too much.

They took seats on opposite sides of the table and got down to business. Carly was glad to see Tee sit calmly beside her while Jason Dooley was fidgeting, crossing and uncrossing his legs, and shifting in his seat. She concentrated on the legalese of the sale as she and Mr. Wilkins went through the papers paragraph by paragraph, outlining the points of the contract. They stopped briefly when a clerk brought in a complete coffee service and set it on the counter at the end of the room. They helped themselves to cups and returned to their seats. Carly noticed Jason Dooley hanging back, trying to get Tee by herself for a private word. This could not be allowed and Carly caught her eye and gave her a slight shake of her head. Tee hesitated but returned to the table and her seat beside Carly. She looked straight ahead and sipped her coffee. Carly leaned close and whispered, "Thank you," into her ear.

Tee swallowed her coffee and gave her a nod. She didn't want her to know how that whisper in the ear affected her. It sent shivers down her spine and her blood pressure went up several notches. She clenched her jaw and tried to concentrate on something, anything else. The meeting continued and soon they were discussing the very last covenants of the sale.

"Okay," Mr. Wilkins said with a big smile. "It looks like we're done. All we have to do now is sign on the dotted line."

Tee straightened in her chair and reached for the pen he extended across the table to her. Carly put a hand on her arm to stop her. "There are still a couple of things," she said.

His eyebrows rose in question. "I don't know what?"

Carly kept her face devoid of emotion only because her job as a lawyer had taught her the wisdom in doing so. After all the time they'd spent on this contract, she'd developed an unfavorable impression of Mr. Jason Dooley.

"If you'll examine the liquor license your client submitted in the package, you'll notice it is not current." Carly picked out the document in question and slid it across the table, turning it so he could read it.

He picked it up and turned to his client. "Jason?"

Jason looked surprised and concerned as he took the paper and examined it. "What?" He stared at it a few seconds longer before shaking his head. "Oh, I know what happened," he said with a nod at his lawyer. "I told Ricky to copy the records last week. He must have copied the wrong license. This is last years. It was renewed months ago." He smiled and nodded at Tee.

"Fine," Carly said with a small smile. She took the paper back and filed it in her folder. "We can expect to see the correct license when?"

Mr. Wilkins looked at his client. "Can we get this done soon, Jason?"

"Certainly," he nodded vigorously. "I'll see about it today."

"Well, that settles that," he smiled again at Carly.

"Not quite," she shook her head. She was afraid to look at Tee now. She knew Tee wanted this deal done but she couldn't let her sign without everything being complete. She would not let her make a bad deal. "I don't see any contract with the NBA, the NFL, or the MLB that allows sporting events to be shown in Mr. Dooley's establishment. Furthermore, there aren't any contracts from any of the major TV networks allowing games to be shown in his bar either." She looked at Jason Dooley and saw him go wide-eyed for a split second.

"It should be in there too," Jason protested. He looked at his lawyer. "I should never have let Ricky do any of this for me."

"No, it looks like you should have taken care of it yourself, Jason." It was clear Mr. Wilkins was not pleased with the way things had turned out. It was a waste of an afternoon's work. He looked at Carly. "I'm sorry, Ms Matthews. I thought everything was in order. I'm sure Jason will have the proper paperwork here as soon as possible."

"Thanks for the coffee," Carly said as she rose and gathered the papers into her briefcase. Her tone suggested she also thought it was a waste of time and that she wasn't pleased in the least.

"Where can we get in touch with you?" Mr. Wilkins asked quickly. He did not want this deal to fall through now.

"Here's my number," Tee said and wrote it on the paper he gave her.

Carly laid one of her business cards on the table. "We'll see ourselves out." She led the way back through the office and out the door. Tee started to speak as soon as the door closed behind them but Carly put her hand on her arm and shook her head. She expected Tee to ignore the warning and was surprised when she kept silent. Carly was grateful the elevator was empty when it arrived. She pushed the button for the ground floor and dropped her briefcase with a thud. "I'm sorry, Tee. I know you wanted this sale to go through today."

Tee was quiet for another moment. "No, you did the right thing," she said quietly. She looked at Carly then and nodded once. "I don't want to inherit any problems, especially costly legal ones."

"That's right." The elevator doors opened and they exited the building.

Tee drove slowly from their parking lot and started back across town. She felt caught in limbo. She wanted this bar but she couldn't fault Carly for doing her job and putting a halt to it. Legal problems were the bane of every business owner and it wasn't smart to go ahead with this deal today. She drove automatically as she went over every word and every action of the meeting in her head.

She parked in the hotel garage and turned the engine off. Now what? Carly was out of the car before she had a chance to start a conversation, if that was what she had been going to do. She didn't know if she had or not. She got out and joined her at the elevator. Carly pushed the button for the lobby when the elevator came. Before Tee could speak, Carly did.

"I need something to eat. I only had a muffin for breakfast." She lifted a hand to press against her brow for a moment. "I'm starving."

Tee didn't know what to do or say. Her panicked flight from the restaurant was the reason Carly had missed lunch. But she hated everything Carly stood for. Didn't she? Then why did she feel so…comfortable with her? With no other plan, she followed her into the hotel restaurant where they took a booth. Tee wanted to smile as Carly ordered. Most women would have ordered a salad or something equally light but Carly was hungry and ordered what Tee called 'real' food. She dug into her briefcase and laid her cell phone on the table. She put her hand back to her head again and leaned an elbow on the tabletop. "How long do you think it'll take them to call?"

Tee had just been watching her and thinking how good she looked and the question startled her. "Uh, I don't know if they will."

"Oh, they'll call," Carly said with confidence. She was still holding her head and not looking at Tee. "Jason wants out from under this bar for some reason."

"He's a drug user," Tee said.

Carly uncovered her eyes then and looked at her. "Is that what you think?"

Tee nodded. "All that moving around, can't sit still, unable to control his energy; those are classic signs of drug use."

Carly stared at her for a moment. "And you would know this because…?"

"Not from using," she assured her quickly. "I don't do drugs." She shrugged. "But I can't say that about other people I've known."

Carly nodded. "I thought he was suffering from something. I just didn't know what." She sat back as the server brought their food. "Thank God," she murmured. Without another word, she dug into her meal. When she was done she sat back and laid her napkin across the plate. "That was good," she said with a sigh. "I may live after all."

"Maybe it'll help your headache," Tee said.

Carly looked up quickly. How did Tee know she had a headache? She nodded though because it was true. Her headache was better already. She reached for her phone and scrolled through the contacts. "I need to talk to Paul and see what he wants to do," she mumbled.

Tee started to reach across the table but stopped. "Uh, why don't you just tell him you're staying here tonight? I mean…we may be making the deal tomorrow."

"I'll see what he says," she said. "He'll have to approve it." She hit send on the phone and waited to be connected to the office. "Hi, Wayne," she said when he answered. "It's Carly."

"Hey girl," he smiled. "How's it going down there?"

"We have a slight problem. There's missing paperwork and we can't get the deal done today."

"Are you staying there tonight or will it take longer than that?"

"That's why I'm calling."

"Let me talk to him," Tee said reaching for her phone.

"Is that Tee?" Wayne asked. "Let me talk to her."

Carly gave up her phone. Obviously she wasn't needed for anything more.

"Hey, Wayne," Tee smiled into the phone.

"Hey Tee. So, tell me…how do you like your new lawyer?" It was obvious by his tone what he was thinking and Tee cringed inside.

"Yes, we'll have to talk about that later. Right now, we need to wait for this Jason Dooley guy to come up with the proper paperwork so I can buy this bar. She thinks they'll call tonight."

"Okay. Go ahead and tell her to get a room for tonight and just to let us know what's happening tomorrow. Okay?"

"Great. Thanks Wayne."

"Tell her I'll let Paul know too."

"Will do. Bye Wayne."

"Bye."

Tee ended the call and slid the phone back across the table. "Wayne says to stay tonight and call him tomorrow." She looked up as the server laid the check on the table. She picked it up and reached for her wallet.

"You don't have to do that," Carly protested. "I'm the one who needed to eat, not you."

"It would only go on your expense account and I'd end up paying for it anyway," Tee told her. "So I might as well go ahead and pay for it right now."

Carly couldn't tell whether she was kidding or not. "Okay."

Tee put a few bills into the folder holding their check and stood up. "That should take care of it." She looked at Carly. "If you're ready."

"I guess that means I don't get dessert." She slid out of the booth and started for the exit.

Tee felt bad. "If you want dessert, that's fine with me."

Carly looked back over her shoulder with a slight smile. "No, it's fine. I need to arrange for a room anyway."

Tee followed her to the front desk. When Carly had arranged for accommodations she stepped forward. "I can put that on my card," she offered. "It's going on my bill anyway, same as the meal."

Carly hesitated, unsure. "I don't know if that's what Paul would want me to do," she finally said. "I haven't traveled for work with his firm so I'm not sure of the protocol."

"Paul wouldn't care," Tee laughed. "He'd tell you to go ahead and let me pay off my bill right now." She stepped up to the desk. "Put that room on my credit card also, please."

The clerk looked at Carly. She nodded. "Go ahead," she said to him. He took Tee's card and tapped on his keyboard for a minute, then handed over an envelope with two key cards. "Room 512."

"Thank you." She turned away and handed the envelope to Carly. "Now, all we have to do is wait I guess."

"Yes," she nodded. She started for the bank of elevators with Tee following. She pushed the button for the fifth floor and Tee reached past her to hit the button for eight. They rode in silence until Carly exited on her floor. She turned back before the doors could close and stuck her briefcase across the beam, keeping them open. "Will you call me if either one of them gets in touch with you? I have a feeling Jason would like to make a deal with you and bypass the lawyers."

"Yes," Tee nodded. "I'll let you know."

"Thanks." Carly removed her case and the doors slid closed leaving Tee alone and surprisingly anxious. She frowned. She dismissed it as nothing more than anxiety over the failure to complete the sale. If Carly was right, Jason would be calling her tonight and by this time tomorrow, she would be in control of the bar. Then the real work would begin. She exited the elevator on the eighth floor and entered her suite. It seemed empty all of a sudden. She sat at the small table and looked out the window to the boulevard below. People walked on the sidewalk, entering and exiting various shops, but Tee didn't see any of it. She was remembering Carly's perfume. She noticed it in the elevator as she reached past her to push the floor button. It was nice. Very nice. Her brain threatened to continue down memory lane so she jerked to a stop and thought about the bar instead. She needed to think about all the details that she'd need to take care of if this deal went through. She'd already made a mental list but it was something to take her mind off what she was currently thinking.

Carly deposited her briefcase on the table and kicked her shoes off before sitting on the edge of the bed. She sighed. This whole ordeal was tiring. She had negotiated many contracts in her career but being this close to Tee coupled with the responsibility of her needs and wants was exhausting. She took off the suit jacket and folded it across the foot of the bed. It reminded her she had no other clothes than those on her back. She sighed again. *Shit!* Did this whole day have to be fucked up? She wanted nothing more than to just lie down and take a nap but she forced herself back up and into her shoes and coat again. She wasn't going to wear the same clothes tonight and again tomorrow. She pocketed the key card, picked up her bag, and went back out to search for clothing.

Tee flipped through the channels on the TV but nothing caught her attention. She picked up a book she'd been reading but couldn't concentrate on the words and finally threw it back on the night table. She was restless and edgy. Maybe she should just go out to one of the lesbian clubs and have a drink tonight. After all, Jason Dooley might not even call. Yeah, she thought, that's what she would do.

She took a long shower and changed clothes. She checked her appearance in the mirror and decided she'd pass inspection. She slipped her wallet into her pocket along with her key card and left the suite. As she exited the elevator into the lobby, she caught a glimpse of a familiar figure. Tee crossed the lobby and entered the dim bar. Once her eyes adjusted, she saw Carly at the far end. The bartender was just placing a beer in front of her. Tee made her way through the small tables and slid onto the stool next to her.

"I thought all lawyers drank scotch."

Carly stopped, the bottle half way to her lips and turned toward her. Her heart stopped beating for at least three beats before starting up again. Tee was the last person she expected to see next to her. She called upon her training to keep her expression neutral. "I guess there's always someone that screws things up."

"And that's what you do?"

Carly took a long swallow of beer. "Oh yes," she nodded as she set the bottle back on the bar in front of her, "I definitely know how to screw things up. She kept her eyes on the top of the bar.

Tee wondered if she was referring to what happened to them or maybe the botched deal today. She signaled the bartender to bring her a beer and turned back to her. She nodded at the bartender as her drink was delivered and laid a bill on the bar. "I see you went shopping this evening," she said finally.

"Yes. I didn't pack a thing. I thought I'd be back home by now." She idly twirled the beer bottle in circles, still not looking at her.

"I hope you're not missing anything important," Tee said with a flash of guilt.

"No." She gave a quick shake of her head. "Nothing important." She gave a brief thought to Gail who had wanted to go out tonight. Carly had cancelled when she found out she had to travel to San Antonio today. She looked up then. "Did you have plans to take over the bar tonight?"

Tee grimaced and shook her head. "No, not really."

"Where were you going?" Carly looked her over and thought she looked absolutely gorgeous. Then it hit her. Of course. Tee was going out.

Tee ducked her head. For some reason she felt embarrassed about her plans to go to the local lesbian club now. "I was going out," she said. Carly just nodded. "I saw you come in here when I got off the elevator." She took a sip of beer but didn't look at her. She was about to ask Carly what her plans were when her phone rang. She dug it out of her pocket and looked at the readout. She sighed. It was Michelle. Her thumb hovered over the answer key long enough that it stopped ringing. A moment later, it chimed with the tone indicating a voice mail. She continued to hold it in her hand.

"Not someone you want to talk to?" Carly observed dryly.

"No. Not tonight." Tee put the phone back in her pocket without listening to the message. Definitely not someone she wanted to talk to right now. She turned back to Carly. "Did you have plans for tonight?"

"No. I just needed to get out of that damn suit."

"It looked good on you," Tee told her without thinking.

Carly's training saved her once again. Had Tee just paid her a compliment? She didn't have time for more than a passing thought though as Tee's phone rang again. She took another swallow of beer as Tee answered it this time.

"Hello...What's the deal...When...Okay, I'll think about it." She hung up but kept looking at the phone in her hand. "That was Jason. Just like you predicted, he says I can pick up the paperwork at the bar tonight. He says he can't find the TV sports contracts though."

Carly just nodded. "That means he's been operating without them. He probably doesn't have a current liquor license either."

Tee looked at Carly. "You were also right about him in that he hinted that we could get the sale done tonight just between the two of us."

What do you want to do?"

Tee frowned. "What do you mean?"

"I can't prohibit you from buying the bar on your own, Tee. I can only inform you that it would be very foolish to do so and remind you of the legal ramifications if you go through with it."

Tee wanted to laugh. "There's the lawyer coming out," she smiled. "Don't worry, I'm not that stupid. I would never go against my lawyer's advice on a deal like this."

Carly felt herself relax and realized she hadn't been sure what Tee would do. "Good."

"Would you like to see the bar?" Tee asked. "I mean, it would have been a pretty good bar to own."

Carly gave her a small smile. Was she offering an olive branch after all? She cut that thought off immediately. No use in going down that avenue; it was a dead end. Tee was just a nice person and even she couldn't be ice all the time. She nodded. "Sure. I've got nothing else to do tonight."

"Okay." Tee was careful not to show how pleased she was. "Do you need to do anything first? Call someone?" She belatedly realized how that might sound and rushed on. "I mean, your office or…"

"No," Carly saved her from herself. "I'm good to go any time."

"Okay," she nodded. She sat looking at her beer bottle.

"Is it very far from here?" Carly asked as she drained her beer.

"No. I usually walk from here."

"Okay. Are you ready to go now?"

"Sure." Tee stood and waited for her to slide off the stool.

"Just let me visit the ladies room and then I'll be ready."

"I'll be right here," Tee promised. She watched Carly walk away and felt a tug in places she shouldn't have. *Just memories, that's all it is.* She turned back to the bar and gathered her change. She was just showing Carly the bar they were in negotiations for, that's all it was.

They strolled past all the other restaurants and bars along the River Walk and Carly was enjoying herself. Tee did not rush her as she thought she would, but let her linger over outside menus and drink lists. Music warred with each other from outside speakers at almost every place, but instead of being raucous, it created a festive atmosphere. They were nearing The Sports Room and Carly understood why Tee would be interested in owning it. Even from outside she could tell it was full of fun people. The current basketball game was being broadcast over the outdoor speakers and knots of young men and women were clustered around patio tables, drinking and listening to the game.

She looked up at Tee and nodded with a smile. "Yeah, I can see you in a place like this."

Tee couldn't keep the grin from her face and her eyes danced. "Yeah, I thought it would be a good investment."

"Why is Dooley selling it?"

They had stopped at the wrought iron railing surrounding the patio and Tee gestured for Carly to precede her inside. "He says it's because he needs to move back East for family reasons."

"You don't believe him," Carly guessed as they entered the bar. The decibel level rose exponentially as they got deeper into the room and she had to yell over her shoulder to be heard. She was shocked to feel Tee's hand on her lower back, guiding her. *She doesn't even know she's doing it*. The thought didn't do much to calm her racing heart or ease the heat on her skin. With Tee guiding, they took a small table near the back wall.

"Would you like something to drink?" she asked as Carly sat down.

"Beer," Carly nodded.

Tee pushed her way across the room to the bar and Carly could not keep from watching her. It was insane to entertain thoughts of her. Of them. She forced her eyes away and checked out the rest of the bar. Everyone seemed to be having a great time cheering for his or her favorite team. It was hard not to get caught up in the frenzy, she thought with a smile. Tee returned with their beer and sat next to her.

"I saw Jason Dooley when I was up there," she reported. "He was going into the back room." She nodded toward the bar. "He's got a new bartender tonight too. Strange, if he's selling, don't you think?"

"Do you want to see him?" she asked. "Are you thinking he might have the right papers?"

"Let's wait for a minute," Tee suggested. "I'm pretty sure he saw me." She hesitated but finally decided to tell her. "He's running book out of the back room. Maybe the new bartender is involved with that."

"He's a bookie?"

"Yes." Tee nodded. "Don't look so shocked. A lot of bars run book."

"Does yours?" Carly saw no point in being shy now.

"No," she laughed. "Lesbians don't make the best gamblers. At least not enough of them to make it worthwhile. And the restaurant is a class place. I don't need the hassle."

"So...not now," Carly said with a steady stare at her. She went on before Tee could refute the statement. "Would you continue the bookie operation here if you owned it?"

Tee laughed at her. "No. Seriously, Carly, despite what you may think of me, it's not something I want to be involved in." She held up a hand as Carly started to protest. "The bar looks like it makes a good profit." She sipped her beer. "Guys think differently than girls, even lesbian girls. Their buddies tell them they can make a fortune taking some frat boys' money betting on games. It looks like easy money so they say, hell yeah. It just grows from there and soon you got some ugly no neck guys wanting some of the action. It never ends well."

Carly stared at her. "It sounds like you've given this a lot of thought."

"I've been around the bar scene for a long time. I worked as a bartender in college and I saw a lot of things go down. I paid attention."

Carly looked contrite. "I'm sorry for thinking you'd do that," she said.

"I don't blame you," Tee told her with a shrug. "You don't know me that well."

Carly felt like she'd been kicked in the gut. It was true. She had jumped to conclusions about Tee. "I'm sorry, Tee. I can't seem to keep my big mouth shut."

Tee looked away. She didn't want to talk about any of that. Not now when things seemed to be going better between them. "Don't worry about it," she waved it off and nodded toward the other end of the room. "This beer is going straight through me. I'll be right back." She got up and threaded her way to the restroom.

Chapter 32

Tee left the restroom and headed for the bar. She knew now why she'd had a nagging feeling that something was off about this whole deal. Carly was probably right about him not having any contracts with the sports people. That would result in a huge fine if it was discovered. And she would be responsible for it if she bought the bar whether it was her doing or not.

He was behind the bar and she saw him start to raise a hand right before the world suddenly tilted. The explosion came from behind the bar and blew outward into the crowd. The bar itself exploded into a thousand splintered pieces that rained down everywhere. Glasses shattered, the mirror blew into tiny shards, and Tee lifted into the air and flew backward. Pandemonium erupted. Tables, chairs, and people alike were thrown around as the force of the blast dissipated throughout the crowd. TV screens fell from their mountings and into the crowd and the lights went out as the power failed. There was instant panic as everyone who could, tried to get out the door at the same time.

Carly was lucky in that she was at the very end of the room and spared the worst of the blast. She had time only to wonder why Tee was air born before she was thrown against the wall behind her. Her head smashed against the unforgiving brick and she was unconscious before she hit the floor.

She woke up with a monster headache, lying on a gurney in a hall off the emergency room. She was surrounded was similar gurneys holding other people injured in the explosion. The air was filled with the moans and cries of people in pain. It took a few minutes before she remembered what had happened. The wall, she thought, I hit my head against the wall. She lifted a hand to her head and barely restrained the groan that rose to her lips. She felt the edge of a bandage on her head and another one below her left eye. She closed her eyes again and laid her head back against the pillow. Then it hit her. *Oh my God! Tee! Where was she? Was she all right?* She struggled to sit up as it all came rushing back. She flashed on a mental picture of Tee flying through the air along with glass shards and chunks of the bar. Tee was caught in the blast that blew up the bar! She had to get to her, had to know if she was even alive.

"Whoa, where do you think you're going?" A harried nurse put a restraining hand on her shoulder and pushed her back down onto the gurney. "No one gets to leave my care unless I say so." She peered down into Carly's eyes. "How do you feel?"

"I'm fine," she answered. "I need to go."

"The doctor will let you know exactly how fine you are and where do you need to go?"

"My friend was in the bar. I need to find her. I need to see if she's okay." Carly knew her voice was showing the stress and panic she was feeling but she couldn't help it.

"Well, you need to stay right here for a little longer. What's your friend's name? Maybe I can find her for you. Was she sitting with you?"

"No," Carly's voice wavered. "She was at the bar when it…" She couldn't continue. The nurse frowned. The odds that her friend was okay were not good. "Her name is Tee Reed," Carly finally got out. "Can you find out?" she begged. "Please?"

The nurse put a hand on her shoulder again and patted her softly. "I'll see what I can do, but there are a lot of patients in here so don't get your hopes up."

Carly put a hand to her face and tried with all her might not to cry. It made her head pound. What would she do if Tee were hurt or…worse? *Jesus!* She couldn't think like that. She needed to think Tee was okay, that she would be fine. She held onto that thought. She held onto it for dear life.

Carly had been transferred to a room by the time the sun was up. She had a concussion, contusions, and abrasions on her face, neck, and back, as well as a badly sprained left wrist. She was in pain from almost every part of her body from the sheer force of the blast. It hurt just to breathe. She had not heard from the nurse yet about Tee's condition and it was killing her to lie there, unable to *do* anything. It was into afternoon before she thought about Paul and the office. She needed to call them and let them know what happened. How could she tell them she didn't even know where Tee was or in what condition? *Oh God, she couldn't do this!* Her head pounded. She struggled to sit up and her breath caught in her throat from the stabbing pain along her ribcage. She closed her eyes and waited until it subsided. Now what? She had no idea where her clothes were, let alone her phone.

"Good afternoon." The doctor came through the door then. He smiled at her while opening her chart. "It looks like you're feeling better." Carly nodded but slowly. She tried a return smile hoping he would think she was fine. "Well, let's just check and see." He took out his penlight and checked her eyes. "Uh Hmm," he murmured. "Can you tell me what happened?"

"I was in the explosion at the bar last night."

"Which bar was that?"

"How many bars exploded last night?" she asked acerbically.

Instead of being offended, he chuckled. "Okay, it looks like your memory is okay. Just to be on the safe side why don't you tell me the name of the bar?"

"The Sports Room," she told him quickly.

"Where in the room were you when it happened?" He wrote in her chart instead of looking at her or he would have seen the exasperated look she gave him.

"At the back. That's why I'm not as beat up as some." She went on before he could find more stupid questions to ask her. "I was with a friend who was close to the blast though. Can you tell me where she is or how she is?"

"What's her name?"

"Tee Reed."

"I don't recognize the name off the top of my head, but there were a lot of people who had no identification. I'll see what I can find out for you though."

"Thank you," she said gratefully. "She's blond, about 5'11", and has a rose tattoo on her right hip."

"Okay," he nodded. "You get some rest and I'll look into it. Deal?"

"Deal."

Chapter 33

The network news coverage showed the live feed as firefighters battled the resulting blaze and rescue workers dug through the rubble for possible survivors and the bodies of those that perished in the blast. Carly watched from her hospital room, the fear of seeing Tee's mangled and lifeless body pushing her to the very brink of hysteria. She would go crazy if she didn't hear something soon. She jerked when the phone beside her bed rang. She answered it with trepidation, wondering what kind of news she would be getting. To her surprise, it was Wayne Jackson. They had seen the news coverage up in Dallas and he'd tracked her down in the hospital. He was frantic with worry. Carly immediately burst into tears on hearing his voice. Between gulps and nose blowing, she managed to tell him the story, ending with her inability to find any news about Tee's condition.

"Just stay put," Wayne told her. "I'm on my way down there right now. I'll take care of everything."

"Thanks Wayne." She hung up, feeling better than she had in hours.

He arrived a several hours later and kissed Carly on the lips as only a gay man could. "Oh God, Carly, how are you? You look…"

"Horrible?" she guessed.

"No," he shook his head. "You look wonderful. We were so scared when we saw it on TV. It looked like nobody could have survived that." He kissed her forehead. "God, I'm so glad to see you."

"Wayne?" She hesitated, fearful, but continued. "I need to know about Tee. Did you find out anything?"

"I'm sorry. I haven't found her yet. I came straight to your room when I got here." He looked into her eyes and thought maybe there was more than just fear for a client there. "Would you like me to try to find her now?"

"Please," she said quickly. "I've been worried all day and nobody will tell me anything!" "Okay," he soothed her gently. "If you're sure you don't mind me leaving you alone again."

"Go," she told him. *Please find her alive!*

The wait for news was agony and seemed to last a lifetime. She finally turned the TV off, unable to bear another minute of the disaster. She was sitting up in bed with her head down on her raised knees when Wayne returned. She snapped her head up, resulting in a searing stab of pain shooting through her temples. She ignored it as best she could while searching Wayne's face for an indication of the news he was bringing. His face was serious, grave even. Her heart sank and tears instantly threatened to spill. She waited, unable to ask.

"I'm sorry," he said when he reached her bedside.

"Tell me," she said dully, her heart breaking at his words.

"She's in bad shape," he went on, unaware of what he'd just put her through. "She's still unconscious."

Carly's head snapped up and she looked at him with wild eyes. "She's alive?"

"Yes," he nodded. "That's what I said. But she's in bad shape, Carly."

"But she's alive." Carly let the tears run down her cheeks unchecked. *Thank you. Jesus God, thank you.*

"Oh God Carly, you didn't think she was alive?" Wayne finally understood.

"I didn't know," she cried. "I saw her get thrown through the air..." She couldn't get the rest out around a throat that was quickly clogging with emotion.

"Oh honey," Wayne took her hand and squeezed. "I'm sorry. Do you want to know everything I found out?"

Carly nodded. "Please," she whispered. She gripped his hand tightly.

"She's in a coma right now," he said gently. "She's pretty cut up and bruised all over her body. She has broken ribs and a broken leg." He stopped himself there.

"Tell me the rest of it," Carly said, reading his mind.

"She's in intensive care," he admitted. "They're still doing tests to see if any internal organs suffered irreparable damage."

"Okay," she nodded and took a deep breath to calm herself. "Can I get out of here and see her?"

"You'll have to wait for the doctor," he told her. "Right now it's really not advisable for you to even get out of bed. You're suffering a slight concussion yourself. How are you feeling, by the way?"

"I'm fine," she brushed the question away impatiently. "I want out of here."

Wayne smiled at her. "Yes, so you've said, but you'll have to wait for the doctor." He patted her hand. "I need to call Paul and let him know how you're doing. He'll be frantic by now."

"Yes," she nodded. "Go call him. I don't want him to worry."

"Should I tell him Tee owns a pile of rubble?"

"No. We never got the deal done." She raised her eyes to him as he stood. "It's the only good thing I can think of right now."

"Get some rest, honey. I'll call Paul and then I'll be right back."

Carly eased flat again and sighed. *She's alive*. It was the only thought she needed right then. *She's alive*. If she could live through that blast then there was hope. She sent silent prayers to the gods that be, thanking them for her life. She must have dozed off because she awoke to find Wayne sitting beside her bed, the TV muted in the corner. It was dark outside.

"Hey," she croaked out.

"Hey," he answered with a smile. "It's a good thing you woke up, it's almost dinner time."

"Oh goody," she said dully. She checked in with her stomach and decided she could probably eat after all. The constant nausea she'd been experiencing was gone.

"How's your head?"

"Better," she said, but refrained from nodding just in case. "Did you talk to Paul?"

"Yeah. He was worried. I told him what I knew about the bar blowing up and all."

"What are the police saying about it?" Carly asked. "Have they figured out how it happened?"

Wayne looked at her for a second without saying anything. "They're saying it wasn't an accident."

"I don't understand," Carly frowned. "What was it then?"

"A bomb," he said.

"What!"

"Someone put a bomb under the bar." He rubbed the back of her hand. "They're not confirming why, or who they suspect though."

"Someone deliberately blew up the bar?" She was incredulous. Who in their right mind would kill innocent people like that? It was senseless. Then she remembered something Tee had said to her at the bar when they'd first arrived. Jason Dooley was running a bookie operation out of the back room. "Did the owner survive?" she asked.

"I don't think so. At least not from what the TV news reported. I'm pretty sure they said the owner, along with two bartenders, were killed in the blast. Why?"

"Tee said..." she faltered on her name for a moment but pushed through it. "She said Dooley was running a bookie joint."

"Was she sure?" he questioned. "That's something the police should know." He thought about it for a second. "Maybe they already do."

"She talked like she was certain." Carly said. She wanted to talk about her to keep her close, to keep a connection between them. "I asked her if she would continue with that if she bought the bar. I was such an idiot."

"She said no," Wayne said with a smile. "Tee wouldn't think it was necessary and definitely not worth the risk."

"She said no," she nodded. "I insulted her."

"Oh, don't feel bad. I'm sure she wasn't insulted that you asked. It was an honest question, after all."

"God Wayne, what am I going to do if she doesn't...?" She clenched her jaw against the well of emotion. "She has to be okay," she finished with a sniff.

Wayne gripped her good hand tightly. "She's going to be fine," he said. "She's in good health. She's fit and strong and she's hanging in there. Those are all good signs."

Carly sniffed and swallowed her tears. "Yes," she agreed with a watery smile. "She is strong."

The aide entered with her dinner tray then and set it up on the rolling table. She gave Carly an apologetic smile and left. Her meal consisted of chicken vegetable soup, mashed potatoes, and milk. There was lime Jell-O for dessert. A bland diet since she had been in no condition to order a meal for herself. She sighed but picked up the spoon. She realized she was hungry now that the worrying over Tee had somewhat abated. At least it was a hot meal.

"Wayne, I'm fine here so why don't you go get something to eat yourself," she suggested.

"I might do that," he answered. "I need to get a room somewhere too. I could do that right now if you're sure you're okay."

"I'm sure. Take your time."

"I'll check on Tee too."

"Thank you."

"I'll be back soon. Get some rest."

Chapter 34

Wayne stood outside the hospital entrance talking to Paul on his cell phone. "I think they'll release her this afternoon…She's doing very well. She's still sore and her wrist is in a brace but she's feeling much better…I'm not sure. What are we going to do about Tee…Still in a coma, I'm afraid…Okay, I'll call you later. Love you. Bye." He closed the phone and slipped it back into his pocket as he headed to the entrance. It had only been a day and a half but Carly was adamant about feeling well enough to leave. He found her in a pair of scrubs borrowed from one of the nurses. She looked adorable and he smiled. "I'm guessing the doctor has already been in to see you."

"I'm free to go," she nodded. "I do need some clothes though. Mine are missing except for my shoes."

"Ooo, a shopping trip," he exclaimed in a falsetto voice. "Nothing I like better."

"But first I need to see Tee."

Wayne nodded, knowing it was useless to argue but also knowing that it would upset her. "I stopped at the admitting office and made arrangements for them to bill us," he told her. "We can stop in ICU but only one of us will be allowed to visit and then only for a few minutes."

"Okay," she nodded. "Let's go."

They were silent on the elevator ride down to the intensive care unit. The room was divided into cubicles, each enclosed on three sides by curtains. Wayne escorted her to the desk. Each cubicle fed vital information about the patient to the monitors displayed overhead. There were three patients being monitored right now. Carly frantically searched for Tee and found the blond head in the third space. Wayne had been talking quietly to the nurse at the desk and now turned to her.

"You can visit her but make it short."

She nodded and stepped quickly to the third room. Her heart clenched like a lead fist in her chest at the sight of her lying there so pale and helpless. She picked up the one hand that was free of needles and held it in hers. It was warm. She rubbed her thumb over the back of Tee's hand and watched her sleep. She felt as helpless as Tee looked. She'd give anything to be able to do something, anything, for her.

When she returned Wayne took her hand and they left. In the elevator, he put his arm around her shoulders. "Shall we go shopping now?"

"Sure," she said but there was no enthusiasm in her voice.

"She'll be all right," he told her quietly. "You need to keep believing that. Okay?"

"Okay," she nodded and took a deep breath. Wayne was right; she needed to keep a positive attitude. "Right. Let's go shopping then."

Chapter 35

"I'm sure you've heard the old story about the guy who'd been in a coma for a year and then suddenly sat up and said, 'I'll have a cappuccino'." Carly looked over the newspaper at the hospital bed where Tee slept on, still in a coma. Nothing. She returned to the paper in her hand. They had arranged for Tee to be transported back to Dallas when it was determined no further damaged would be done by the move. She was now in a private room in Presbyterian Hospital. She had a variety of bandages on her face and around her neck and chest area where she'd suffered cuts from flying glass. Her left leg was in a cast supported by a pulley system to keep it elevated and she knew under the flimsy hospital gown her torso was bandaged against several broken ribs. What was visible was marred by a hue known only in deep bruises, a bluish purple mixed with green and yellow around the outer edges. It was painful just to look at her.

Carly worked at the office during the day and at the end of office hours, she went to the hospital and sat with Tee. Markie visited during the late afternoon and she and Carly had taken to chatting together as they met in her room. They were becoming quite close from sharing the tragedy that affected both of their lives. Markie had originally wanted nothing to do with Carly but she just couldn't ignore how deeply Carly seemed to care for Tee. It was painfully obvious she was devastated.

"How is she today?" Carly asked when she entered Tee's hospital room to find Markie sitting beside her bed.

"She's still sleeping." Markie didn't look at her but at the bed.

"Do you think...?" Carly had been unable to continue past the tears that threatened spill.

Markie did look at her then. What she saw on Carly's face couldn't have been manufactured. She was distraught and frightened. Without thinking she hugged her tightly. "She's going to be just fine," she said softly. "We can't think otherwise." Carly hugged her back so hard Markie was afraid she'd crush her. "And you must not come in here and talk to her when you're crying. It'll only upset her."

"You think she can hear us?"

"Yes, I do. She's just resting; getting well enough to wake up. And when she does she'll know we've both been here and that we...care for her."

"You're right," Carly sighed and wiped her eyes with a tissue. "I'll be okay now. Thank you."

"How are you doing?" Markie asked. *She eased her away so she could look at her. "You look a little pale, if I may say so. And how's your wrist?"*

"I'm fine," Carly waved her concern off. *"It's her we need to concentrate on."*

Markie could see she was still a bit battered. She was pale and thin and there were dark circles under her eyes as well. "You know, you should get some rest yourself. It won't do her any good for you to wear yourself down. Okay?"

"I'm fine," she said automatically. *"I'll just sit with her tonight in case she needs something."*

That had been the beginning of a shared tragedy friendship; one Carly was coming to count on. Tonight Carly read the paper to her. It was the third night she'd been back in Dallas. It marked a week since the explosion. She folded the paper with difficulty due to her sprained wrist and laid it on the floor. "Shall I tell you about what happened?" she asked. She scooted her chair closer to the side of the bed and took Tee's hand in hers. "You know that fun bar you wanted to buy? The Sports Room?" She squeezed Tee's hand. "It blew up—with both of us in it. Do you remember any of that? It was awful. Just as you were approaching the bar to talk to Jason Dooley it exploded." She took a second to let that sink in—if it was. "We were both taken to the hospital in San Antonio and then a few days later we had you brought back home. You're in Dallas now. The doctors say you have a severe concussion. That's why you're still asleep. And that's okay. You're just healing and you need time to do that." She absently rubbed the back of Tee's hand with her thumb. "Do you remember that day? Do you remember seeing me for the first time when you thought it would be

Paul you were meeting?" She squeezed her hand again. "I was so afraid you would tell me to leave. I knew you hated me." She felt Tee's hand move ever so slightly in hers and she held her breath, but Tee slept on. "Do you remember the woman you saw me with in Chicago? She is my *ex-girlfriend*. We've been apart for more than six months now. She's...unstable. She was diagnosed as being bipolar and that night she was missing some of her meds. I didn't know it. I'm sorry. I...I knew I had to control Kim or she'd go completely crazy. That's why I told you to let it go." She stopped, unable to go on. She knew tears would show in her voice. She continued to caress Tee's hand softly. "Anyway, I know I told you this all before but I wanted to apologize again. I miss you terribly, Tee. You were the best thing that ever happened to me. I'd do anything to have you back in my life again." Her voice cracked again and she blinked hard to keep the tears away. Tee's hand moved in hers again and she sat up straighter, leaning closer. "I mean it, Tee. I'd do anything to have you back." She held her breath, waiting, but no other movement was forthcoming. "Okay, you get some rest and we'll talk again later. I'm going to be right here for a while longer so, if you need anything, just let me know. Just squeeze my hand." She sat back in the chair and picked up the paper with the hand that was still in a brace. It was doing better but she had been advised by the doctor to continue wearing it for at least another week.

It was getting late when the nurse poked her head in the doorway. "It's almost time for you to be going, isn't it?" she asked with a smile.

"Yes," she smiled back. "It's that time again." She stood and folded the paper up once again. Without thinking, she leaned over the bed and kissed Tee on the cheek. "I'll be back tomorrow," she whispered. She joined the nurse in the hall. "She moved her hand tonight," she reported.

"That's good," the nurse smiled up at her. "I'll make a note of it on her chart so the doctor will know."
Carly left the hospital and drove home. She was bone tired. Between work and sitting at the hospital, she was wearing down. She wouldn't give up though.

Chapter 36

"Good morning," Carly said as she arrived at the law office. She carried three cups of gourmet coffee in a cardboard carrier and placed one on Wayne's desk. "Cappuccino for my buddy and Mocha for the boss." She put one of the two remaining cups on his desk also. "Is he in the office today?"

"You are a Goddess," Wayne sighed as he took his cup. "And, yes, Paul is in the office today, at least for now." He picked up his phone and punched a button. "Paul, there's coffee for you out here, thanks to our favorite girlfriend."

Paul appeared in the doorway to his office, a smile on his face. "Good morning, Carly." He came forward and took the coffee from Wayne. "This is great. Thanks." He took a sip and sighed in appreciation. "How's Tee?"

"She moved her hand last night," Carly told them with a smile. "It may not mean anything but it's the first time she's done it."

"That's good," Wayne spoke up. "Did she move her hand because of stimulus or was it just random?"

Carly thought back to her one-sided conversation. Had Tee moved because of her confession? "I'm not sure," she said. "I was talking to her at the time though, so maybe."

"You've been talking to her?" Paul asked.

"Yes. The nurses said it sometimes helps." She sipped her coffee. "I read the paper to her sometimes too."

"What did you read to her last night?"

"Just the box scores. But she moved her hand when I was telling her…something else."

"Oh?" Wayne asked with an arched eyebrow. "And just what were you telling her?"

"Uh…I can't remember."

Paul smiled at the blush creeping up her neck and nudged Wayne in the back. "I have to get some work done. Thanks for the coffee, Carly." He disappeared back into his office.

"Carly, can I ask you a question?" Wayne asked when he'd gone.

"What?"

"Did you and Tee…get, uh, together down in San Antonio?"

"Jesus Wayne! I was only there one day and that evening the bar blew up! How fast do you think I move?"

He grinned, not in the least offended by her perceived outrage. "Maybe not that day but there is something there. I could see it when I went down there to get you." He calmly sipped his coffee. "Had you met her before that?" Carly hesitated and that was all the answer Wayne needed. "Ooo, tell me." He leaned over his desk and took her arm. She made a face and was about to refuse when the phone rang, saving her. He answered and she went into her office and closed the door.

She was going over a contract at her desk that afternoon when Paul stopped in her office. "Can you spare a minute?" he asked.

"Sure. Come on in." She laid the contract aside and leaned back in her desk chair. "What do you need, boss?"

Paul gave a brief smile at her use of 'boss'. "I just got a call from Jane Canton over at Sylar Industries. She needs some advice concerning some issues over there. Do you think you could take a look and see what you think?"

"Sure," she nodded. "Who exactly is Jane Canton and where can I find her?"

"She's Tee Reed's executive assistant. Tee's office is on the top floor of the Reed Building. Jane's been running things since the accident. I think it's getting to be a bit overwhelming for her."

Carly nodded. "Is there anything I should know before I go over there or is it just to make sure nothing is about to fail?"

"She's got a couple of contracts with suppliers coming due and there are people wanting to negotiate for some renovations she wanted done in the spa. Jane just doesn't want to get taken advantage of because Tee isn't there right now."

Carly nodded. "No problem. I'll take a look and see how I can help her. I'll finish this contract up and then run over there."

"Good. Thanks Carly." He turned to leave. "Let Jane know we're here for her."

"Will do."

It was late afternoon before Carly made it over to the Reed House but Jane made it clear she was happy to see her. She had several contracts laid out on Tee's desk for her to go over.

"I think I know what Tee would do but I don't know as much about this as I should and I didn't want to make a big mistake."

"It's fine," Carly assured her with a smile. "May I?" She indicated the chair behind the desk.

"Make yourself at home," Jane urged her. "Anything you need just let me know."

Carly sat behind the desk and realized she was sitting in Tee's chair. She immediately felt a hitch in her heart rate. She reached for the first contract and began reading. She was deeply engrossed in the legal language when Jane entered and put a cup of coffee on the edge of the desk.

"Do you take anything in your coffee?"

"Oh, thank you," Carly smiled up at her. "No, black is fine."

"How are you doing?" Jane's voice was anxious.

Carly nodded. "It looks good so far." She looked up at the clock. "Are you about to leave for the day?"

"No, stay as long as you want." Carly was about to tell her she wanted to leave herself when there was a knock on the doorframe. Jane's face broke out in a big smile. "Fiona, this is Ms Matthews. She's the lawyer who's going to help me with some of the legal issues while Tee is out. Ms Matthews, this is Fiona Nix, our IT person."

"It's nice to meet you," Carly said and stood to shake her hand as she came across the room.

"Nice to meet you too," Fiona nodded. She dropped Carly's hand and turned to Jane. "I guess this means you'll be here for a while longer?"

"Yes…"

"Actually," Carly interrupted her, "I was thinking of calling it a day myself." She looked at Fiona with a smile. "I can be here again tomorrow morning if that works for you, Jane."

"That's fine," Jane told her. "I'm just grateful for your help." She turned to Fiona. "Fee, can you get Ms Matthews a keycard for the elevator by tomorrow?"

"I can do better than that," she said with a grin. "I can have one here in a few minutes if you'd like to wait."

Carly laughed. She liked the spunky, outspoken, tattooed woman. "I'm waiting then." She waited until

Fiona disappeared back out the door. "She's quite…exuberant," she noted.

"Yes, she is," Jane nodded with a laugh. She turned to Carly and her countenance was serious. "How is Tee doing? I didn't get over there today."

"She moved her hand for the first time yesterday," Carly smiled. "Hey, how did you know I've been going to see her?" she asked with a quick frown.

"Markie dropped by earlier this week and she said you were sitting with her at night."

"Oh," she nodded. "Yes, we've crossed paths."

"She said you care about her." Jane reached out to touch her hand briefly. "I'm glad. She needs someone who cares about her right now."

"Well, it's a little…"

"Here you go," Fee came through the doorway holding out a keycard. "Your very own personal entry card, Ms Matthews."

"Please, call me Carly, and thank you."

"Just use it in the elevator and you'll be able to get up to this floor without calling first."

"Thanks, Fiona." Carly slipped it into her pocket. "I'll be here first thing tomorrow morning if that's okay with you, Jane."

"That will be fine," Jane nodded. She watched as Carly tidied the folders on Tee's desk. "Give Tee a kiss for me tonight."

"You're going to see Tee?" Fiona asked.

"Yes, I'm on my way there now."

"That's great. Kiss her for me too," she laughed.

Carly carried a magazine with her from the waiting area into Tee's hospital room. Markie was sitting beside the bed and smiled as she entered.

"Hi."

TEE with Carly

"Hi," Carly smiled back. "How is she tonight?"

"She's starting to get restless," Markie said. "She's been moving around and making a few sounds now and then."

"That's great! I mean, it's a good sign, isn't it?" Carly asked anxiously.

"Yes. The doctor was in earlier and he said it means she's getting closer to waking up."

"Oh God, that's good news," Carly said quietly, but Markie saw the glint of tears in her eyes before she blinked them away.

"Sit down," Markie said gently. "I'd like to talk to you for a moment if I could."

"Sure." Carly stepped to the side of the bed and took Tee's hand before leaning over to kiss her on the cheek. "Hi, Tee. It's Carly. Markie and I are both here right now. I'll be here for a while so let me know if you need anything." She stepped away from the bed then and took the chair next to Markie's.

"Carly, can I ask you something?"

"Sure," she answered. "What do you need to know?"

"It's about Tee."

Carly sighed. She knew it would come up eventually but she was still unprepared to deal with it. She looked up to see Markie watching her intently. "Let me save you the trouble of asking the hard questions," she said. "I was with my ex-girlfriend in Chicago. We haven't been together for months but her sister convinced me to come up for a visit." She sighed in frustration. "Kim was, is, bi-polar. She evidently decided that day was a good one to stop taking her meds. I was unaware of it. We happened to be in the same bar as Tee. She saw me and came over. Kim saw it. Needless to say, she went a little nuts." She shrugged. "I needed to get Kim under control and told Tee to go so I could calm her down."

Markie reached over and took her hand. "Is that all there was to it?" she asked gently.

"Pretty much," she nodded. She wouldn't try to make it seem anything other than what it was. "I called to explain but she wasn't answering her phone. I left a message; more than one. She returned with a message of her own that pretty much told me to fuck off."

"Carly, I don't think Tee understood the situation," Markie declared.

"I don't know. I think she...I don't know. She was really angry with me. And then when I got back home my law firm fired me on some trumped up charge." Carly choked up and stopped. Markie waited patiently until Carly could continue. "I had a pro bono case I wanted to work," she began. "My firm just wanted me to plead it out and be done with it. My boss kept after me to close it and move on. I wanted to actually defend the man. That was when I first started seeing Tee." She stopped for a moment. "She was so good to me. I told her how I was having trouble with the case and she gave me some advice. Mostly though, she just let me talk. She always made me feel like whatever I said really mattered." She took a big breath and let it out slowly. "We went out on a Friday night and she didn't leave until Saturday night."

"Honey, that is *so* not like Tee. She stayed the night with you?"

"Yes, and I'm not ashamed to say it was the best night of my life," she said, her eyes still on the floor.

"Go on. What happened then?"

"A woman at the firm came on to me one day in the middle of all of this. She hinted that I could advance quickly in the firm if I slept with her. I lied and told her I was seeing someone but that I was flattered. It seems she was pissed. The other women in our group said I'd committed career suicide by turning her down. Anyway, it was that Friday that I was locked out of the office system and then I got a call telling me my services were no longer needed." She dropped Markie's hand so she could wipe her eyes. "It seems my pro bono case got e-mailed to every name on the company list. That is cause for dismissal and could have resulted in my being turned in to the ethics committee. I didn't do it. I can't prove it but I think it was either the same woman or my boss. I got the feeling they were looking for a reason to get rid of me."

Markie watched her silently for a moment. "It sounds like you were pretty overwhelmed by a very bad situation, honey."

"Yeah, but losing Tee was worse. I thought we really connected Markie, and I let that special feeling get away. She'll never trust me again." She sniffed. "I know that. But God, I miss her so much."

Markie put an arm around her shoulders and hugged her. "Carly, Tee is a reasonable woman. I think she was a little shocked at her feelings for you. She hasn't had deep feelings for anyone in a very long time. Maybe that's the reason she reacted so strongly. In fact, I'm sure it is."

"Yeah, maybe." Carly's voice indicated she thought it was hopeless.

Markie hugged her again and then released her. "Keep your chin up, honey. Just take it one day at a time and see what happens." She stood and gathered her things. "Let me know if she wakes up tonight."

"Will do," Carly nodded. She stood as Markie bent to kiss Tee's cheek.

"She's getting more kisses while she's unconscious than when she's awake," Markie laughed. "I'll be here tomorrow," she said and gave Carly a kind smile as she went out the door.

Carly stood for a long time at the side of the bed just looking at Tee as she slept on. She was pale and thin but seemed to be comfortable. She caressed her cheek softly.

To her surprise, Tee moved her head into her touch. Carly froze for a second.

"Hi, Tee," she finally got out. "Are you feeling better tonight? I spoke to Jane and Fiona today and they both said I should give you a kiss for them." She waited but Tee remained still. "I went to your office this afternoon. You have a great place. Jane is feeling a little bit overwhelmed and Paul wanted me to go see if I could lend a hand. You have some stuff that needs attention so, until you're able to take care of things, I'm going to be helping her out. Is that okay with you?" Tee frowned and the leg beneath the blanket moved slightly. Carly held her breath. The frown on her face deepened and she moaned a bit. "You're going to be fine, Tee." Carly wanted her to know that above all else. Tee seemed to sink back into the coma and was still once again. Carly finally took the chair beside her bed and settled in. "Okay, you need a little more time. That's fine. You take as much time as you need. We all just want you to get well." She reached out, took Tee's hand, and entwined their fingers. "Shall I tell you what the San Antonio police found out about the bomb in the bar? I've been reading the paper from down there. The police know about the bookie operation Jason was running. They suspected he was dealing drugs as well. So they think the bomb was placed by a drug lord he might have been skimming money from or by one of those ugly, no-neck guys that he owed for gambling debts. You were right on all counts, Tee. I swear, from now on, I'm going to believe everything you say. I will never doubt you again." She fell silent as she thought back to the explosion once again. It made her stomach roil, the memory of Tee being thrown through the air as fresh as the instant it happened. She swallowed with difficulty and cleared her throat. "I'll never forget that night, Tee. I thought you were…" She faltered and had to stop. It still affected her deeply. "Did I tell you I still have nightmares about that night? I do.

Some times after I have one of them I'm afraid to go back to sleep. I'm exhausted but...anyway, I hope you're not having any. You need some restful sleep so you can heal." She felt Tee's fingers tighten around hers and held her breath.

"Uhh," Tee rasped hoarsely.

"Oh," Carly stood quickly. Tee's eyes were mere slits against the light. "Tee?"

"Water," she croaked.

"Here, just a second." Carly fumbled with the carafe of water and poured some into a plastic glass. She stripped the cover off a straw and inserted it. "Here you go. There's a straw so just open your mouth a little." Carly held the glass low and touched the straw to her lips. She sucked once on it and swallowed.

"Thanks," she said weakly. Her eyes closed and Carly thought she was asleep again.

"Oh God," Carly sniffled. "You woke up." She held her hand and let the tears roll down her face. "You woke up," she repeated in wonder.

"More." It was still hoarse but clear enough to understand. Carly quickly brought the straw to her lips again and held it while she drank. "Head hurts," she mumbled when she was done.

"You had an accident," Carly said softly. "You're in the hospital." She set the glass on the small table with a trembling hand.

"What...happened?" Tee's eyes were unfocused and half closed.

Carly hesitated. How much should she tell her? She didn't want to upset her but she had to tell her something. "You were in the bar down in San Antonio when it happened? Do you remember being there?"

"No..." Tee's eyes slid all the way closed and she was asleep.

Carly's heart fluttered in her chest. She woke up! She reached for the call button and pressed it. She didn't want to leave her bedside now. When the nurse arrived, Carly told her how Tee had awoken and wanted water. The nurse checked her vitals quickly and then smiled at Carly. "She's doing very well. She'll be in and out like that for a while so don't let it frighten you. I'll make a note for the doctor."

"Thank you." Carly stood for a long while after she left, holding Tee's hand and stroking her arm. "I'm going to call Markie," she said aloud as she placed her hand back on the bed beside her. "She wanted me to let her know if you woke up." She pulled her cell phone out of her bag and punched in Markie's number.

"She woke up," she said when Markie answered. "It was just for a minute, but she woke up…She asked for water…The nurse said she would tell the doctor…Yes…I'll be here for a while longer just in case she wakes up again. I don't want her to be alone if she does…Okay, I will. Bye." She closed the phone and sat back down beside the bed. "Markie says for you to rest up and get well. She'll be back to see you tomorrow."

Chapter 37

Tee woke up slowly, the pain in her head making it impossible to sleep. She opened her eyes and quickly closed them again as a shooting pain lanced through her head. *Christ! She'd never had a hangover this bad...ever.* She took a deep breath and another pain shot through her chest. Was this all a bad dream? Was she was back on the floor after trying to beat up her workroom? She needed to sit up. She needed a drink. She needed...something. She tried to push up to a sitting position and found one leg unresponsive. *What the hell?* She forced her eyes open again and squinted against the harsh light. *"What the...?"*

"Hey," came a soft voice from beside her. "How do you feel?"

"My skull is exploding," she moaned.

"Just lie back," Markie said. "Does anything else hurt?"

"Fuck yeah, everything hurts," Tee moaned. "What the hell happened?"

"You were in a bar when it blew up," Markie answered. "Do you remember?"

Tee searched her memory but it was too painful and she gave it up. "No."

"You were in San Antonio," Markie explained slowly, hoping as she went on that Tee's memory would fill in the blanks. "You wanted to buy The Sports Room. Do you remember that much?"

"Yeah, the bar on the River Walk." Tee kept her eyes closed, frowning as she tried to follow the conversation.

"You were down there for several days checking it out." Markie didn't know whether to tell her about Carly being there with her or not. She couldn't very well tell the story without it though so pushed on. "Carly was there too. The seller was not current on his license and she put a stop to the sale until he could bring it up to date. Do you remember that?"

Tee was silent for several moments. "Yeah. She didn't know...Yeah, I remember. We had a meeting at the lawyer's office."

"Yes," Markie said and nodded even though Tee couldn't see her. "You were both in the bar that night when it...exploded." She waited for that to sink in.

"I...we were...at the hotel." The strain of trying to piece things together was making her head pound and she raised a hand to her head. She encountered bandages and scabs of healing cuts. "What is this?" she asked urgently, her voice panicky. "What's wrong with me?"

"You have a few cuts on your face," Markie told her quickly. "Leave the bandages alone, okay?"

"Where am I?"

"You're in the hospital. In Dallas."

"What? How? I don't remember!" Her frustration was evident.

"You were transferred here from the hospital in San Antonio." Markie kept her voice calm and hoped it would help her do the same. She held her hands to keep her from touching her bandages and also to keep her from panicking.

"What's wrong with me?" Tee opened her eyes again and suffered the stabbing pain. Her stomach rolled and she immediately closed them again. "Tell me," she demanded in a shaky voice.

"You have a concussion, a few cuts on your face from flying glass, two broken ribs, and a broken leg." She waited a beat for it all to sink in. "Other than that, you're in great shape."

Tee kept silent as she processed it all. "Yeah, that's great."

"It *is* great," Markie told her. "You could have been killed." She reined in her emotions and continued. "The owner and two of the bartenders *were* killed," she explained. "They were right in the middle of the explosion."

"I'm sorry," Tee whispered. She freed a hand and raised it to her head again and felt the various bandages, trying to visualize what she looked like. "I don't remember."

"That's to be expected," she told her. "It's because of the concussion. The doctor said you would probably get your memory back in time."

"Fuck," Tee groaned.

"Let me get a nurse," Markie told her. "Maybe she can give you something for your head."

"Hey." Carly smiled at Markie as she entered the hospital room that evening. She automatically looked at the bed to check Tee's condition. "How is the patient tonight?"

"Hi. She woke up again today."

"Yeah? That's great!"

"She was even talking a bit before she went back to sleep."

"What did she say? Did she remember anything?" Carly asked anxiously. She stopped by the bed to look down at Tee for a second.

Markie took note of the fact that she didn't automatically kiss Tee on the cheek this time. Interesting, she thought. "She doesn't remember the explosion at all. She did, however, remember being in San Antonio to buy the bar."

Carly gave her a quick look. "That's good, right? She remembers being there and why. That's good."

"Yes, I think so. She was in some pain, of course. I told her about her injuries. I think it panicked her a little bit when she found all the bandages on her face."

"She looks good," Carly said instantly and missed the smile on Markie's face. "The purple is almost all gone and the swelling is down. Everything else will heal in time."

"Make sure you tell her that," Markie said.

Carly looked panicky at that but nodded. "I will. Yes, I should tell her she looks good." She sat next to Markie.

Markie touched her on the arm. "It'll be fine," she said soothingly. "She's going to make a full recovery."

"Yeah, I know that."

"Are you nervous about talking to her?"

"Maybe a little…Yeah. She hates me." Her voice was small and forlorn. "Maybe it would be better if I wasn't here when she wakes up."

"Stop that!" Markie told her sharply. "You need to be here for her." Markie hesitated but decided to tell her the story so she'd understand. "Let me tell you something about her. Tee had a girlfriend in college. That's where we first met. Anyway, it was serious, even though I could tell the girl was no good for her. She led Tee around campus like a prize bull. Tee was the best looking lesbian in school and she loved showing her off."

"I can imagine what she was like in those days," Carly smiled fondly. She thought Tee was possibly the best looking lesbian even today.

"They were hot and heavy for a couple of semesters, until Tee found out she was cheating on her with another girl and had been all year long. When she realized it, it broke her heart. She never fully recovered from the whole thing." Markie waited, watching Carly for her reaction. She wasn't disappointed.

Carly buried her face in her hands and bent from the waist, rocking in her chair. "Oh God," she moaned. She was devastated. "She thought I treated her the same way! No wonder she hates me. I can't believe this!"

"So, now you know the story," Markie went on. "She thinks she's a lousy judge of character. She put me in charge of getting her a date because she didn't trust herself."

"You got her a date?" Carly's stomach felt as if it was trying to turn itself inside out.

"Yes, but I don't think it was working out." She touched Carly's arm again. "She just did it because I said she needed to get out there again."

"I'm sure there are thousands of women who'd love to date her." Carly struggled not to show the agony she was in, thinking about someone else in Tee's bed. She couldn't look at Markie. "She'll find someone," she said dully.

"Well, she was wrong to put me in charge of her dating," Markie told her. "And I'm not going to fix her up with anyone else." She waited but Carly kept silent. "I'm surprised Michelle hasn't been up here."

"Is that who she was dating?" Carly forced herself to ask.

"Yes."

"Maybe she doesn't know what happened," Carly suggested. "I had to replace my phone so I'm sure hers was lost in the rubble too."

"I didn't give that a thought," Markie admitted.

"Maybe you should give her a call," Carly said. "I'm sure she's wondering what happened."

Markie gave Carly high marks for that. Not many women would be so considerate of the competition. "I should let her know," she said with reluctance, "especially since I was the one who introduced them."

Carly stood. "I'm going down the hall for a cup of coffee. I'll be back soon." She might be able to do the right thing but she wasn't strong enough to stay and listen to the call.

Markie watched her walk out the door with mixed feelings. She had hurt her best friend, deeply. She remembered how devastated Tee had been. Nevertheless, she also knew, now, how Carly really felt about Tee. All she had to do was watch her eyes when she looked at Tee in the hospital bed. She drew her cell phone out and scrolled down to Kathleen's number. Kathleen offered to call Michelle for her and she took her up on the offer. Kathleen knew her better after all. She told Carly when she returned to the room.

"Well, in that case, maybe I'll go on home and tend to a few things that I've been neglecting." Carly stood looking at the still figure on the bed.

Markie saw the wistfulness in her eyes. "We don't know if she's even going to be here," she told her.

"That's true," Carly nodded. She also knew that if it was she who got a call saying Tee was in the hospital after not hearing from her in a week, she'd break her neck to get to her. She'll be here," she said quietly. "I would be." She stood a moment longer just to look at her. She sighed finally and looked back at Markie. "You'll keep me informed?"

"Carly, you don't need to leave," Markie said firmly. "She knows you've been here." She stood beside her.

TEE with Carly

"She'll be happy to see her girlfriend." She picked up her bag and impetuously hugged Markie. "Thanks Markie." She released her and started for the door. "Call me."

Markie watched in dismay as she disappeared. She knew in her heart that Carly cared for Tee. She also knew Tee wasn't all that interested in Michelle. At least she didn't think so.

Tee woke up a short time later. Markie heard her and got up to bend over the bed with a smile. "Hey good lookin', how are you feeling?"

"Water," she croaked.

"Hold on a second." Markie got the water glass ready and held the straw to her lips. "Here. Just suck."

Tee wanted to laugh but could only manage a smile. "Suck?" she asked weakly.

"Stop it," she admonished her, but she was smiling as she said it. "How do you feel tonight?"

"What time is it?"

"It's about eight o'clock."

Can I sit up?"

"Well, let me see if I can figure out how to operate this thing." Markie made some adjustments and found how to raise the head of the bed. "How's that?" She shifted the pillows behind Tee's back and neck.

"Thanks." She looked around the room. Her stomach heaved at the motion and she quickly closed her eyes. Her head throbbed and she waited for the worst to pass. "Isn't it late for you to be here?" she asked at length.

"Yeah, but no one has come to kick me out yet so I thought I'd hang around a while longer." She was afraid to mention either Carly or Michelle, not knowing how she would react to either name. "How do you feel?"

"Better," Tee said, but was careful to keep her head still. "I'm tired of sleeping."

"Does your head hurt?"

"Some, yeah." She stopped just before nodding. "I feel a lot better this time."

"Good," Markie said with a smile.

"What does my face look like?"

"Don't worry about that," she said quickly.

Tee looked down at the leg suspended in its sling. "I must really look bad then. What's the verdict on the leg?"

"You look fine," Markie scoffed. "You have a broken leg and it will heal fine in a few weeks."

"What else?"

"A couple of broken ribs."

"That would account for the painful breathing," she acknowledged. "Now, tell me about my head."

"You have a concussion." Markie said. "You also have several cuts and scrapes from all the broken glass flying around. None of them deep enough to leave a scar though. So, you'll be just as pretty as you ever were."

Tee tried to smile at her best friend. "Tell me what happened. Please."

Markie kept her face from showing her distress at answering the question again. "Why don't you tell me what you remember and I'll try to fill in the blanks."

Tee frowned, struggling with a faulty memory. Her head pounded but she pressed on. "I was in San Antonio," she said finally. "I was going to buy that bar. I remember that." She closed her eyes. "He was running book," she added and her eyes opened again. "The bartender was stealing too." She smiled up at Markie, pleased with her recalling of events.

"That's right," she nodded at her in encouragement.

"I didn't buy the bar, did I?"

"No." Markie waited for her to remember.

Tee frowned again and put a hand to her head. "Carly." It wasn't exactly a question and Markie waited. "Carly was there." She looked at Markie.

"Yes, she was there."

TEE with Carly

"She was…why was she there?" She looked to Markie but she just waited for her to work it out. "I called Paul to come down for a meeting. I think." She laid her head back against the pillows with a grimace. "It hurts to think."

"Just relax, honey," Markie told her. "It'll come back to you, just give it some time." She laid a hand over Tee's on top of the blanket. "You just need to rest."

"Tired of resting," Tee huffed from behind closed eyes. "Tell me."

"The bar blew up," Markie said, knowing withholding the information from her would only hurt and frustrate her.

"It blew up," Tee murmured softly, trying it out in her mind. "The bar blew up," she said again. She opened her eyes. "Yeah. I was on my way to the bar when everything went crazy." She smiled in triumph at the memory. "I was looking at Jason when it happened." Her eyes darkened. "Did he survive?"

"No, he didn't," Markie told her. "Both he and the bartender died that night."

"I'll ask Carly about…," she said and then stopped in surprise. She looked once again at Markie. Her eyes went wide. "Is she okay?" she asked anxiously. "Wait…she was here. Wasn't she?"

"Yes. She's been…siting with you at night." Markie wasn't sure how much she should tell her.

"Not…"

She was interrupted by the arrival of Michelle. She entered amidst a cloud of perfume and hysteria. "Oh my God, Tee!" she exclaimed loudly as she rushed to her bedside and leaned over the bed to hug her. "Don't worry, darling, I'll be here to take care of you. Don't worry about a thing."

Tee winced as Michelle's attentions jostled her ribs and made her head throb. She groaned without realizing it. "Michelle…"

"Michelle, maybe it would be better if you didn't move her," Markie said. "She has some broken ribs and a concussion."

"And a broken leg?" she exclaimed. "Oh my God, Tee." She turned to Markie. "Kathleen said there was an explosion!" She turned back to Tee. "What in the world were you doing in a building that blew up?"

Tee closed her eyes and winced at the onslaught of questions and emotions flying around the room. Markie saw it and eased Michelle away from the bed. "Sit down. She's feeling better tonight but she needs to stay calm and quiet." She hoped Michelle would take the hint. When she had gotten her into the chair, she turned to Tee. "Honey, I have to be going. Are you going to be okay tonight?"

"Of course she'll be okay," Michelle spoke up. "I'm going to be here." She shot a look at Markie. "I said I'd take care of her."

Markie looked at Tee with a worried frown. "Honey? I'll stay if you want me to," she whispered.

"No. Go ahead and go. I'll be fine," Tee assured her. "Will I see you tomorrow?"

"Yes. I'll be here."

Tee looked like she might say something else but then just squeezed Markie's hand. "Be careful."

Chapter 38

Carly slid her card key through the slot and keyed the elevator for the third floor. The construction crew was working on the remodeling of the spa today and Jane had called. It had been two weeks since returning to Dallas from San Antonio and she had just been to the clinic to have her ribs probed and her wrist re-evaluated. She still had a wrap around her ribs but her wrist was free of the restraining brace. The bruises around her face and neck were also improving but she was anxious for them to be gone completely. It had also been a week since she'd been at the hospital to visit Tee, although she talked to Markie frequently and knew she had been released. The constant nag of worry about her had vanished. It had been replaced by an ache in her heart she knew would never be healed. She trembled with the effort of controlling thoughts of Tee as she stepped through the doorway into a swirling cloud of tile dust and grit. She waved a hand ineffectively in front of her face to clear the air. Just concentrate on the problem and you'll be fine, she told herself.

"Carly." Jane was walking toward her across the expanse of the spa foyer. "Thank God you're here."

"Man, what a mess!" Carly coughed. "I got your message. What's going on?"

"These guys are trying to put down the wrong tile. I've told them a million times it's wrong but I'm not getting through to them."

"Do you speak Spanish?"

"No."

"Do they speak English?" Carly was looking around the dusty room trying to locate the crew chief. "Do they nod and smile a lot?" she asked. "That's a sure sign they don't understand a word you're saying."

"Then they don't speak English," Jane said morosely.

"Well, let's see what we can do." She stepped into the center of the room. "*Jefe!*" she shouted. "It means chief," she said quietly to Jane. A stocky man wearing dusty jeans and a work shirt with a blue bandana around his head looked up. "*Aqui, por favor.*" She waited for him to cross the foyer to her. "*ordenes.*" She held out her hand for his order form.

"*Si, si,*" he nodded and retrieved his clipboard from amidst the jumble of tile boxes, tile saws, and grout. "*Aqui es.*" Here it is.

Carly read over the order form and showed it to Jane. "What is the name of the tile Tee originally selected?" she asked.

"Caspian Blue is what she ordered. I remember it because it was one of the ones I liked when she was showing me samples."

"This says Cerulean Blue."

"Well, that explains it then." Jane looked at her hopefully. "What do we do now?"

"We call the tile company and ask them what happened and they'll decide what to do about it. It'll mean a delay in getting the job done though." She sighed. "When was the spa scheduled to re-open?"

"We didn't have a firm date but Tee wanted it back in operation as soon as possible. Every day it's closed we lose money."

"And possibly clients. Okay." She nodded and turned back to the crew chief. "*para ar por hoy.*" Stop for today. "*orden incorrecto.*" Wrong order.

"Si, senorita." He nodded and shrugged as if it wasn't on his shoulders if the crazy American woman wanted his crew to stop working.

Carly motioned for Jane to follow her back out into the hall where they could breathe. "It's not their fault," she said with a shake of her head. "His crew is laying the tile that's on his work order. I'll call the company and get it straightened out if you want."

"Yes, please," she blew out a frustrated breath. "I've been trying to get the monthly reports done all week and it seems like something is always interrupting me." She reached out to squeeze Carly's arm. "I'm sorry to keep calling on you to get me out of a jam."

"Don't worry about it," Carly grinned. "I didn't have anything planned anyway."

"I see you aren't wearing the brace on your hand. Is your wrist all healed?"

"Yep," she grinned. "My ribs are still a little sore but I feel good." The elevator arrived and together they ascended to the fifth floor and the offices. "Can I use her office?"

"Of course."

Jane returned to her work and Carly went on into Tee's office. She shook the work order out over the trash can to clear it of dust and then smoothed it out on the desk surface. She hesitated before calling the number on the form. She would be remiss if she didn't check first. She picked up the phone and punched the intercom button. "Jane?"

"Yes?"

"Do you have the original order form or contract or something from this tile company?"

"Yes. I'll bring the file in to you."

"Thanks." She hung up and re-read the form just in case she'd missed something but there was no mistake. Jane appeared a minute later and handed a thin file folder to her. "Okay, let's get this straightened out. Thanks Jane."

"No, thank you, Carly." She gave her a smile and returned to her own office.

Carly went through the order form in the file and it was simply a mistake between what had been ordered and what had been written on the form from the Federal Tile Company to the work crew. She dialed the number on the Federal Tile papers and went through the interminable phone menu until she was ready to pull out her hair. Obviously, they weren't prepared for any mistake to be addressed, as there was no option for speaking to a real person. She fumed behind the phone and finally slammed it down in frustration. "Idiots!" she exclaimed out loud. She picked it up again and re-dialed. This time she pushed the button for billing inquiries. When she was eventually connected to the billing department she was ready to explode. The clerk assured her there could not possibly have been a mistake and that was the wrong thing to say to Carly at the time.

"Then make no mistake about this," she said through gritted teeth. "As her attorney, I have the authority to tell you to cancel the entire order. My client will not be held responsible for your sloppy, disorganized operation. Moreover, I will advise her on selecting more honest and qualified business partners in the future. Quality is not something she will tolerate…No sir, there is absolutely nothing you can do that will change my mind. The very fact you tried to wiggle out of your mistake tells me you're running a sloppy company. Cancel the entire order, recall your workers, whom I suspect are illegals, and clear out of this building. *Now*." She hung up the phone and then put her face in her hands. "Oh God, she's going to kill me," she moaned.

"No, she's not." Tee's voice came from behind her.

Carly whirled around in the desk chair, a hand to her heart. "Jesus! You scared the hell out of me!" Tee was leaning on crutches just inside the door to the back hall. She must have entered while Carly was ranting on the phone. She was thin and pale but gorgeous nonetheless.

"Sorry. I didn't mean to frighten you." Tee looked around her office once before returning her gaze to Carly. "I didn't know you were here." She hesitated and Carly saw the confusion in her eyes.

"How could you?" she tried a small smile. "Jane just called me a little while ago and asked if I could assist her for a moment." She stood up and swiveled the office chair toward her. "Sit down. It *is* your office."

Tee stood for a second but finally hobbled to the chair and eased into it with a sigh. She sensed Carly was about to bolt. "Could you please fill me in on what that was all about?"

"Certainly." Carly leaned over to pick up the file and Tee got a whiff of something that smelled vaguely like eucalyptus. It was wonderful and she took in a deep breath to catch more of it. She instantly regretted it as her ribs protested. She unconsciously put a hand on her left side and a small moan escaped her lips. "Tee!" Carly cried out and, without thought, put a steadying hand on her shoulder. "You shouldn't be at work."

"I'm fine," she said through tight lips. "I just forgot about the ribs for a moment." She eased back in the big chair and relaxed a little. "I won't be forgetting again anytime soon." She looked expectantly at the file still in Carly's hand. "You were saying?"

"Are you sure you're okay?"

Carly sounded worried and it made Tee feel good for some reason. "Yes. I just…forget sometimes that I'm…not fully healed yet. Please, continue."

"Federal Tile," she said and her disdain was apparent. "They started putting down the tile in the spa today. The wrong tile, as it turns out." She laid the open folder on the desk in front of Tee and pointed to the appropriate section. "Jane tried to tell them they had the wrong color but they're just the crew and none of them spoke enough English to understand her. She called me and I came over to see if I could lend a hand. I speak just enough Spanish to tell the guy to stop when I saw the error."

"And the phone call?"

Carly sighed and stepped back. "I told them to cancel the order," she said quietly. She put a hand to her forehead as she felt another headache begin. "I'm sorry. I lost my temper."

"Sit down," Tee said and waited until she had taken a chair across the desk from her. "Why are you sorry?"

"I cancelled the order and now the project is going to be behind schedule. You're going to lose time and money because of it." Her head pounded but she resolutely brought her eyes up to meet Tee's.

"Did they offer to fix the problem?"

"No. They told me the tile was what had been ordered and they would charge Sylar Industries for it. That's when I lost my temper."

"So why are you sorry?" Tee asked. "They were wrong and refused to alter the order. I heard you tell them you had the authority to cancel the order. And you are right about that as long as you were acting as my attorney."

"I was," Carly nodded slowly. "I cannot abide sloppy or dishonest work. Customer service is a forgotten art these days, I'm afraid."

"You're right and I would have been pissed if I came back to the wrong tile in the spa." She gave Carly a smile. "I would rather suffer a delay and get what I want than settle for someone else's mistake. Thank you for doing the right thing."

Carly looked at her in surprise. "You're okay with my decision?"

"Yes," she nodded. "I would have done the same thing if I had been here." She shifted her cast forward a little more and sighed. "I hate this damn thing."

"How are you feeling?"

"Much better," she answered. "Why did you stop coming to see me in the hospital?"

The blunt question took Carly off guard and she scrambled for an acceptable answer. "I...well I thought..."

"Do you still think I'm only good for an occasional roll in the hay?" Tee kept her pinned to the chair with her intense eye contact.

"No!" she protested immediately. "I don't think that. I never did." She dropped her eyes then because she couldn't stand the heat. "I'm sorry about that night. I didn't mean it like you think."

"Then what did you mean?" Tee's voice was harsh with the need to hear it.

"I was frightened that Kim was too emotionally unstable. I was worried she'd do something to get us thrown out and arrested. She was off her meds." She looked at her hands clasped in her lap. "I told you when I called that night."

"And now I'm supposed to believe it was all just a big misunderstanding?"

Carly's shoulders slumped. "No," she whispered. "No, you don't need to believe that." She rose from the chair without looking at her. "This is why I quit coming to see you at the hospital. I knew you didn't want me there." She walked to the office door and Tee let her leave.

"Boss!" Jane opened the office door and looked in. "You're back!"

"Hey Jane. Come on in." Tee smiled as her assistant crossed the room with a huge grin on her face.

Jane rounded the desk and though she threatened to hug Tee hard, she actually kept her embrace gentle. "Man, it's good to see you!"

"Thanks, Jane." Tee matched her grin. "It's great to actually be back."

"I should tell you Carly has done an absolutely great job of helping me out," she said. "I just needed some help now and then. Was that okay?"

"That was very okay," Tee assured her. "I commend your ability to recognize a need and to take steps to solve it. Very good move, Jane."

"Thanks." It was obvious how much Tee's praise meant to her. She beamed with pleasure. Then her countenance fell slightly. "Umm, boss? I saw Carly leave and she seemed...upset."

"Yeah," Tee nodded with a sigh. "That's my fault. I upset her and I shouldn't have. It has nothing to do with her work for you though so don't give it another thought. You did great."

"She's really been a big help, boss," Carly persisted. "If you upset her you should apologize. I would have drowned here without her."

Tee nodded and finally smiled. "Yes, you're right. I should apologize. I will apologize." She nodded again.

"Great," Jane grinned. "Do you want me to give her a call?"

"No Jane, I can dial the phone myself." Tee laughed for the first time since she'd awoken in the hospital with a monster headache and pain in every other appendage.

"Okay, good." Jane grinned at her. "Are you staying here?"

"Yes. I'm in the same suite as before. I came up here to let you know when I ran into Carly. I'll probably need the suite for at least a few more weeks."

"I'll put it on the schedule," she nodded. "How did you get here? Did Markie bring you?"

"Yes. And, by the way, Fee needs to give her an access card."

"I'll take care of it. When will she be back here?"

"Later tonight. She's packing up some of my clothes and bringing them by."

"Okay, I'll get Fee on it right away. Is there anything else I can do for you, boss? Would you like some coffee or maybe some lunch sent up?"

"I would like some coffee," Tee admitted.

"I'll be right back."

There was a knock on the door to her suite and Tee called out for Markie to come in. She was on the couch with her leg propped up on a pillow on the coffee table. She wore a tee shirt and warm up pants. The zipper on the left leg was wide open to allow for the bulk of the cast and Markie had gotten a sock to cover her toes in the hospital.

"Hey girlfriend," Markie greeted her. "You look comfortable." She deposited the large suitcase she'd pulled in behind her next to the small desk. "I hope I got everything."

"It'll be fine whatever you got," Tee told her. "I'm just glad I have a good friend who'll run these errands for me."

"Yeah, well, I'd be most grateful if you didn't hurt yourself again for a while. I'm getting tired of seeing you banged up and having to live here." She flopped next to her on the couch and reached for her hand. "How do you feel?"

"I'm good," she nodded. "Tired," she added when she saw the look in Markie's eyes, "but good. I just wanted out of that hospital."

"I know, but you will let me know if your headache gets worse, won't you? Please?"

"Yes, I'll let you know," she promised with a sigh to show how unnecessary it was.

"Have you talked to Michelle since you've been back here?" Markie asked as casually as she could.

"Uh, actually there won't be a need to talk to Michelle any more," Tee said. "We had a conversation in the hospital room the other night and decided to part ways."

"Oh?"

"Come on," Tee gave a short bark of a laugh. "You knew it wasn't going to work out for us."

"Well, I know you weren't ever going to love each other," Markie admitted. "You did say she was the right kind of woman for you though, if I remember correctly."

"Yes, I said that," she nodded. "I was wrong, of course. You knew that too."

"What kind of woman do you need then?" Markie asked with interest.

"The kind that I can trust," she said simply and then held up a hand to halt any further questions. "That's the end of it. Okay?"

"Okay," she agreed. "You'll let me know if you meet one?"

"I'll let you know," she vowed.

"Have you talked to Carly lately?"

Tee snapped her head around to stare at her. "What are you talking about?"

"You know she was beside your hospital bed the whole time you were in a coma. I just thought now that you're out of the hospital you might have talked to her." Markie tried for nonchalance but failed miserably.

"As a matter of fact I talked to her this afternoon," Tee told her smugly.

"Oh really? How is she? I miss talking to her."

Tee frowned at this bit of new information. "You talked to her?"

"Every day," Markie confirmed as she suddenly found a nail that needed her attention.

Tee warred with herself but finally asked, her need to know greater than her need to keep things private. "What did you talk about?"

"Oh, you know, the usual stuff women talk about."

Tee clamped her teeth together in an effort not to scream at her friend. "Markie, just tell me what you talked about," she ground out.

"You, of course. We talked about you, honey. What else?"

"And what, exactly, did she say?"

"Well, let's see." Markie pretended to ponder the question just to irritate her. "She told me how she got fired from her old law firm for wanting to prosecute some free case she was working on, and getting into trouble for refusing the advances of a senior attorney." She glanced at Tee next to her. "It sounds to me like she really got a bad deal from that place."

"Some senior attorney made sexual advances to her?" Tee asked in shock. "That's crazy. Especially for a law firm."

"Yeah, you'd think they'd know better than that, wouldn't you?"

"Why didn't she turn him in?"

"She was busy trying to figure out how her free case got e-mailed to everyone on the company's list and defending herself. And it was a she not a he."

"What?"

"She got hit on by a female," Markie clarified. "Not a male."

"Christ!" Tee jerked upright with the need for action but, of course, there was nothing she could do. "What the hell happened?" She forgot she wasn't supposed to care.

"She got fired," Markie told her calmly. "She had her computer hacked, a female attorney with seniority felt rejected and reacted with vengeance." She squeezed Tee's arm. "But by then she was busy trying to figure out how to clear up the misunderstanding in Chicago. You remember, the one about the *ex*-girlfriend."

"Jesus," Tee moaned. She slumped back against the couch and put a hand over her eyes. She knew Carly had been fired but that's all she'd been able to bare before shutting everything else out in a cloud of her own pain. "She must have been so…" Words failed her. She felt the misting of tears behind her eyes. "Is this what she told you?"

"She said she was innocent. She thought it was her boss or the rejected woman. She was utterly devastated by the whole thing."

"How do you know if it's true?" Tee hated having to ask.

"You remember my new girlfriend, Kathleen?"

"Yeah."

"She also works at Brown, Hardin & Simon," Markie told her. "She's an attorney in a different section." She squeezed Tee's arm again. "She asked around and confirmed most of it. I guess it's common knowledge that this particular attorney likes younger women. She thinks no one knows. And Kathleen's pretty sure about the hacked file too since it's impossible to e-mail *everyone*." She let that information sink in. "So, it looks like she was a victim," she added.

Tee groaned as a pain greater than any she'd ever known before ripped through her. What had she done? She had been so hurt by her past experiences that she'd completely blocked out anything else about Carly. Blocked it so she could wallow in self-pity. She hung her head. "Jesus, she must have been so fragile," she whispered, forgetting Markie was even there.

"Maybe you could talk to her again," she suggested kindly. "Maybe tonight." Markie stood and moved to the door. "I have a date with Kathleen tonight but I'll call you tomorrow in case you need something." She opened the suite door. "Goodnight."

"Night," Tee looked up with eyes dark with sorrow. "Thanks, Marks."

"You're welcome, sweetie."

Tee sat for long moments after she left, her mind a complete blank. She stared at the floor while trying to put a coherent thought together. She had been an asshole, a gigantic asshole. She could at least have given her a chance to explain. She flashed back to San Antonio and seeing Carly go into the hotel bar. She had followed her because she felt that irresistible pull of her. Even as she professed to hate her, she still wanted her. *Just hold on*, she thought. *So what if Carly had been the victim? That didn't necessarily mean she wasn't also a serial dater.* She tried to hold on to that thought as to a lifeline but it wouldn't work. She couldn't keep the anger inside her. It leaked from her soul in rapidly escalating drips. Carly pulled at her like a magnet. It was something she had never experienced before. She continued to sit silently, unable to make the one move that might save her from drowning in her own misery. Was it stubbornness or fear keeping her from reaching for the phone? Only when she could admit it was fear did she pick up the phone and dial the number she still knew by heart.

"Hello?"

"Uh...it's Tee," she finally got out.

"Is there something wrong with the tile company?" she asked quickly. "Whatever it is, I'll see to it tomorrow morning. I promise."

"No, no," she said immediately. "It's not about the tile."

There was a moment of silence. "Then what is it?"

"Uh, I...would like to talk to you." Tee hadn't thought this would be so hard. What if she had blown it forever? What if Carly was tired of having to explain herself?

"Okay."

"Oh...not on the phone."

"Well then, do you want me to come to the office tomorrow? I can arrange that."

"No." Tee knew she couldn't go through the night like this. "Could you possibly come to the Reed House tonight?"

"I...guess so," she answered slowly, unsure of where this was heading. "Your office?"

"No. I'm staying on the third floor in one of our suites." There was silence on the other end of the line. "I can't drive and it's close to the office," she offered in explanation.

"Okaaay," Carly finally said in obvious confusion.

Tee suddenly realized how all this must sound to her. "How about this?" she suggested. "Would you like to have dinner downstairs with me? My treat."

They agreed on dinner in an hour and Tee exhaled in relief after she hung up. Jesus! Getting an actual date had never been this nerve wracking! She thumped into the bathroom and began the arduous task of cleaning up and changing clothes. She was restricted in what she could wear because of the cast but she changed into a clean pair of warm ups with a matching jacket. She called down to the restaurant and reserved the table in the back corner where it was secluded and private. Now all she had to do was get herself downstairs. She slipped her keycard into her pocket and left the suite. Her nerves began working on the short elevator ride down to the restaurant and, by the time she entered through the back, she was already a wreck. She stopped to chat briefly with Chef William and to let him know she would be in the dining room with a guest. She didn't expect any extra service but she didn't want him worrying about why she was there. She made her way through the room and reached the reserved table just as Gregory, the host, caught up with her. He quickly set the table for two and poured water. Tee knew she shouldn't drink but ordered a beer. She needed something to calm her nerves. She wiped her palms on the napkin and contemplated what she should say just as Gregory appeared with Carly. Tee wished she could stand to hold the chair for her but she had to settle for a smile as Gregory did the chair thing instead.

"Hi," she said and immediately felt inadequate.

"Hello," Carly answered. She looked up at Gregory and ordered a scotch. When she looked back at Tee, there was a question in her eyes.

"Thanks for coming," Tee said.

She nodded. "Thanks for a free dinner." She looked around the restaurant with interest. "This is really nice."

Tee nodded and smiled. "You've never eaten here before?"

"No. I did eat at the gay ball though and that came from here, right?" She used the informal term for the GLBT annual ball.

"Yes." Tee grinned and relaxed a little. "Our catering staff did a pretty good job, didn't they?"

"It was wonderful," Carly assured her. She smiled her thanks at Gregory as he delivered her scotch. She took a small sip and looked silently at Tee, the question in her eyes.

"Uh, I wanted to talk to you…" She was interrupted by the arrival of their waiter. Once they had ordered, she tried to think of the best way to approach what she wanted to say without sounding like an idiot. "Carly…I need to apologize for what I said to you this afternoon. I was out of line. You didn't deserve it and I apologize."

Whatever Carly had thought this was going to be about, it wasn't that. She kept her lawyer face on but her eyes reflected her surprise. She exhaled a slow breath. "Thank you."

Tee knew she hadn't expected that. "I want you to know…" She looked away and closed her eyes for a second to gather her strength. "I've treated you unfairly and I feel badly." She stopped. This wasn't going the way she wanted. She leaned over the table. "You tried to tell me what happened and I didn't want to hear it. I was wrapped up in my own self-pity and I didn't give you a chance to explain."

Carly couldn't believe what she was hearing. "So, why are you telling me this now?" She realized how that sounded and softened her tone. "I mean, after this afternoon…What made you change your mind?"

Tee blew out a big breath but kept her eyes on Carly's. "I talked to Markie, for one thing."

"She told you to apologize?"

"No. She reminded me that I can be a real jerk." She looked at the table where Carly's hand lay and entertained the idea of taking it in her own. She was saved from embarrassment by the arrival of their food. When the waiter had retreated, Tee watched as Carly began to eat. She seemed not the least affected by Tee's apology. She stabbed at her own salad in silence for a moment.

"How are you feeling?" Carly's unexpected question brought her back to attention.

"I'm fine," she answered automatically. She stabbed and chewed. "How about you?"

"I'm good," she nodded. "I got the brace off my wrist earlier today and it feels great." She looked up. "Your bruises are fading."

"Yeah, yours too." She looked around the room. "We must look like crash victims to everyone else."

"It was a hell of a crash," Carly said quietly.

Something in her voice alerted Tee. "It was," she agreed. "Do you think about it very often?"

"Oh." The fact that she did hit her like a punch. She looked away and didn't answer immediately.

"I've only been conscious a little over a week," Tee continued to give her time to recover, "but I still think about it." She looked up then. "At least the parts I remember."

"You still don't remember everything?" Carly asked. She was grateful for even the slight change in direction.

"Not all of it," Tee admitted. "I get flashes every now and then of things that I can't quite recall but nothing that hangs together enough."

"I'm sorry to hear that," Carly said. She took a bite and chewed, her gaze unfocused on the middle distance. "How much *do* you remember?" she finally asked.

Tee gave it some thought. "I remember parts of the meeting in the lawyer's office but not all of it." She was frowning as she thought about it. "I remember being in the hotel bar. That was later that day, right?"

"Yes," she nodded. "How much of that do you remember?"

"Uh, I remember…" She let her voice trail off as she thought about whether or not she should tell Carly everything she remembered.

"What?" Carly prompted. "What were you just thinking about?"

"I was thinking about when I came downstairs from my room. I saw you go into the bar."

"And?" she asked. "You followed me?"

"Yes."

"What else do you remember?" She continued eating, seeming not to notice that Tee had just admitted to following her.

"I remember having a drink at the bar with you."

"And?" she prompted.

"And then there are these sort of flashes. Things that don't connect." Tee put her head down and began eating again.

"Can you describe any of them?" she asked quietly.

Tee brought her head up when she heard the slight quaver in her voice. "I don't know. I haven't tried." She lifted her shoulders in a small shrug. "Maybe." They ate in silence until they were both finished. "Dessert?"

"Oh, I don't think I can," Carly shook her head. "That was a fabulous meal though. Thank you."

Tee saw her chance of any meaningful conversation slipping away. Carly was clearly getting ready to leave. "You're welcome." She impulsively put her hand over Carly's on top of the table. "Please…"

Carly looked at her in surprise. "What?"

"I…would you come upstairs with me?"

If it hadn't been for the look of panic on Tee's face Carly might have misunderstood her plea. She should leave. She should just thank her for the apology and the meal and be on her way. There was no good reason to prolong her misery by being close to the one woman she craved and couldn't have. It was settled. "Okay," is what came out of her mouth.

Tee let out a pent up breath and smiled. "Thank you." She reached for her crutches and Carly waited until she was on her feet, or foot, in this case.

"Would you mind leading the way?" Tee asked. "I'm a little awkward yet."

TEE with Carly

"Sure." Carly chose the path of least resistance and they reached the elevator without mishap, although she thought Tee looked a little tired.

Tee slid her card through the reader and punched the third floor button. They were silent until they reached the suite and Tee used her keycard to open the door. "Please don't look at the mess," Tee joked. "I just arrived today and the maid hasn't been in yet."

Carly looked around the room with interest. She'd heard about the suites, of course, but had never been in any of them. "This is very nice," she said.

Tee thumped her way to the kitchen. "Would you like something to drink?" She saw the look on Carly's face. "Coffee?"

"Coffee would be good," Carly nodded.

"Make yourself comfortable." Tee opened one of the lower cupboards but before she could extract the filters, Carly's hand reached past her and pulled both the filters and the coffee from the shelf.

"Let me do this," she said matter-of-factly. "It's much easier for me and faster." She turned to the coffee pot on the counter. "Why don't you make yourself comfortable? You look like you could use it more than me."

Tee inhaled Carly's scent and her mind went hazy. As always, she couldn't think when she was this close to her. "Thanks." Tee turned and thumped her way to the couch and lowered herself heavily onto it.

"It shouldn't be long," Carly said from the kitchen. She thought Tee looked tired but she pushed the thought away. It really didn't matter to her, did it? She found coffee cups in another cupboard and, when the machine finished spitting out its dark aromatic liquid, she filled both and carried them into the small living area. She handed one of the cups to Tee and took hers to the chair facing her. She sat and looked at her, waiting. There was a reason Tee wanted her here and now it was time to find out what it was.

Tee felt her scrutiny and struggled not to fidget. "Carly..." she leaned forward and placed the coffee on the small table. "Would you...I'd like to know what happened."

Carly settled back into the chair and sipped her coffee. She didn't really want to talk about the explosion but what recourse did she have? "We went to The Sports Room that night because Jason Dooley called you and said he had the papers we needed for the sale. Do you remember? He didn't initially have his liquor license current and there were no professional sport contracts for permission to show the games in the bar?"

Tee nodded slowly, frowning. It was coming back to her. "Yes, I remember that now. He was talking about getting me to sign off on the deal at the bar." She looked up with a smile. It was something she hadn't remembered before.

"Yes. We walked along the River Walk to the bar and went inside." She waited to see if Tee would comment but when she didn't Carly continued. "We had a beer and you said you were going to the restroom. I saw you come out of the back hall and you started to walk toward the bar." She stopped and swallowed hard. She was breathing quickly now as the memories flooded her brain. Her hands shook so badly she spilled coffee. "Damn it!" she exclaimed and quickly set the cup on the small end table beside her chair. She rose and went into the kitchen for a paper towel to clean it up.

"Carly, have you talked to anyone about this?" Tee asked kindly when she had returned.

"Well, I talked to Wayne." She mopped up the spill. "You probably don't know this either. He heard about the...explosion on the news and drove down to get us." She threw the paper towel away in the kitchen garbage and returned to her chair but didn't pick up the coffee cup again.

"That sounds like Wayne," she said fondly. "He's such a big teddy bear."

"Yes, he is," she agreed. "Anyway," she steeled herself to continue the story. After all, she was the only one who knew what actually happened that night, and Tee deserved to know. "You were on your way to the bar when it exploded." She pushed on before the memories could interfere again. "I saw you..." she clamped her jaws together to fend off tears. "First, I saw you fly through the air. And then there was glass and parts of the bar flying everywhere. And then it seemed like there was a wall of air that hit me and I was slammed back against the back wall." She waited until she could continue. The worst part was over now. "I must have hit my head on the wall because that's all I can remember."

Tee watched her face and that alone convinced her how horrible an experience it must have been. She looked stricken even today. "Markie told me Jason was killed in the blast."

"Yes. Him and at least one other bartender. I never heard for sure whether it was one or two. You know how news reports get things like that wrong half the time. I do know that Jason was killed though." She took in a big breath. "The last I heard the police thought he was the intended target because he was either skimming money from the gambling operation."

"I knew he was a bookie." She frowned at Carly. "Didn't I?"

"You did," she nodded. "We talked about it at the bar. I asked if you would continue once you owned the bar. You said no and I questioned that. It was insulting to you and I'm sorry for it.

"I don't remember that."

Carly gave a slight shrug. "It was a conversation we had that night once we got to the bar."

"What else do I need to know?"

"You were in a coma from that moment on. Wayne came down and we stayed with you until they said it wouldn't hurt to move you. You were in ICU down there. We hired an ambulance to transport you to the hospital here." She gave her a small smile. "You should be getting all the bills pretty soon. It wasn't cheap but I...we couldn't leave you down there all alone."

"And then?" Tee wanted it all.

She knew what Tee wanted now. "And then Markie visited you during the day and I visited you after work. You do remember I work for Paul Carrington now?"

"Yes. I remember you were in my room the first time I woke up." She kept her eyes on Carly's. "But then you stopped coming. Why?"

"I told you," Carly tried not to snap the answer at her, her emotions still very near the surface.

"You said you didn't think I wanted you there. Why did you think that?"

"I would think that was pretty evident," she said. "You had no use for me. Plus, your girlfriend was on her way. You certainly didn't want or need me in the way."

Tee nodded in understanding. "I see."

Carly picked up the coffee cup and returned it to the kitchen sink. "Now you know what happened," she said as she returned. She started for the door. "Let me know if you have more questions."

"Carly, wait." Tee struggled to get up and reached for her crutches. She stopped near the door where Carly waited expectantly. She inhaled and her brain went fuzzy again. "Uh, I would like to, uh, talk to you again." *She sounded so stupid! What was the matter with her?* "I'm sorry for being so horrible to you this afternoon. I'm an idiot and I need to keep my mouth shut." Carly was looking at her as if she'd lost her mind. "I'm sorry." She gave her a hangdog look. "Please, can we talk again?"

"Of course," Carly nodded. She'd do whatever she could to help Tee remember that day.

"Great. Thanks."

Tee's body was floating toward her. Carly wanted to reach out for her but her arms wouldn't move. Tee was looking at her with sad eyes and then she began screaming as her body began falling apart. First a leg fell off and then an arm. Tee pleaded with Carly to help her. Carly struggled with all her might but she couldn't get her body to move, couldn't reach her.

She awoke to the sound of screaming—her own. She jerked upright in bed, her chest heaving, and her throat raw. She was drenched in perspiration and her sleep shirt stuck to her chest. She took several minutes to calm her breathing before stepping into the bathroom for a much-needed shower. Maybe tonight she'd finish that autobiography she'd been reading. She was not exactly surprised she'd had a nightmare tonight. Having dinner with Tee was bound to bring everything back to the surface again.

She slipped into a fresh shirt and went into the living room. She curled into the corner of the couch with her book but didn't open it right away. She thought about Tee instead. It was something she usually fought against thinking about but tonight it was inevitable. Tee had looked tired and thin, but still good. She would make a full recovery and that was great. Once Tee was healthy and Carly explained everything she could remember about the explosion, what then? There would no longer be any reason to see each other. Maybe then she'd quit having nightmares. She resolutely opened her book. It was a pretty steep price to pay for sleep.

Chapter 39

Tee sat in her office chair and tried to relax. She was already tired of lugging the cast around and she kept forgetting about her bruised and broken ribs. It led to bouts of breath stealing pain that she could certainly do without. Before she could reach for the phone, her inner office door opened and Jane entered with her morning cup of coffee.

"It's so good to have you back, Tee," she smiled.

"Thanks, Jane." She sipped the coffee with relish. It was another thing that signaled her life was returning to normal. "How have things been since I was out of it?"

"There were moments when I wanted to rip out my hair," she admitted with a laugh, "but I called Carly and she always rescued me."

Tee nodded. It seemed Carly had made a friend in Jane. "I'm glad she was able to help out."

Her phone rang and Jane answered it before Tee could. "Sylar Industries...Yes, she is. Hold on a moment." Jane put the caller on hold and handed the receiver to Tee. "It's Markie."

"Thanks." She hit the hold button as Jane left. "Hey Marks…yes, I did…No, not exactly…We talked about other things though and she agreed that we can talk again." Tee sighed loudly enough that Markie would hear it. "Give me some time, will you? This isn't as easy as you seem to think…Soon. I'll let you know or maybe you want to arrange it yourself?" Tee was beginning to get irritated. "Look, Marks, it's between us, okay? I know you do…Yeah, I'll call you later…I know. I love you too…Bye." She hung up and sighed. She leaned back in her chair and thought back to their conversation the previous night. Carly had been cautious and Tee couldn't blame her for that, especially after what she'd said to her that afternoon. She just couldn't seem to let go of her anger. And that was what was holding her back, she realized. She'd let Carly think she wanted to talk about the explosion so she didn't have to talk about how she'd reacted so badly to the situation between them. She was a coward and a jerk. Great. She finished her coffee while staring at the phone. If she apologized to Carly, then what? They'd magically go back to the way they were before? No. That wouldn't happen. What then? They would at least be civil to each other. They were that already. She rubbed her hands over her face in frustration.

"Fuck!" she said out loud. "Fuck, fuck, fuck." She was further frustrated by not being able to pace. "Damn it!"

Jane appeared in the doorway. "Boss? Are you okay?"

"Yes," Tee sighed. "I'm just throwing a tantrum."

"Can I do anything for you?"

"No. Yes." She waved a hand at the phone. "Would you get me Paul's office, please?"

"Right away." Jane returned to her office and a minute later she sent the call to Tee's phone.

"Wayne?"

"Tee? Is that really you?"

"Yeah," she laughed. "I finally got out of the hospital."

"And you're back to work already? Why don't you take some time, honey? No one would blame you for taking some time off."

"I'm not doing much of anything," she said. "I'm just sitting behind the desk while Jane does all the actual work."

"She really stepped up," Wayne said. "You should be proud of her."

"That's what I've heard. I'll have to give her a raise."

"What can I do for you, Tee?"

"First of all, I want to thank you for everything. I hear you took charge of taking care of me and getting me back here from San Antonio."

"I had help," he said quickly. "Carly was adamant we had to get you back up here. She arranged everything."

"Is she there? I hear she works for you guys now."

"No, she's out of the office today. Do you need something? I can call her or we can set up an appointment."

"No, I don't need an appointment," she assured him. "It was just…I'll call her later."

Chapter 40

Wayne hung up the phone and rang into Carly's office. "Hey Carly, I just got off the phone with Markie. She and Kathleen are going to the Rawhide tonight and wanted to know if we'd like to meet them there."

"What's the occasion?"

"Nothing. They're just going out and hoped for some company. What do you say? We can kick up our heels. I mean, if you're feeling up to it."

"I feel great," she assured him. "And yes, I'd love to go out dancing. Is Paul going?"

"Yes. For once, I got him to forget about work. Shall we pick you up or do you want to meet us there?"

"Pick me up," she said. "What time?"

"Markie says they're going to dinner and then on to the Rawhide so they should be there about nine or nine-thirty."

"Hey, how about we go to dinner with them?" Carly suggested. "That would be fun."

"Oh, yes it would," he laughed. "Let me call Markie back and set it up." He buzzed her back in less than ten minutes. "It's a go," he told her. "We're meeting at Snookie's on Cedar Springs at seven-thirty."

"She was okay with us joining them?" Carly wanted to make sure they weren't imposing on a romantic dinner or something private.

"She was excited," Wayne told her. "Said she should've thought of it herself. So, we'll see you tonight."

"With bells on," she laughed.

The group entered the bar together laughing and jostling each other. Dinner had been fun and they'd only had to walk down the block to the bar. Markie had introduced Carly to Kathleen with care, not knowing how she would react to the fact that Kathleen worked for Carly's old employer. Carly didn't even hesitate to hug her and say she was glad to meet her. There wasn't a trace of hostility or stress in her actions and she seemed genuinely happy to meet her. They commandeered a table and Paul volunteered to buy the first round.

"Hey Carly, I think you have an admirer," Markie nudged her with a shoulder as they sat next to each other. She pointed her chin toward a table along the wall from theirs. A woman was leaning past her companions at their table to get a look at Carly. Kathleen leaned back behind Markie to look at Carly. "She's definitely interested," she said with a big smile. "What do you think?"

Carly tried to look without being obvious. "I'm not sure I've had enough to drink yet," she laughed at Kathleen.

"You might want to think about it," she advised. "I think she'll be coming over here pretty soon."

She was right. The woman in question soon detached from her group and approached their table. She didn't look at anyone but Carly. "Would you like to dance?" she said loud enough to be heard over the noise. Carly hesitated only a moment before leaving her chair and joining the woman, who took her hand and led her onto the dance floor. Kathleen kissed Markie on the cheek and whispered in her ear. "She's good looking, don't you think?"

"Excuse me?" Markie asked with an arched brow.

"You have nothing to worry about, love. You know that." Kathleen slid an arm around her shoulders and nuzzled her neck.

"Girls!" Wayne shouted. "Public display!" Where upon he promptly kissed Paul and they all laughed.

Tee was just taking a seat at the bar and their laughter drew her attention. She made her way across the room to their table and ran a hand across Markie's shoulder from behind. "Hello, beautiful."

Markie looked up and squealed in delight. "Tee! Oh my God, you're walking!"

"Yeah. I got the cast off this morning," she grinned. She spied the empty chair next to her and sat down. She looked pointedly past Markie with a question in her eyes.

"Tee, I'd like you to meet Kathleen. Kathleen, this is Tee, my best friend in the whole world."

Tee reached past Markie to shake her hand and gave her a genuine smile. "It's nice to meet you." Wayne and Paul returned then with drinks for everyone and Tee rose to give and receive hugs all around.

"God Tee, it's so good to see you out and about and all in one piece," Wayne said with emotion. "How does the leg feel?"

"It's a little weak but, damn, it feels good to get that cast off," she laughed.

"Are you here alone tonight?" Markie leaned over to ask.

Tee was struck by the odd question. Why would Markie ask her something like that? She knew she was no longer dating Michelle. She looked at her and opened her mouth to reply. A prickling sensation ran up the back of her neck and she slowly turned to look at the dance floor. Carly was there with a strange woman, dancing. She wanted to turn back to Markie and tell her that she was, indeed, here alone tonight. She wanted to carry on a conversation with Wayne about getting her cast off that morning. She wanted to talk to Kathleen and see for herself if she treated Markie well enough to deserve her. She could do none of those things. She could only stare at Carly on the dance floor. She looked fabulous in blue jeans and a red shirt that dipped just low enough to show the beginning swell of her breasts. Her hair was down and fell in thick, lustrous waves down past her collar and over her shoulders. Tee watched her move and felt the pull of her. It was strong, much stronger than she could have imagined. She was unable to look away until her dance partner put a hand on her hip and moved closer until their thighs were touching. She stood then. She thought she heard Markie saying something about staying calm but she brushed it aside. "Who is that?" she asked with a clenched jaw.

"I don't know. She just asked Carly to dance a minute ago." Markie didn't know if that was a good thing or not, but by the look on Tee's face it wasn't going over well with her. She smiled to herself. She'd known Tee still had strong feelings for Carly. Maybe now she'd do something about them.

Tee stepped free of the table as the song ended and another began. As if sensing her gaze, Carly turned. Their eyes met and held. Carly wasn't aware that her dance partner was speaking to her. She started toward Tee as Tee started toward her, each locking eyes with the other. They met and stood silently just looking at each other.

"Hi," Carly finally spoke, her voice thin with nerves.

"Hello." Tee started a slow sway to the beat and Carly followed. "My name is Tee," she said. "I own Sylar Industries."

"I'm Carly Matthews," she played along. "I'm an attorney and I have a crazy ex-girlfriend who forgets to take her meds."

"I'd like to dance with you but I just got my leg out of a cast this morning."

"Can I do anything to help?"

Tee shook her head. "No." She moved closer until she could smell Carly's shampoo. "It just takes time for things to heal."

"Yes," she agreed with a slight nod. "Time is a healer…of many things."

"May I buy you a drink?" Tee's voice was deep and rich and wafted over Carly's ear like a soft breeze on a summer's night.

"Yes, that would be nice." Carly thought this was as close a proximity of their first meeting as they could make it. She remembered their first dance, how they seemed to connect immediately. She didn't know where this might be going but she wanted to find out. She followed Tee to the bar and took an empty stool while Tee leaned on the bar next to her. Tee ordered them both a beer and handed one to Carly. "Thank you."

Tee was having a hard time thinking clearly, her head buzzing with Carly's nearness. She felt the tingle in the pit of her stomach and the heavy fullness between her legs. She would embarrass herself if she wasn't careful. She wanted to touch her but was afraid. She wasn't entirely sure her touch would be welcome. She took a deep breath in an effort at calmness. "Would you like to play a game of pool?"

Carly gave her a smile that did nothing to ease the throb in her jeans. "Yes."

Tee used it as an excuse to take her hand. The first contact shot a current through her and she had to concentrate not to lose it. What she wanted to do was put Carly on one of the pool tables and take her right then and there. What she did was put her money on one of the tables for the next game. Once again, they played a soft game of pool, teasing each other, just happy to be together. Tee had only to sink the eight ball to win the game and she leaned over the table and pointed to the corner pocket to call her shot.

"Are you sure?" Carly asked, leaning against Tee's backside as she lined up the shot.

Tee dropped her head as a rush shot through her and she lost her breath. She felt Carly's breasts push against her back and her pelvis against her ass. "No fair," she managed to get out.

"Since when is anything fair?" Carly pushed against her and moved her hips just enough to keep her off balance and unable to think.

"Jesus! Those two could cause global warming all by themselves!" Kathleen gulped to Markie. The whole table had watched the progress of the two since Tee had stood up.

"There are a lot of unresolved issues between them," Markie remarked.

"It looks like they might be able to resolve at least a few of them," Wayne added with a smile. "They look good together, don't they?"

"Yes, they do," Markie agreed. "I just hope they *are* good together…this time."

"They've been together before?" Wayne asked.

"Yes."

"I knew it!" Wayne clapped his hands together in excitement. "I knew there was something going on." He turned to Markie. "Tell me!"

"Oh, I don't think I should," Markie hedged. "It's her place to either tell you or not."

"Sure," Wayne nodded. Then he smiled. "I think this is the one who's spicy."

"Spicy?" Markie asked in confusion.

"Yeah. Carly once told me she quit dating someone because she was too sweet but that she'd let one get away that was *the one*. I asked her if that one was spicy. I think Tee is Ms Spicy."

Markie laughed. "Well, she is that."

At the pool table, Tee could barely breathe let alone make an easy shot. She scratched by putting the cue ball in the side pocket, thus giving Carly the win. Carly stepped away and laughed as Tee straightened up. She turned and gave Carly a look that could have started a fire.

"It seems you win," she said. Carly's antics at the pool table let her know exactly where she stood. Her eyes caressed her face before moving down to her breasts. She licked her lips and let her tongue linger for just the barest of moments on her bottom lip.

Carly sucked in a breath and was unable to look away from Tee's mouth. Jesus! She remembered what that mouth could do to her. She felt everything inside her turn molten. Her panties were going to be ruined by the gush between her legs. She stood, trembling, not sure her legs would support her for much longer.

"What…" She had to stop to clear a throat that was suddenly dry as dust. "What do I win?"

Tee noticed how breathy Carly's voice was and that she had to swallow repeatedly before she could speak. "What do you want?" she asked, moving away from the table toward her.

Carly retreated as Tee advanced until she was against the wall with nowhere left to go. She broke eye contact as Tee finally stopped well within her personal space. "I…"

"Yes?" She put an arm against the wall next to Carly's shoulder and leaned in to brush the question against her ear. "What is it you want, Ms Matthews?"

Carly couldn't seem to catch her breath now. She couldn't think. She was just one big raw nerve, pulsing with need, her need for this one woman. "Tee…" she looked past her shoulder in an effort to break the spell. "I want…" She was trembling so hard she could barely speak. She struggled to get air into her lungs. "Jesus, Tee," she finally blurted out. "I want you." She brought her hands up to cup Tee's face.

Tee closed her eyes and took a step back, fearing she might lose control and do something totally inappropriate. She didn't see the look of anguish on Carly's face. When she opened them again, Carly had tears rolling silently down her face. Only then did she see that Carly had misunderstood. "No, no, no." She rushed forward until she was against her this time. She put her arms around her. "I…we're in a public place." She placed a soft kiss in front of Carly's ear. "Jesus Carly, I was afraid I wouldn't be able to control myself." Carly was afraid to believe it, afraid it was all just a cruel joke. She kept her arms at her sides as Tee pulled her face against her shoulder and held her tightly. "Don't think that, Carly. Please, don't think that I'd do that to you." Tee put her own wanting aside as she concentrated on what Carly needed to hear. She put her lips against the side of Carly's neck and kissed her softly. "I…we need to go somewhere more private." Carly didn't respond and Tee really began to worry. "Please, Carly. I want this to be a new start. For us." She leaned back and bent until she could make eye contact with her. "I swear on my mother's grave. Please, can we go somewhere and talk?"

Carly drew in a deep breath and pulled away. She searched Tee's face for any sign of duplicity but found nothing there but compassion and honesty. She tried to smile as she wiped the remaining tears aside. "Is that what you want? To talk?"

Tee's heart lifted instantly. "Oh God, baby," she breathed. "You're killing me." She leaned forward until her forehead rested against Carly's. "We can do anything you want. Anything."

"Well," Wayne remarked as he watched them leave together. "I guess that settles that."

Markie smiled and nodded. "Yep. I guess it does." She leaned over and kissed Kathleen on the cheek. "You'll get to meet her again. I hope you like her."

"From what I just saw I think I'm going to get along with her just fine," Kathleen laughed. "Maybe I can pick up a few pointers from her."

"Oh honey, you don't need any pointers," Markie said with a waggle of her eyebrows.

"Okay, you two, enough," Wayne protested. "Men present at the table."

"He uses the term loosely," Paul interjected with a laugh.

Tee swiped her keycard and waited for Carly to precede her inside. Carly looked around the small living room as Tee closed the door behind her. On the way from the bar to the Reed House Tee had all she could do to keep her hands on the wheel and her eyes on the road. She had smelled her though and the scent drove her crazy with need. She was beginning to sweat with the effort of holding it together by the time they pulled into the garage. They stood just inside the door now and looked at each other for a moment. "Can I get you something to drink?" Tee asked. She was breathing hard, her core trembling with the need to touch Carly. She was certain she would perish if she couldn't feel her skin against her own and soon. At Carly's inquisitive look she added, "You might want to hydrate." Carly's mouth dropped open. Tee strode across the room, her eyes telegraphing a warning of what was to come. She scooped Carly up in her arms without slowing down and kissed her hard while walking them into the bedroom. She felt Carly's legs wrap around her hips and her arms around her neck. Her tongue was sucked deeply inside Carly's mouth. By the time Tee reached the side of the bed they were both breathing hard. "Out of your clothes," she gasped between kisses. "I want you naked. Now."

Carly's legs dropped to the floor and she released Tee to fumble with the buttons on her shirt. Tee unbuttoned Carly's jeans and jerked the zipper down then peeled them off her hips. They pooled on the floor just as Carly dropped her red shirt behind her. Tee caught her breath. Clad only in a black thong and a matching black silk bra, Carly was truly breath taking. With a deft twist of her wrist, Tee unhooked the clasp on her bra and freed her breasts. She slid the straps over her shoulders and tossed the garment on the floor with her shirt. She cupped both breasts in her hands, her thumbs and forefingers grasping and tugging on her nipples.

"Tee. Oh God, Tee." Carly arched into her touch, throwing her head back and exposing more of her neck for Tee to kiss.

"Get on the bed," Tee growled. She bit Carly's neck and spun her around, shoving her face down. She leaned over and grabbed her ass, squeezing roughly. She took the waistband of the thong and jerked it down to her thighs.

"Oh," Carly gasped.

Tee ripped the flimsy garment off her legs and threw it aside. She put a hand on the small of Carly's back, keeping her down, while she kicked out of her boots. "Let's see if you're ready for me tonight." Her voice was harsh in Carly's ear as she climbed onto the bed to lie fully on top of her. She rocked against her ass as she pulled Carly's arms above her head and held them with one hand. She bit her neck at the base where it joined the shoulder and heard Carly let out a small yelp. "I know you like things rough." Carly whimpered and Tee felt her move her ass up against her. "Oh yeah, I remember that, little one." She bit and kissed her way along her neck and shoulder while she worked her hand under Carly to squeeze her breast. Carly lifted her torso as much as she could to allow her access and Tee smiled. She liked things rough, yes indeed. She pinched the nipple between her fingers with a twist and heard the groan Carly tried to stifle. "I'm going to fuck you, little one," she whispered, her lips brushing against her ear. "I'm going to fuck you like you've always wanted to be fucked, like you've always dreamed of being fucked." Carly groaned and writhed beneath her. "Are you wet, little one?" She rolled her over and Carly immediately spread her legs. "Let me check." Tee put a hand between her legs and discovered an absolute flood of desire. "Oh yeah," she breathed. It was all she could do to keep her composure. Carly was pushing frantically against her hand so she entered her with two fingers only to discover it wasn't nearly enough and pulled out to add a third. She pushed deep until she could go no farther. She straddled her thighs and let her fingers slip out slowly.

"Tee." It was a plea.

Tee massaged her opening, allowing just the very tips of her fingers to enter her. She was careful not to touch her clitoris. Carly was frustrated and spread her legs wider in an effort to let her need be known. Tee wrapped her left arm around Carly's waist and plunged into her. She went deep and rubbed against her inside walls, which sent Carly into a torrent of heightened sensitivity.

She cried out and bunched the sheet in her fists. She was shaking with the unleashed emotions of a pending explosion that snaked along her spine. It was almost more than she could bear.

"Not yet," Tee growled in her ear as she bent over her. "Do not come yet." She slid back out and reached for the lube in the dresser drawer. She quickly drizzled the liquid over her hand and wrist. She then re-entered her with four fingers folded together. Carly grunted with the width and Tee held her knuckles just outside, waiting. She took her other hand and caressed Carly's breast, pulling and twisting her nipple and putting her lips along her neck to suck and nip. It had the desired effect of distracting and arousing Carly once again and soon Tee's hand slipped past the tight ring and fully into her.

"Oh God," Carly moaned beneath her.

Tee moved slowly, wanting to touch her as deeply as she could. Carly was panting heavily now but seemed frozen in place. "Just relax," Tee whispered in her ear. "You're mine, little one, and I'm going to fuck you until you can't stand up." Carly moaned again but Tee felt her muscles relax a little and a new flood of wetness oozed down her arm. She continued her attentions to her breast and began a litany of soft words in her ear while moving her hand deeper and deeper. When she was buried to her wrist, she very gently caressed her from the inside. "Relax, baby. I've got you." She slowly massaged the spot she knew would drive her crazy.

Carly cried out and began short pumping strokes, straining for release. "OhGodOhGodOhGod." She didn't know who or what she was. She couldn't think of anything other than her need to come.

Tee dropped her hand from her breast and stroked slowly down her belly.

Carly rocked faster the closer she got to her clit and, when Tee's fingers slid on either side of it, she went off, screaming as the first wave of her orgasm hit with a force beyond any previous experience. The subsequent waves crashed into her with slowly diminishing vigor until she was limp with exhaustion.

Tee carefully slid out of her and moved to cover her with her own body, feeling the continued quivering as Carly rode out the aftermath. She kissed a line down her neck and across her shoulder, knowing Carly probably never noticed but needing the connection for herself. When the shaking and trembling stopped, Tee rolled to the side. Carly was out cold. Tee covered her and left the bedroom on wobbly legs. She was swollen and tight with her own need. She undressed in the bathroom and turned on the shower. When she stepped under the spray, her hand was already between her legs. She stroked lightly since she was already so full and stiff. She tried to make it last but it was impossible. When she realized the hand she was using was sticky with Carly's come and it was mixing with her own wetness, she bucked hard and came against her own hand.

Chapter 41

It was well past two in the morning when Carly awoke. She was momentarily disoriented. Lying quietly, she tried to figure out where she was. When it hit her, she sucked in a quick breath and jerked her head to the side. Tee was asleep next to her. She let out the breath she was holding and relaxed back against the bed. It was true. Tee had...Jesus! She jerked upright with the memory of what Tee had actually done to her. She swung her legs over the side of the bed and stood up. A trip to the bathroom and an inventory of her body told her it hadn't been a dream. She was sore but completely and utterly sated. She felt as if her bones were made of rubber as she made her way back to bed. She crawled under the covers and Tee reached out an arm to pull her into an embrace without opening her eyes. "You okay?" she asked softly as she fitted Carly into her side and pulled her head down to her shoulder.

Carly slid an arm and a leg across Tee's body and placed a soft kiss against her neck. "Yes."

"Sleep." Tee rested her cheek against the top of her head. Carly drifted for a moment, safe in the cocoon of Tee's embrace. As nice as it was though, she stirred and pulled away. "What?" Tee muttered thickly.

Carly kissed her shoulder and then the side of her neck as she eased on top of her. "Tee," she murmured softly, "are you asleep?" She kissed the other side of her neck while her hand drifted down to cup her breast. Tee took in a deep breath but her eyes remained closed. "I think you're playing opossum," she said and bent to take her nipple between her lips. It puckered instantly and Carly took it between her teeth and pulled gently.

Tee's breathing changed and she cupped the back of Carly's head, keeping her there and urging her on. "Oh, that's good," she murmured. "So good."

Carly hummed around a mouth full of her breast. She sucked and bit gently until Tee was writhing beneath her. She slowly kissed her way down her belly and Tee brought her knees up, and lifted her hips. "Oh no, baby, not so fast," Carly told her. "I want some more time with you." She lifted her head and smiled up at Tee. "Just relax and enjoy it."

Tee groaned in frustration then jerked as Carly ran a hand through the moist blond curls between her legs.

"Oh yes, baby," Carly whispered. "You're so ready for me, aren't you?"

Tee was always quick to ignite with Carly. "Yes," she rasped out hoarsely. "Only for you." Her hips were lifting, pushing against Carly's hand, needing the contact.

Carly teased her opening, pushing in just enough to feel the warmth of her before withdrawing to rub along her length. The scent of Tee's arousal was intoxicating. She entered her finally, fully burying two fingers in her and Tee pushed back at her, pumping her hips. Carly let her dictate the pace for a while before putting a hand on her soft belly to hold her down and withdrawing from her totally.

Tee moaned and lifted her head to look down at her.

"Easy, baby. Just hold onto it for a minute." Carly climbed on top of her and kissed her hard, pulling Tee's tongue deep into her mouth. She released her and slid onto her back, beckoning to her. "Come on, baby, climb on."

Tee straddled her and rubbed herself against her stomach, coating her with evidence of her need.

"Grab the headboard and lift," Carly urged her. When Tee had, Carly positioned herself beneath and entered her.

Tee's eyes slid closed and she began pumping her hips, her hands wrapped tightly around the headboard.

"Oh yeah, baby," Carly cooed to her. "You feel so good." She allowed Tee to continue until she showed signs of nearing the peak. "Lift up, baby."

Tee ignored her and kept pushing to her summit.

"Baby," Carly spoke sharply and broke through her haze. "Easy, baby. Trust me," she said more softly.

Tee dropped her head and gripped the headboard with white knuckles but stopped.

Carly withdrew to a pitiful whimper from above. She eased down just enough to guide Tee's center to her mouth.

Tee was very close to losing it now. She felt Carly's tongue flick over her clit and then enter her. She felt her clit twitch in warning and held very still, panting and trying to stave off the climax that was dangerously close. "Close," she rasped out. "So close."

Carly withdrew her tongue and waited for it to pass. When she felt Tee's legs lose some of their tension she began again, licking her length, going inside, and flicking over her clit.

Tee dropped a hand to the top of Carly's head. "Right there. Stay right there," she managed to get out. She rocked against Carly's face, her hips pistons against her tongue. She did not last long before a shuddering climax claimed her at last. Her hands still clutched the headboard, her legs trembled, and her head hung between her outstretched arms as she came down slowly. She finally became aware that Carly had resumed licking her length, slowly exploring every inch of her. She moaned as Carly hummed against her oh so sensitive clit. The vibration sparked a surge of renewed arousal she hadn't thought possible. "Oh," she whispered.

Carly lifted her head and slipped her fingers between them to fill her. "Do you like this?" she asked as she wiggled them inside her.

"Yessss!" Tee hissed, her heart rate ratcheting up immediately. She began rocking slowly. Carly seemed to know what she needed and let her set the pace as she began to climb again. "Go easy, baby," she murmured. "Make it last this time."

"Can't," she panted. "It's already…too close." She could feel the ribbon of her eruption slithering up through her legs, warming her as it teased its way upward toward her core. "It's..." She broke off as her clit pulsed and threatened. "Suck me."

Carly pulled her clit between her lips, sucked hard once, then once again, before Tee cried out, and convulsed as wave after wave washed over her. She collapsed finally, spent.

Carly caught her and eased her down the bed until she settled with her head on her shoulder. She kissed the top of Tee's head gently and felt tears behind her eyes. This was it, she thought. Nothing could ever compare to this.

Chapter 42

"Have another strawberry," Tee said and held the small plate out to Carly. They were both dressed in the plush robes provided by the Reed House and had just finished a room service meal. They were at the small table near the kitchen and Tee got up to open another bottle of wine. She poured for Carly first and felt her gaze rake hotly over her body. She grinned and took her own seat. "Something you like?"

"Oh yes," Carly nodded her head. "Definitely something I want." She kept her eyes on her breasts as she said it.

Tee's smile turned sultry and her tongue snaked between her lips to swirl around the edge of her wine glass. "Maybe I should tell you that we here at the Reed House, offer every service available for our valued clients."

"Oh, really?" she arched an eyebrow in question. "And are these services rendered by the staff here?"

"Some are," Tee nodded, her eyes sparkling with merriment. "And some are outsourced to…private parties."

"I see." Carly seemed to ponder this. "Whom would I talk to about arranging service of a, shall we say, delicate nature?"

"Delicate, you say." She nodded as if to herself. "We may be able to accommodate that, you being a most valued customer. I shall take care of your request myself to ensure you are…satisfied."

"You are a most kind host." Carly gave her a smile that was equal parts wicked and charming. "I will take this under advisement."

"I look forward to…servicing you." Tee gave her a wicked grin right back as she let her eyes roam down over her breasts.

"Oh, you are evil," Carly laughed in delight. She held out her wine glass and Tee reached across the table to tap hers against it.

Carly took a sip and set the glass down, her eyes now trained on the tabletop. "Tee?" Her smile was gone now. "I want you to know how sorry I am." She looked up then. "I don't want you to have any fear about how I feel."

"How do you feel?"

"I feel as if a part of me that I didn't know was missing has been found, and now I'm complete. I feel whole." She looked as much fearful as earnest. "I love you."

Tee stared at her so long Carly began to worry. Then she reached across the table and took Carly's hand in hers. "I felt a connection to you the first time we danced. When we're together, I can feel your heart beating in my chest. Whatever has happened to us, or will happen to us, we are connected in a way that can't be broken. And, just so you know, I love you too."

Carly's eyes shimmered with tears as she squeezed Tee's hand tightly. "Can I call you Thelonious?"

TEE with Carly

Tee threw her head back and roared with laughter. "I declare my love and all you want is permission to call me by my given name?"

"If I have your love I don't need anything else."

Tee's smile could have lit up the entire city. "I love so you much, Carly Matthews, but no, you may not call me Thelonious." At the look on her face she continued, "Thelonious Monk was a jazz piano player that my mother loved with a passion. She told me she listened to his music every day when she was pregnant with me. And, or some unimaginable reason, when I was born that's the only name she could think of. Lucky me, huh?"

"I think it fits you," Carly declared. "You need a name that's not ordinary because you are definitely not an ordinary woman." She made a mock fearful face. "What's your middle name?"

"Sylar," Tee said promptly. "It was my grandmother's name."

"You named your company after her then." Carly kept rubbing her thumb over Tee's knuckles as they talked.

"Yes. She was a strong influence in my life." Tee watched Carly's gaze slide to their hands on top of the table.

Carly only dimly heard the last statement as her thoughts drifted to what those hands could do to her. Those knuckles had given her such pleasure. She felt a twitch between her legs and her heart rate kicked up a notch.

"What are you thinking about, Little One?" Tee asked softly.

"Oh." Carly felt the rush hit like a hammer. She looked up into Tee's eyes then. "Do you know what that does to me? When you call me that?"

Tee smiled. She knew exactly what it did to her but she wanted to hear her say it. "What does it do?"

"Oh God, Tee. When you call me that I can't..." she faltered and stopped to take a calming breath. "I can't think about anything except..." She stopped to press her legs tightly together under the table.

"You think about me fucking you. Isn't that right, Little One?" Tee turned their hands so she held Carly's in hers and pressed her thumb into her palm, rubbing in circles.

"Yes. Oh God, yes." Carly's voice was shaky with need.

"I love fucking you, Little One." Tee rubbed her palm harder. "I love how you want me. I love *knowing* you want me."

"Oh God, Tee, I do," she gulped.

"Would you like me to take care of that right now?"

"Yes." It was all Carly could do to get the word out.

Tee stood, still holding her hand, and led her back into the bedroom. She knew Carly was ready but, instead of taking her right then, she stopped her next to the bed and wrapped her arms around her. She put her lips on Carly's neck and kissed her softly, trailing a line up to her ear. Tee loosened the belt on Carly's robe and let it fall open while she continued to nip at her neck. Her hands slid inside the robe and she caressed Carly's belly. She could feel the rapid pulse against her lips increase as her hands both dipped and rose, one to brush against the thatch between her legs and the other to heft a breast. Carly moaned softly and her hips thrust forward in hope of further contact. Tee eased the robe from her shoulders and tossed it aside. She added her own to it and wrapped her arms around Carly again and this time they were skin to skin. She took her time letting her hands roam over Carly's body, loving the feel of her skin trembling beneath her fingertips. Her mouth moved over Carly's shoulder, kissing and nipping. She could feel Carly waiting for whatever she would do to her.

"I love having my hands on you," Tee whispered in her ear. "I want to touch you absolutely everywhere."

"Oh, yes," Carly breathed.

Tee slid a hand down over her ass, squeezing and massaging her before dipping to caress her inner thigh. "Sit on the bed," She whispered in her ear. "On the edge." Tee dropped to her knees in front of her and wrapped her arms around her as they kissed. Carly circled her arms around Tee's neck and the kiss deepened. Tee slowly ran a hand over her breast and tugged on her nipple as Carly sucked on her tongue. Their breathing increased immediately and when they were forced to break apart for air, Tee dipped her head to take the other nipple in her mouth.

"Ohhhh," Carly shuddered with pleasure and put both hands in Tee's hair. "Oh baby, your mouth feels so good."

Tee switched to the other breast and took the nipple between her teeth to tug gently. Carly's gasp above her was reward enough. She trailed her fingers over Carly's stomach and felt the muscles there tighten and jump beneath her hand. She continued the ministrations to her breast as she slowly allowed her hand to stray lower. She brushed against the tangle of fine hair and moved on to caress the silken skin of her inner thigh. She eased her hand between her legs and they parted immediately, inviting her inside. She stroked her length slowly, coating her fingers, and massaging her softly. She lifted her head to kiss Carly once again and entered her just as their tongues met.

Tee stroked slowly but steadily with both tongue and fingers and soon Carly was groaning into her mouth and thrusting her hips into Tee's hand. Tee released her mouth and trailed a line of kisses down her torso, stopping to suckle each breast briefly before continuing down to the soft skin of her belly. Carly's muscles jumped beneath her lips and she knew she was driving her wild with desire.

Tee dropped lower and pushed Carly's legs apart to kiss the tender insides of her thighs. Her tongue snaked out to lick the length of her and Carly's legs jerked in response.
Carly was panting with anticipation as she leaned back on her elbows. She looked down the length of her own body to see Tee's blond head between her legs. The sight of her lover pleasuring her was almost enough to send her over the top. Tee's lips closed around her clitoris and in an instant Carly was flying, soaring into a powerful orgasm that shook her to the core

Chapter 43

"Boss?"

"Captain IT, how are you?" Tee leaned back in her office chair and smiled into the phone.

"I want to come back home."

"Does that mean you were successful in your latest project?"

"Affirmative, boss. I got everything you wanted. You were right, as usual. These people are real scumbags."

"E-mail everything you have and I'll take it from here. However, I do need you to stay there for a while longer. It shouldn't be more than a few more days though. Okay?"

"Whatever you say, boss, but I really want to come home."

"You will and with a raise for all your good work. Seriously, Fiona thanks for everything."

"You're welcome, boss. Actually, it's been kinda fun. I don't get this kind of challenge every day."

"Don't get used to it. I want you back home soon. Keep your cover intact for a while yet and I'll let you know when its time to act."

"Will do. Later, Boss.'

"Thanks, Captain."

"Wayne? It's Tee."

"Hey Tee. What's up?"

"I'd like to make an appointment with Paul and Carly."

"Both of them?"

"Yes. Can we do that soon?"

"Well, let's see." Wayne browsed through the schedules for both attorneys. "Actually, they're both in the office for the rest of today and I don't see any appointments scheduled. Do you want it that soon?"

"What time today?"

"Any time after two o'clock."

"Great. I'll be there at two."

"Can I tell them what it's in reference to?"

"Tell them we're going to score one for the good guys. See you soon."

Tee walked into the offices of Paul Carrington and Carly Matthews and leaned down to kiss Wayne on the cheek. "Hey there, hotshot."

"Hey Tee," he smiled fondly at her. "They're wondering what's on your mind. You're being very mysterious."

"No mystery," she declared. "I have some documents they'll be interested in, that's all. Are they ready to meet?"

"Yes. Go on into the conference room and I'll get them for you."

Tee had barely set her briefcase on the table when Carly and Paul entered, questioning looks on both of their faces. She gave them a big smile. "Hi."

"What's going on, Tee?" Paul asked before Carly could.

"I happened to come across some papers that might be of interest to you." She looked directly at Carly. "It has to do with your former employer, Brown, Hardin & Simon." She opened her case and extracted a file folder which she placed on the table before her.

"What about them?" Carly's voice was clipped, the anger barely contained.

"I have proof that your work computer was hacked and your files tampered with while you were working there." Tee slid a sheaf of papers across the table and they both pounced on them immediately.

"Where did you get these?" Paul asked in shock.

"Let's just say a friend."

"Not good enough," he shook his head. He looked at Carly. "We need to know before we go off and do something stupid."

"He's right," Carly nodded. "Where did you get these papers?"

Tee sighed but knew they were right. "Fiona has been working at Brown, Hardin & Simon for the last two weeks in their IT department. She put together everything you have there."

"Fiona?" Paul asked with a raised brow.

"Fiona Nix," Tee answered. "She's the head of Sylar Industries' IT department."

"She hacked into Brown, Hardin & Simon?" Paul exclaimed, practically coming out of his chair.

"No. She works for them so it's not hacking," Tee told him quickly. "Their data is her job."

Paul stared at her. "Are you serious?"

"Tee, what if they find out? Fee could be in serious trouble for this," Carly said urgently.

"The worst they could do to her is fire her," Tee reassured them. "And that's exactly what we want them to do." She proceeded to lay out the plan she'd developed over the last few weeks.

Chapter 44

"Would you like more coffee?" Tee smiled at Carly. They were all back in Paul's office conference room a week later. Paul had drawn up the proper paperwork to sue the firm of Brown, Hardin & Simon for wrongful termination, fraud, unfair hiring practices, theft, and slander. On Tee's advice, he sent a copy of the paperwork to Hardin via courier the night before.

"Are you sure about this, Tee?" Paul asked again.

"It's really up to Carly," she told him. "If she wants to go ahead and sue them, it's her decision." She took Carly's hand in hers on top of the table. "But I think they'll want to do some negotiating and it could be monetarily beneficial to her." She looked at Carly. "It's up to you, babe."

"I think this is best," Carly nodded. "I don't really want to go through a big trial and drag this out for years. And they would drag it out that long, trust me."

"What if they don't call?"

"He'll call," Tee said with conviction. "Mr. Hardin is not someone who will take this quietly. He thinks he can do whatever he wants with impunity. He'll try to bluster and threaten her into going away." She nodded. "He'll call."

It was afternoon when the call came. Wayne answered as he usually did and put the call through to the conference room. Paul hit the button for the speakerphone before answering. "Paul Carrington."

"This is Mr. Hardin of Brown, Hardin & Simon." He emphasized the name. "You might have heard of us," he said snidely.

"Yes, Mr. Hardin, I've heard of you," Paul said easily. "We're suing your firm, in case you haven't received the paperwork." Butter would have melted in his mouth.

It was all Tee could do not to laugh out loud. She grinned across the table at Carly and she smiled back but Tee could sense she was nervous. She put her hand over hers on top of the table and gave it a squeeze.

When Carly looked into her eyes and saw the love there, she relaxed. Hardin couldn't hurt her any more than he already had. Nothing could hurt her as long as Tee was beside her. Nothing. She squeezed Tee's hand in response and grinned back at her. Hell, after what she'd been through with Tee, this was nothing.

"You can't be serious!" Mr. Hardin's voice came over the speaker with force. "It's your client that should be sued by *our* firm. I knew I should have turned her into the ethics committee!"

"I'm sure you thought so at the time, Mr. Hardin," Paul replied evenly, "but my client says your company hacked her work files and distributed her case log to other people in the firm to have an excuse to fire her. We're sure it was the other way around and we're willing to go to court to get it settled. My client wants her reputation back."

"Her reputation was based on where she worked. *We* were her reputation!" He fairly sputtered with indignation.

"The court will take that into consideration," Paul answered calmly.

"We'll countersue! We'll ruin you and your little piss ant operation! You won't be able to get a job as a janitor in this city when we're done with you!"

"That is your prerogative. However, I would advise against that course of action. Once we get into court, your firm will be made to show your files, all your files, and perhaps there's more you wouldn't care to admit than what we have uncovered so far."

"What have you uncovered?" he screeched. "What do you *think* you have?" he quickly amended.

"We know for a fact you hacked into Ms Matthews work computer and that's all I'm prepared to say at this time." Paul remained calm and let the silence stretch as Mr. Hardin tried to ascertain his intentions.

"I'll get back to you after I've advised the other partners." He hung up.

"Well, that went well," Paul said dryly as he hit the button on the speakerphone to hang up.

"You did great, Paul," Carly told him with a big smile. "I've never heard him sputter like that. He was rattled."

"Yeah," he laughed. "I kind of liked that."

"Now we'll see just how stubborn he is," Tee said. "Will he actually go to the partners with this or will he try to make it go away by himself?"

"I think he'll want more information before he commits one way or the other," Paul said and Carly nodded in agreement.

"He can't afford to let the other two partners know how badly he screwed up," she said. "They'll sacrifice him if they think it's the best course for the firm."

"Great," Tee grinned. "Now, we just sit back and wait for his next move.

"Tee, Carly is on line two," Jane said over the intercom.

"Thanks, Jane." Tee swiveled to the phone and punched the button. "Hey beautiful."

"I hope you know it's me when you answer that way," Carly remarked.

"You're the only one who gets that particular greeting," Tee laughed. "How are you today?"

"He called."

"Hardin?"

"Yes. He wants to meet with us."

"That's good," Tee nodded. "He's doing exactly what we thought he would. Are you ready to face him?"

"Yes," she answered immediately.

Tee liked the steel in her voice. "I want to be there too," Tee reminded her. "I want to watch that bastard squirm."

"That's why I'm calling. He wants to meet today."

"Wow, that's fast. It means he's anxious to see what we have."

"That's what Paul and I thought too. Can you get away this afternoon?"

"I had a couple of things scheduled but they'll have to wait. I wouldn't miss this for the world. What time?"

"Two-thirty."

"I'll be at your office by two o'clock."

"Good. See you then."

"I love you."

"I love you too," Carly answered. "With all my heart."They entered the eighth floor office of Mr. Hardin precisely at two-thirty in the afternoon. Mrs. Nolan quickly rose and led them into Mr. Hardin's office without a word. Carly swept past her without a glance.

"Good afternoon," Mr. Hardin said formally and indicated he wanted them to sit in the arrangement of couches and chairs to the side of his desk.

"I think we'd all be more comfortable at a conference table," Carly said before anyone could sit. "This is not a social meeting." Her face was absolutely devoid of emotion and she looked directly at him.

Tee wanted to cheer. Her lover had taken the home court advantage away from him and put him on an even playing field. They stood waiting.

"I don't know if there is one available at the moment. We have several meetings with important clients today," he blustered.

"Fine," Carly answered and turned for the door. "Call us when you can arrange a proper meeting if you need to discuss *your* situation." Her use of the word need and the emphasis on 'your' was her way of showing strength.

"Wait," he said immediately and Tee had to turn away to hide her smile. "Just let me check first. Maybe I can find one open for a short time." He tried to recover with the 'short time' caveat but no one was buying his act. He left them in the office to go out to Mrs. Nolan's desk. It was another sign. If he weren't worried about their lawsuit, he would just have called out to her desk and asked for a room to be held in his name. They waited in silence. He returned quickly to escort them down the hall to conference room C.

"What can we do for you, Mr. Hardin?" Paul asked when they were seated at the conference table. He, Carly, and Tee were on one side, Mr. Hardin on the other.

He looked questioningly at Tee. "May I ask your name?" he asked in an effort to regain control of the meeting.

"My name is Thelonius Sylar Reed," Tee said and held his eyes.

"My I inquire as to your status at this meeting?"

"Actually, you may not," Tee answered before Carly or Paul could. "Suffice it to say I'm here as an interested party and leave it at that."

He stared at her a moment but couldn't find a valid reason to protest her presence. "Very well," he conceded without a shred of grace and turned to the two lawyers instead. "I can understand your situation," he began with false confidence. He looked at Carly. "You feel you were unfairly terminated. I'm sure we can arrive at an equitable solution without wasting the court's time on this."

"What did you have in mind?" Paul asked with a frown.

George Hardin frowned but wiped it quickly from his face. He was sure Carly would take the lead on this and tip her hand. No matter, he thought. He'd make mincemeat of this no-name lawyer.

"I've heard Ms Matthews was unemployed for quite some time after she was terminated from this firm." It was evident from his tone that he was amused by this thought.

"How does that affect the situation?" Paul asked.

"I think we could come to an agreement as to some sort of compensation for her lost time," he went on. "I could probably talk the partners into a small monetary package." He looked at Carly. "Because you had such a difficult time gaining employment, we might be able to see our way clear to making up for that situation."

Tee stiffened in her seat but kept a tight rein on her emotions. She wanted nothing more than to put a fist in his ugly, smug, sanctimonious face.

"That's most kind of you," Paul nodded easily, "especially since the illegal actions of this firm were the cause of that situation. Not only did you fire Ms Matthews for something you did, but you also influenced other law firms throughout the city to deny her employment. I'd say paying her for her lost employment is the very least your firm will do." He looked George Hardin in the eye. "It is definitely not the most you'll be able to do, however."

Mr. Hardin was nonplussed. Where was the anxiety? Where was the fear? Did they not comprehend the power of this firm? "Perhaps you don't understand how much pressure this firm can bring to bear upon your firm also, Mr. Carrington." He said it with the confidence of long use.

"Oh, I'm sure you think you can pressure me," Paul answered easily. "You'd be wrong though. Have you even read the papers we sent to your office? If you had, you'd know we have every intention of suing this firm for all the allegations spelled out therein." He sat forward and put his elbows on the table. "Make no mistake, Mr. Hardin, you will not win this battle. You hacked Ms Matthews' files and sent them to everyone in the company in order to fire her. You threatened her with the ethics committee so I'm positive they'd be interested in what you've done also. Even your firm cannot pressure the state board of ethics. Then there are always the newspapers. I'm sure I could find some reporter that would love to take a shot at this story." He paused to stare coldly across the table at him. "Are you positive your high profile clients would retain your services once the story is out? Really, Mr. Hardin, think about it. Are you even sure your partners would accept your continued employment here?"

"What do you have as proof of all these allegations?" he barked out. "It's ridiculous to think our firm would have to resort to something of that nature. No one will believe her word against ours!"

"They won't have to, Mr. Hardin," Paul sat back in his chair. "We have proof of the hacked files; proof that came from your own company files. You were very sloppy, Mr. Hardin. Technology is unforgiving in its nature to record everything."

"What proof?" he questioned belligerently.

Paul opened his case and extracted a thick file folder from which he took a sheaf of papers. "These are copies, obviously. But these are the tracks left behind when you accessed Ms Matthews's computer, copied her case file, and sent it to every e-mail address on the company roster." He slid the papers across the table in front of him.

"I'm not a computer specialist," he sneered. "How would you know what all this gibberish means?"

"I know what it means because a computer specialist brought it to me and explained what it meant."

"Who?" he demanded to know. "How could anyone get this information?"

"It's straight from your company network," Paul said with a sneer of his own.

"That's a lie! If any information came from this company's records, it was obtained illegally! It would not be allowed as evidence of anything!" He was triumphant.

"I can assure you it did come from your network," Paul assured him calmly. "It was given to me by a member of your staff. She discovered what was going on and wanted to protect herself."

"Who?" he demanded once again and this time his voice shook with repressed anger.

"Her name is Fiona Nix. She works in your information technology department. By law, she is required to report any illegal act."

He slammed his chair back against the wall and stalked to the telephone at the other end of the room. Within seconds he was back, but remained standing. "I've sent for this technology person and we'll get to the bottom of this." He continued to stand as they waited for Fiona to arrive. Soon enough the door opened and Fiona entered.

"You wanted to see me?" she asked, looking at Mr. Hardin.

"Yes," he said flatly. "Are you responsible for this?" He held up the papers Paul had shown him.

Fiona made a show of crossing the room and looking closely at the papers. She then handed them back to him and stepped away. "Yes, I am responsible for that."

His face turned purple with rage. "You're fired!" he screamed.

"I'll hire you," Tee spoke up quickly and grinned at Fiona. "Be at Sylar Industries tomorrow morning." She shrugged. "Or any time you want to show up. Maybe take a week off if you want."

"What!" Mr. Hardin screamed across the table at her. "You can't hire her! This is insane!"

"You fired her," Tee shrugged. "I hired her. Everybody heard it."

"You can't get away with this!" he continued to yell.

"No, it's you that can't get away with this," Paul told him calmly. "Your own employee found evidence of a crime and reported it to me to protect herself from you. I think that about sums it up.

"Oh, one more thing," Paul spoke again. "When you're figuring out how much you're willing to pay Ms Matthews for all your, shall we say, misconduct, you might want to figure in the fact that we can and will include sexual harassment in the lawsuit."

"What are you talking about now?" he screeched, spittle flying out of her mouth. He was still standing and began pacing in short strides behind his chair.

"Don't tell me you were unaware Ms Phillips made an unwelcome sexual advance to Ms Matthews? From what we can tell, everyone in the firm knows she goes after younger women with less seniority at the firm. She's known for it, I'm told."

"That's not my concern," he shook his head. "I can't control what other people do around here!"

"Oh, but you can," Paul told him. "In fact, it's your job as a partner to ensure a safe working environment. That's federal law." He stood up and both Carly and Tee followed his lead. "I think you have a few things to consider, Mr. Hardin. We'll be interested in hearing from you if you want to settle this out of court." He turned at the door. "Or perhaps your partners will be interested in settling this if you're not." The threat was not lost of him. Pay up or the partners would hear about this and his employment would vanish. "I'll be available for the next twenty-four hours, Mr. Hardin. Good day."

They all left and Fiona followed them down the hall, each one silent until they had exited the building. "Yes!" Fiona was the first to break. She pumped her fist in exhilaration. "Shit! That felt great!"

They laughed and then all started talking at once. It was pandemonium, which only made them laugh harder as they made their way down the street.

Chapter 45

The next day they all waited anxiously. Carly tried to keep busy with other things but it was hard to keep her mind on work. She went down the block for coffee and returned with pastries as well. She knew they'd gotten something when she stepped through the door. There was electricity in the air and Wayne was smiling.

"What?" she asked.

"He sent an e-mail to Paul," Wayne said quickly. "Let him tell you."

Carly hurried into his office. "Paul?"

Paul was grinning up at her. "How does it feel to be the newest millionaire in Dallas?"

"You're kidding?" Her mouth dropped open in shock. "Are you serious?"

"Yes, Ma'am," he laughed. "He sent the offer just a few minutes ago. Of course, we aren't going to just take his offer."

"We're not?" Carly asked, still in shock.

"Hell, no. What kind of lawyers would we be to settle that easily? If he's willing to give you a million then there's more to be had."

"Wow, Paul," Carly said. "I can't even think straight right now."

"That's my job," he told her. "Go shopping or whatever and let me handle this."

Four hours later Paul emerged from his office. Carly and Wayne were both huddled in the outer office, talking and giggling together.

"We're celebrating!" Paul announced when they looked up. "Two point five," he yelled. "Wow!" Wayne jumped up and hugged Carly and together they jumped up and down.

"Hey, how about me?" Paul asked. "I'm the one who did all the negotiating."

They grabbed him and pulled him into their joyful dance around the room. "You're the best, honey," Wayne told him and gave him a big kiss. Carly kissed him next and they began laughing.

"I have to call Tee," Carly shouted. "She's waiting." She disengaged from the two men and picked up Wayne's phone. "Jane, is she there?" She held on while Jane sent the call through.

"Hey," Tee's voice came on the line.

"We're celebrating!" Carly shouted. "Paul got him up to two point five million. What do you think of that?"

"I think it's wonderful," Tee laughed. "Congratulations."

"Why don't you come on over and celebrate with us?"

"I'll do better than that. Tonight Reeders Row is hosting the celebration, all drinks on the house! Tell them to bring anyone they want and let's party!"

"You're the best!" Carly laughed in delight. "But you don't need to do that. We'll be fine with getting burgers and beer."

"Please let me do this for you," Tee said. "I want to."

"Okay," she relented. "Whatever you want, love."

"Great. Tell the boys to get ready to let loose. We're going to party tonight!" Tee hung up with a smile on her face. She'd known they would win. She knew George Hardin's type. He thought he was above the law, or more worrisome than that, thought he was the law. It felt good to be able to help take him down a peg or two and get some justice for her lover as well. She picked the phone back up and called over to Reeders Row to alert the bartenders as to what was about to happen that night.

The music was rocking the house and it was packed to the rafters with people dancing, drinking, and laughing. There were platters of food lined up on catering tables against one wall and a large cake on another table at the end. The normal bartenders had been supplemented with additional help and everyone seemed to be having a great time. Tee stood at the end of the bar sipping a beer and watching Carly on the dance floor. She was so happy. Tee smiled to see her so carefree for a change. Their eyes met and Carly gave her such a sweet smile it made her heart sing. Additionally, it made other parts of her anatomy pulse. Whew! She'd better think about something else. She was browsing through the food table when she felt arms encircle her waist.

"Who might be so bold as to touch me when it's clear I belong to the most beautiful woman in the world?" she asked.

"Sweet talker," Carly laughed softly in her ear. She kissed the back of her neck and hugged her. "Thank you."

"It's nothing," Tee scoffed. "I think everyone's having a great time, don't you?"

"Yes," Carly hugged her tighter. "Thanks to you. Did I ever tell you how much I love you?"

"You might have mentioned it," Tee smiled. "But it wouldn't hurt to tell me again." She turned in Carly's arms to face her. "You are so beautiful."

Carly leaned up to kiss her. "I love you."

"Right back at you, babe."

"Would you like to dance with me?"

"I'd be delighted to dance with you," Tee said. She took Carly's hand and pulled her onto the dance floor. "Remember our first dance?" Tee asked as they fell into the rhythm.

"Oh yes," Carly answered with a smile. "I'll remember that dance for the rest of my life."

"So will I," she nodded and moved closer until their thighs were touching. "I knew then you were something special."

Carly snuggled her pelvis against Tee's and watched her eyes darken. She put her hands on Tee's hips and moved in tandem with her. Tee's eyes told her what she was doing to her and she smiled. "I love dancing with you."

"Yes," Tee answered absently as her eyes strayed to her breasts. "Will you stay with me tonight?"

"Yes. Do you need to ask?"

"I don't want to ever take you for granted." Tee's hands roamed up and down her back as she spoke.

"Don't worry," Carly told her. "I won't let you." They danced for another minute. "Thanks for everything, baby. You were amazing. You got Fiona a job at Brown, Hardin & Simon just so she could dig out the dirty little secrets that Hardin was keeping. He paid big to keep his job and cover his ass with the other partners."

Tee smiled down into her eyes and kissed her lightly on the lips. "You are welcome, lover. You are just ever so slightly wrong about the pay off though."

"What do you mean?"

"He paid you and Paul to keep his little secret from the partners. He did not pay me to keep the secret." She grinned when Carly looked up at her in surprise and shock.

"Oh my God! You…aren't going to tell them, are you?"

"I wouldn't dream of telling Brown or Simon. At least not until that little bastard's check clears his bank."

"Thelonius Sylar Reed…I love you so much."

"As I love you, my little one."

Made in the USA
Lexington, KY
25 August 2012